DECEIT

A NOVEL

AVA HARRISON

Deceit: A Novel
Copyright © 2019 by Ava Harrison
Published by AH Publishing

Deceit: A Novel
Cover Design: Hang Le
Cover Photographer: Jon Wong
Cover Model: Christian Hogue

Line Edit: Lawrence Editing, www.lawrenceediting.com, Editing4Indies
Proofreader: Marla Selkow Esposito, My Brother's Editor
Formatting: Champagne Book Design

Dedicated to all the women who have fallen for the wrong men over and over before finally finding their prince charming, this one is for you!

"To live is the rarest thing in the world.
Most people exist, that is all."

—Oscar Wilde.

CHAPTER ONE

Oliver

"WHERE ARE YOU?" MY MOTHER'S SHRILL VOICE HISSES through the phone. This is a daily occurrence, and sometimes I wonder why I even bother to answer.

Because she's your mum, and she raised you. Because deep down, under her icy facade and lectures, I know she does, in fact, love me even though she drives me bonkers.

"You know damn well where I am, Mother." I sigh, closing out the window on my computer. There's no use trying to work right now, not when my mother has something to go on about. I turn away from my desk and face the window.

"London again." She pauses before continuing. "I see." Her voice is low, and all the muscles in my back tighten at her tone.

"You know I do business here."

"Don't you think it's high time you come home and manage business here?"

Not this again. No matter what, whenever I speak to my mother, she stresses the importance of my moving in full time at my estate, also known as Pembroke Manor. "You're perfectly capable of handling the estate business. You've been doing it for years."

"You're right. I have because I knew you were young and had other pressing matters."

She means to say sow my wild oats, but she's too proper. She'd be right, though. I've certainly had my fair share of exploits to give her that belief. "But now it's high time you come home and do your duties. This is your estate. Your title. Your legacy."

As she speaks of titles and family obligations, it feels like an invisible noose tightens around my neck, cutting off my blood flow. I tug at the collar of my Armani dress shirt, allowing more oxygen to rush into my lungs.

Fuck the title. Fuck the responsibilities. Fuck the obligations.

I haven't asked for them, I'm not ready for them, and I have a feeling I never will be.

To most people, home is where they go back to in order to recharge.

To me, home is filled with bad memories and sorrow. My father may have died years ago, but I still hate going to the estate, even if it is mine *now*.

Many years passed before I was able to claim my inheritance and my title after his death, but luckily for me, as I was escaping the responsibilities of my youth, my mother was running the everyday aspects of our estate.

The title was something I never wanted any part of.

Tainted by a memory of my father and the man he was.

He died when I was young, but I still remember the yelling, the drinking.

He was rarely around, but when he was, Mother would tell me to go to my room. I wouldn't listen to her, though. Instead, I would creep down the stairs . . .

And that was when I would hear him yell and her wail.

Then one day, I was sent away to boarding school and only came home occasionally for visits.

So no, being the Earl of Lockhart was always bittersweet.

"I know what my responsibilities are, Mother." My eyes close of their own accord, images flashing that, even now, I don't want to see. I shake my head and banish the mental pictures of my father aside.

"Then start acting like it," she grits out, and the words are enough to snap me out of my haze and replace the sadness with anger.

Yes, I love my mother, but she knows how to push my buttons. "I'm always careful, and I'm diligent about avoiding the paparazzi," I bite back. If there is one thing my mum can't fault me for, it's my need for discretion, so the fact she's harping on this infuriates me.

"Being an earl is more than just avoiding being photographed looking like an arse," my mum retorts. "I need you here to help take care of family business."

"I do take care of family business . . . *here*. Since I have taken over the finances in London, I have doubled our wealth."

"It's not always about money. I need you here dealing with something else." When I let out an audible puff of breath rather than pressing her, she continues, "The Prices are up to something."

"Don't be ridiculous, Mum. No one has touched the land in . . . well, ever."

She scoffs as though she's speaking to an irritating child. "I have it on good authority, there is an appointment, and that James Price is coming into town, Oliver. What do you make of that?"

I don't humor her with a response.

"Stop acting like your father. Your gallivanting and drinking are worrisome enough, but the women . . ."

Her words hit their intended mark because my father has always been a sore spot.

He was a drunk, and what he put us both through was more than I cared to think about. If my mum's intention was to make me feel like a complete and utter wanker, she succeeded.

"I need you here, Oliver," she says again, her voice breaking this time. "I can't see that man. Price ruined my life."

"What are you going on about?"

My mother doesn't sound like herself. It actually sounds like she might be crying, but that can't be. I've never seen her cry. My mother has never shown emotions like that.

"Are you crying?" I ask.

"Everything happened because of him," she mumbles away from the phone, and I'm not even sure she's talking to me. I know she hates the Prices, and I know it's the only land of the original entail property she has never been able to buy back, but why would that have ruined her life? So what if the property was passed down from generation to generation through the act of entailing it to the male heir?

The notion is ridiculous in this day in age.

"Mum, what happened? And because of who?"

"Just come home, okay?"

Her voice has me rattled, so I let out a sigh because as much as I don't want to leave London, I have to. Out of habit, I pull out my lucky coin. The one I acquired from the headmaster during my first year of boarding school.

At a time when my life was shit, I hated my dad, and I believed in nothing.

"Not everything needs to be chance. We can make our own luck," he had said and then placed the coin in my hand with a wink.

I flip it once in the air.

Heads.

Home it is.

Duty calls, after all. No matter how much I fight it, I know I need to do what's right.

For my family.

For my title.

"I'm on my way."

CHAPTER TWO

Addison

One day earlier . . .

MY FINGERS TAP RHYTHMICALLY ON THE KEYBOARD. Early morning correspondence is a necessary evil, so someone has to do it.

After I respond to the last email from this morning, I stretch my arms to the ceiling, letting my palms open and close and moving my fingers around to get the feeling back. I need coffee and a break.

I close out the window on my computer and load a news site instead. Jasmine won't be here for another thirty minutes. Jax and Grayson aren't here either, so I might as well see what's happening in the world.

As soon as the website loads, I realize the mistake I've made.

Picture after picture.

There they are. The one thing I was trying to forget is screaming back at me. I told myself to lie low and try to forget.

I told myself I was strong enough to attend my ex's wedding.

But how could I ever think that? This weekend has been haunting my every moment. Even if I tried to pretend it hasn't.

I've known this day was coming, but with my extensive business travel, I have kept preoccupied long enough for it to actually escape my mind. Now, being back in New York, I realize my mistake and know I shouldn't be here. I should still be lying low. I lied to myself, thinking I'd be okay when the time came. Now looking at the words and the photos, I know I won't be.

"Hotelier Spencer Lancaster to marry supermodel turned successful model scout Olivia Miller this weekend."

Quickly, I close the page, but it's too late. Unfortunately, the images of the happy couple have burned my retinas. How Spencer Lancaster's handsome face looks adoringly at his fiancée.

I'll never be able to undo it.

Emotions bubble inside me as the feelings I had pushed down rise to the surface. Before I can stop myself, I refresh the screen and bring the image back up. *Why am I doing this?*

Everything blurs in front of me. My lungs burn, and a suppressed sob lodges itself in my throat. Lifting my hand, I run the pads of my fingers on my skin and find them dampened by the tears that must have escaped.

With a deep breath, I walk into the bathroom in my office and stare at my reflection. From the unobservant eye, I might look fine. My brown wavy locks are perfectly blown out, and my makeup is flawless, but for someone who knows me, who really knows me, they'd know.

Spencer would know.

My eyes are flat.

I can't let anyone see me. I've worked so damn hard for everyone to take me seriously. Having spent my life in a man's world, I might not have had to kick and scream my way to the top, but I still had to prove I could lead like my father and not let my emotions get in the way. In the end, through hard work and perseverance, Grayson and I both took over. I'm the CEO, and Grayson is the CFO of Price Enterprise. Jaxson, our youngest brother, is the COO.

The truth is, after a bunch of mistakes in my early years, I realized I didn't want to be that girl who let a man dictate her life, but that was another lie I told myself. Because, all it took was one online headline, one damn article, for everything I have built to fall apart around me. Every wall around my heart to crumble.

No. I can't fall. Not here. Not now. They can't see me—not my brothers and not my employees.

Turning on the water, I grab a towel and dab my face, making sure to wipe away any remaining smudged makeup. I freshen myself and pull my shoulders back.

Cool and collected Addison Price.

It only takes another moment, but now, back in front of my desk, I check the time. Jasmine should be here now but not Jax and Gray. I might be able to get out of here before they realize.

I need to go somewhere.

Get out of this damn city.

My brothers will expect my presence at the wedding if I'm in town. They will expect me to smile and cheer.

I can't, though, so I have no choice but to leave.

But where?

Sitting back in front of my computer, I pull up my files and rummage through the properties. *Where can I go?* I need to leave under the guise of working because I can't let anyone know. I'm a strong woman, and I won't allow any man to bring me to my knees like this. At least not publicly.

No. If I get out of here and leave the country to "work," I'll be away from the discerning eyes of the people who know me best and have time to rein in my emotions. The plan is solid, but now I need to figure out where I'm going.

Picking up my phone, I dial the intercom. “Jasmine, can you please come into my office?”

“Of course,” she says through the line. A few seconds later, she walks in wearing a smile on her face. She stops midway into my office, and her smile fades, a frown replacing it as she takes me in.

Jasmine has been my assistant for a few years now, but before that, she was an intern. We met during a speaking engagement I gave to an NYU graduating class of women. I spoke of empowering women in business over lunch, and when she asked me a list of very pointed and discerning questions, I was instantly impressed. I offered her a position during dessert.

We bonded instantly, and before long, I promoted her to my assistant. But she’s so much more than that, and when she looks at me right now with her chocolate eyes narrowed and her head cocked, I know she sees past it all.

She sees my pain.

“Are you okay?” she asks.

“Yeah,” I lie. “I just wanted to tell you I’m going away on business.”

She steps farther into the room, closer to where I’m sitting behind my imposing desk. If she gets any closer, she’ll know for sure.

“When?” Her jaw twitches as she waits for my answer.

“Today. Soon.”

A fine line forms between her brows as she continues to stare at me, and I know she knows I’m lying.

“What business?”

Since I have no idea yet, I falter.

“What’s going on?” she asks.

“Close the door,” I say as I cover my face with my hands.

Squeezing my eyes shut, I will my heart to stop beating so fast. I really don't want to lose my cool at the office, but I need to talk to someone, and Jasmine has proven herself loyal time and time again. Having her know and understand will help me.

"Spencer is getting married this weekend," I say with my eyes still closed. I was clearly in denial, thinking maybe something would happen or maybe it would come and I wouldn't care . . .

I was wrong on both accounts.

I open my eyes and see her sitting in the chair in front of me, her eyes watching my every move.

"I know."

Everyone knows.

"I'm going out of town," I say again.

"I understand. Where are you going to go?" she asks, leaning on my desk and resting her hands on the surface.

"I'm not sure yet. All I know is Grayson and Jax can't know why I'm leaving town."

"Don't you think your brothers are smarter than you give them credit for?"

"Well, of course, but if I can give them a plausible reason . . ."

"And what would be plausible?" She cocks her head, and I let out a sigh.

I have no idea. So much for a well-thought-out plan.

"Surveying a property?" Jasmine responds before I can come up with an idea.

"Okay. That could work. Hmm. What are some of our clients looking for?" I ask.

Jasmine stands, and I watch as she struts out of my office. A minute later, she returns to the same chair, but this time with an iPad on her lap. She starts to move her hand around. "Blue Coast Industries is looking for a commercial spot to build their new headquarters."

I shake my head. "Still in America. Too close." I can still see the news in America. The truth of the internet means I can see the news anywhere . . .

A shudder works its way through my body at the thought.

I just won't go online.

Jasmine tracks my movements with a nod. "Okay, America is out. Any other prerequisites?"

"Someplace off the beaten path maybe. I need quiet, but I also need to be able to work."

"Got it."

I watch as her eyes widen.

"What?"

"Nothing," she says too quickly, and I know she's holding back.

"Tell me, Jasmine." My hands twist beneath my desk, waiting to hear what she has to say.

"The Lancasters are looking to build a new line of hotels . . ."

I let out a long-drawn-out and completely melodramatic groan. *The Lancasters.* Will I ever be rid of him? "No!"

"Just hear me out." She lifts her hand passively, so I nod for her to continue. "You want your brothers to think you don't care? You want them to think you aren't hiding? This is your perfect cover story. If you cared, would you be working for him?"

I think about what she suggests, and as much as I hate to admit it, it makes sense. "Okay," I mutter reluctantly. "What are they looking for?"

"These will be very exclusive luxury estates. Cities are off-limits."

"So we need a big piece of property on the beach or in the country. What do we have available? Not in America," I say because if I'm going to be traveling under the guise of work, I want to be far, far away from Lancaster, even if he's my cover story.

"There are a few in Spain and France."

"What else?" I shake my head; too many memories exist in both countries with Spencer. He has hotels on my properties there. Jasmine continues to type and swipe.

"Hmm. This one actually might be perfect."

"Where is it?" I ask, leaning forward on my desk.

"Wiltshire," she responds as she turns her iPad to me. There's no image on the iPad—just words that I can't make out from where I'm sitting.

"Where?"

"Wiltshire. England. Cows. Green hills. Hot Brits. You know."

"Really?" I had no idea we even had property in Wiltshire. Hell, I don't even know where Wiltshire is.

"Apparently, it was one of your father's first purchases, but he never built on it. It wasn't even in the portfolio."

"I wonder why," I say out loud, but then it hits me. If it was Dad's first, he wouldn't have touched it. He was nostalgic like that. Me, not so much.

"Doesn't say. But there is no price attached to the land, so maybe he inherited it."

I shrug. I'll have to ask Mom one day. "Tell me about this property."

Jasmine spends the next forty minutes discussing the area, and by the time she's done, I decide it's exactly where I need to go. The property is a little over two hours outside of London, so there's no way I'll see any newspaper articles regarding the wedding, and since I have sworn off googling him, it shouldn't be a problem.

"That's where I'm going. It's perfect. If Gray asks, it makes sense . . ." I say more to myself than to her.

"What do you need me to do?"

"Book me a place."

"Got it." She types again, probably a note for herself on her to-do list. She loves making lists. "When do we leave?"

Her comment makes me cock my head to the side and look at her. "I'm going by myself."

She rolls her eyes at me.

"What?" I shrug.

"You never travel to locations without me. You don't think that will be a red flag?"

She's right, and I hate that she's right. Any other time, I would just say I need to get away, but since I never get away, and since this trip coincides with the weekend of the wedding—a wedding my brothers are going to—I have to make this believable. I always travel with my small team on business, so I'll have to take them.

"Fine, book us a place. Tell Marcus to come too," I say. Marcus, my driver, doubles as security if we are ever in an unsafe location, but seeing as this is not that type of trip, I'm really bringing them both for show.

With the mood I'm in, I'll probably check out the property once and spend the rest of the weekend sequestered in my room with a pint of ice cream.

Then, when the coast is clear, and Spencer is off on his honeymoon, and some new gossip litters the pages of *Exposé*, I'll fly home and pretend none of it happened.

It's a solid plan.

What can go wrong?

A lot can go wrong.

A ton.

Every single thing, actually.

I thought that leaving New York would silence the voices in my head, but it didn't. I still remember how I hurt him. I still feel the regret and guilt for how I treated him, and I still remember the pain of seeing him with her.

Years later, I know I was never the right person for Spencer. I know he's meant to be with Olivia, and while a part of me is happy for him, a part of me I don't like to think about is also jealous of that happiness. Jealous he was able to move on, and I haven't.

Instead, I'm torturing myself with endless thoughts of all the what-ifs, and my brain is firing rapidly, screaming at me to check the internet, but I know I can't. That would be stupid.

Heading downstairs, I see Marcus and Jasmine in the kitchen. "I'm going out," I say before I can stop myself.

Jasmine pops her brow. "Umm, okay."

"I'm going to see if there is a place to get a drink."

"I can head into town and get you—"

I raise my hand. "I need a change of scenery. I'll just drive into the village we passed and see if I can find a place to grab a drink."

"I'll drive you." Marcus moves to stand, but I shake my head.

"Don't be ridiculous. I can drive myself."

"And have a drink?" he leads like a father.

"I'm a big girl, and what's one drink?"

He doesn't look happy, but I don't want to be around them, or anyone who knows me for that matter. Taking the keys, I walk toward the door.

"Remember, they drive on the opposite side of the road," Jasmine says.

I turn around and glare at her. She holds back her laughter as I exit the cottage.

CHAPTER THREE

Oliver

T*his is exactly what I needed.*

The scotch travels down my throat and it helps to loosen up everything inside me.

I arrived at my estate earlier today, but as soon as I walked in the door, my mother found me and started running down a list of everything I needed to know while here. Then she started to drone on and on about the land—the damn piece of property she was never able to purchase back.

With one of the Prices coming into town, she wants me to find out what he's up to and get to the bottom of what the real estate mogul plans to do with it. He won't be here for a few days though, so knowing I'm about to star in one hell of a shitshow; I decided to loosen up with a few drinks down at the pub.

What's the harm in a little downtime? Besides, I have my reputation as a drunken womanizer to keep up, *apparently*. I groan at my mother's words replaying in my head.

Now I find myself at The Carpenter's Arms, taking a swig of my drink. Surprisingly, it feels good to get away from the hustle and bustle of London. It feels good to be home. I stayed away way too long.

I often found it easier to allow my mother to handle Pembroke Manor, and if I'm being honest, the need to go out and party, drink, and have a good time was all I could think about for way too long.

After sitting for a few minutes to enjoy my drink, I finally look up to see Robin, the bartender, looking over my shoulder with wide eyes. Even in the dark and musky bar, I can tell he's in shock. *I wonder what he's looking at.*

I take another swig, but eventually, curiosity takes over, and I find myself turning around. What greets me leaves me wide-eyed as well.

Who is *that*?

She's gorgeous. Probably the most stunning woman I have ever seen. She's tall and lithe like a ballerina with long brown hair that sweeps over her shoulders to fall below her full breasts.

I'm sure I've never seen her. I would have, without a doubt, remembered such an exquisite creature.

I scan her over, perusing her body. It's clear she doesn't belong here, and it's not just her clothes that make her out of place. She's not in the normal attire one would expect in a pub like this—jumper and whatnot.

No. She is in heels, at least five inches, and wearing a pantsuit. But what makes this woman stand out even more than her clothes are her eyes.

She looks uneasy as her gaze sweeps across the space, and she scrunches her nose. My brow furrows with curiosity as I continue to watch her. With what appears to be a hesitant step, she walks toward the bar.

Halfway through the space, she stops, and then with a shake of her head, she must think better of her decision because she moves to turn back around and leave.

"Going so soon?" I ask in my gruff, come-hither voice, still looking at her over my shoulder.

She looks up from where her eyes were staring previously at the floor, peering around the space to find who had spoken to her.

Seeing as I'm the only one sitting at the bar, it shouldn't take her long to figure it out. Well, that's not true. Harry is here too, but he's pissed and passed out with his head on the bar, so I can assume she knows he didn't speak to her.

It only takes her a few seconds to find me, and when our eyes meet, hers widen, but she doesn't say anything. She just stares at me dumbfounded.

"You just got here," I continue. It's not often a woman like her walks into a pub like this. Having her here could be interesting.

A good distraction at least.

"And I was just leaving," she replies in a curt tone, taking a step back as if just being in this location will give her a disease or something.

"Oh, come now, stay." My words come out playful, and I turn on my chair to get a better look. She stares at me in surprise, but she doesn't move back, so I lift my hand and then pat the bar. Her gaze follows my movement, and her beautiful face distorts, her full lips puckering.

I hold back a laugh because I know why she's grimacing. Dried liquor and spilled beer make the vile bar sticky beneath my fingertips.

She glances back down, but now she's looking at the floor, which quite possibly has never been swept by the looks of it. From where I'm perched, I can clearly see rubbish littering it and even a few balled-up napkins.

"It is quite vile, but in my opinion, it adds to the ambiance." I wink. "Fancy a drink?" I point at the bottles against the wall. "Looks like you need one."

"And you know this because . . . ?" Her voice is heavy with sarcasm as her eyes narrow, challenging me.

"I'm well-versed in what stress looks like. So come on, take a seat, and let me buy you one."

"I'd rather not . . . but thanks for the offer." She moves to take a step back but then stops. "Are there any other restaurants—"

I know where she is going with that, so I lift my hand and cut her off. "Not particularly. Plus, why would you want to go anywhere else but here?

"The Carpenter's Arms is not only the best pub in town but well, it's actually the closest one in fuck knows how many miles." I shrug and squint as I try to gauge the proper distance. "Thirty? Forty tops."

"You have got to be kidding me," she mumbles under her breath, blowing out a puff of air that makes the wisp of hair hanging over her face float up.

"Not kidding. I'm British, and we don't do that." I chuckle, and that just makes her scowl. She's quite pretty even with the scowl plastered to her face. Now that she's close, I allow myself to really take her in.

She's American. I caught that from what little she's said and from the look of her fitted trousers and blazer, well-heeled at that.

She stands perfectly still and tall, the curve of her neck long and inviting. She looks like she stepped off a runway and into a boardroom.

Stunning.

But that still doesn't answer the question lingering in my mind. What is she doing here? In my local pub? Does she know James Price?

"Come sit, have a drink. It's better than not drinking at all." I shrug, not just because I'm bored and lonely, but rather because I'm intrigued.

First, I want to see if she might know the Prices, and if so, maybe she can be useful in obtaining information on them.

Second and most importantly, I'd very much like to allow this disarming beauty to help me pass the night.

"I can't." Her brow furrows again.

"Oh, come on . . . live a little," I jest. It doesn't help lighten the mood, though. If anything, she is more on edge. "I promise you"—I lower my voice—"it's perfectly safe in here."

"I'm not worried about safety as much as I'm worried about catching a disease." Ah, there it is. She points at the counter to clarify.

"You won't catch anything."

She steps closer and touches the surface, testing it out herself this time. She slowly lifts her fingers back up, and although you cannot hear the sound of her finger touching the sticky surface, I imagine she hears it in her mind by the way her face twists again.

"You're right. I might not catch anything, but I might die."

"I also promise you won't die. And if by some strange chance you do, at least you did it in a great pub. Here, everyone will treat you like family. We'd give you a proper burial."

"That is so reassuring." She shrugs and pulls her purse higher on her shoulder.

"Have it your way. But you're missing out . . ." I trail off before turning to the bartender in front of me. "I'll have another, Robin," I say to the older man standing across the bar from me.

His weathered face holds back any emotion, but I know he wants to let out a chuckle. He's been serving me scotch since long before I was even allowed to be here. This man has seen me at my best and worst.

"I'll have what he's having," the feisty American says from beside me as she lets out a sigh.

When Robin moves to get us the scotch, I turn to my left and meet her eyes. She's been watching me, and by the red flush spreading across her cheeks, her thoughts weren't proper.

The color suits her.

It makes me conjure up thoughts of spending my night with her. It's a much better thought than what awaits me at my estate.

I lift my gaze back up, and she's still staring.

Her large eyes are green but not the typical shade of green. More like amber. Like a cat. She narrows them at me in speculation. I want to lift my hands, and say, "I come in peace," or something similarly ridiculous, but I opt for indifference. What I've learned in my thirty years of life is that women often like to work for it. So instead of pressing the issue, I turn back to the bar.

Once our drinks are set in front of us, I lift the glass tumbler to my mouth. "Aren't we going to say cheers?" she asks, leaning into me, and that makes my lip tip up. Just as I suspected, indifference always works with the Americans.

Like leading a lamb to the slaughter.

With slow precision, I turn to face her again, lean forward, and tip my glass to hers. "What are we drinking to, love?"

"Love?" she asks. "Really?"

"You are quite lovely," I respond but maintain my indifference.

Leaning into me more, she cocks her head. "Does that ever work?"

"I'm not trying to make it work. I'm just speaking the truth." I shrug and take another swig. The liquid flows down my throat, searing me with its warmth. "Plus, I'm British."

"And . . . ?"

"We call everyone . . . love."

"Well, that's wonderful," she deadpans before she looks back down at her glass—her *full* glass.

"So what should we cheer to?" I ask. "Quiet pubs that bring all sorts?"

With that, she laughs, and her shoulders soften. She shakes her head at me.

"That won't do?" I ask.

"No. Something better." As she warms up to me, she becomes even more enticing, if that's possible.

"To drinking our problems away?"

She nods with vigor. "Much better." She smiles up at me and brings that glass to her lips. "To drinking our problems away." She tosses the entire contents down her throat, then swallows hard and licks her lips.

Brilliant. Very few women can drink scotch with such ease. "Another?" I ask as I follow suit and chug my entire glass.

"Yes." She sighs with relief. "Another, please."

"You're quite serious?" I say, dismayed.

"Yes," she drawls, looking at me with wide eyes. "I'm having a bad day."

"That's apparent. Are you sure you feel safe drinking like that? I mean, this pub is full of riffraff." Her eyes scan the room, and I can't help but grin at her wary expression.

"I jest. As I said before, you're quite safe."

"Something tells me I'm safe with everyone but you." She smirks.

"Darling, you have no idea how right you are." I wink before motioning to Robin for more drinks.

Once she's three drinks in, she's more relaxed. Her purse

sits on top of the bar, and her body is not as tense as it was when she first walked in. She stares up at the cobwebs, and I wonder what she's thinking about.

I certainly hope it's not how she's had too many drinks and will probably throw up all over the floor. The least she could do if she's about to be sick is find the loo.

When she stiffens, I move my hand and touch her back. "Are you all right there?" I ask, now concerned that maybe she, in fact, couldn't handle the scotch.

She turns her head to me, and I can clearly see she's upset. Whatever was haunting her when she stepped into the bar has returned, and it matters to me. I want to change the look in her eyes because I see too much of my own ghosts in them.

"So now what?" I ask.

She tilts her head at me. "What do you mean? I had my cocktails, and now I go back to my house." Her eyes are hazy, and I know she's feeling the buzz.

"House?" *Interesting.* I was certain news of an American living here would travel quickly. "Do you live here?"

"No." She shakes her head and cracks her neck from one side to the other.

"Then what do you mean *house*?" I ask, fully intrigued now.

"I'm renting a house for a week. There weren't many hotels to choose from."

"Try none." I laugh. "Other than the room above the pub and the inn, but you don't want to stay there."

"Oh, really?" she deadpans.

"It's a bit dodgy. As is the room upstairs."

She glances down at the beer-stained counter. "You think?" She laughs again, and the sound has my lips tipping up. She's gorgeous, but even more so when she smiles and laughs.

"So what brings you to our humble abode? It's not often that we have American visitors."

"I can't imagine why." She rolls her eyes, and a full chuckle escapes my mouth. "Must be the lack of options," she assesses.

"Must be." I incline my head. "The truth is, we don't want the hustle of Londoners." I might love the city, but here . . . this is a sanctuary. "The fewer outsiders, the better." With the exception of this intriguing specimen, we rarely have visitors. Although looking her over, I'm not unhappy to have her here.

She could be a great distraction while I'm settling the estate business.

When I have to get away or have business on the property, I seldom have fun distractions. The trips for business are usually terrible, but this woman has the potential to change that.

"So you never said why you're here," I say.

"I'm here on vacation." She doesn't offer any more information about herself, so I do what any bloke would do. I press.

"Are you at least going to tell me your name?"

She nibbles on her lip as Robin pours us our fourth round.

"Oh, come on, love, you can tell me."

She actually groans. "I'm going to have to." Her eyes narrow at me as if I've annoyed her.

"And why is that?"

"So you stop calling me love," she quips and takes a small sip of her drink.

"Again, I'm British . . . it's our version of sweetheart." I lift my own glass, placing it just under my nose to inhale. The aromas make my mouth water as I then lower it and take my own swig.

"But I'm not your sweetheart." She waggles an eyebrow at me. "Fine." She pauses, her eyes looking up as if she's rummaging through her brain to pull out a fake name. "Addy. My name is Addy."

It makes me laugh. "You sure? You don't look too positive."

"It's Addy," she says forcefully.

"Well, Addy"—I let the word trickle off my tongue—"I'm Oliver or Olly, if you like."

"Oliver is fine."

I stare at her for a second, and she opens her mouth. "What?"

"You don't look like an Addy."

"What do I look like?"

"I went to school with an Addy. She was a horrible, mean girl. Awful, really. I was a late bloomer, so I was a few inches shorter than she was, which meant I was her punching bag. You don't strike me as an Addy. You look like a . . . love."

"Jeez, you're impossible." This elicits a chuckle from me. "Call me Addison. Is that better for you? Do I look like an Addison?"

"Yes. Much better. How about another round, Addison?"

"I'm not sure . . ."

"If you're worried about driving, I can give you a lift home."

"One, that doesn't help at all because then you'd be driving drunk. And secondly, I have transportation." This woman gets more fascinating, which is a dangerous complication from just trying to get her in my bed.

"Well then, there's no issue now, is there? Just stay and have one more cocktail. Live a bit."

She lets out another sigh. "Okay."

"Brilliant." I turn back to the bar. "One more round."

One more turns into three more.

Which turns into the most fun I've had in a long time.

Addison tinkers with the dated and completely out of place jukebox in the corner while I sit at the bar waiting for her. The jukebox has been here for as long as I can remember. Apparently, the owner of the pub picked it up on a trip to America, but from the horrible selection, it should have stayed across the pond.

I watch as she makes her choice. She's different from most of the women I know. Sure, when she came in here, she seemed high and mighty, but deep down, I can tell she's different. She's not pretentious. She's actually quite delightful.

When she sits, she smiles a devious smirk that makes her look even more endearing. "What's so funny?" I ask, and then I hear it. The god-awful song she chose. The singer croons about their heart with a Southern accent, and I can't help but laugh too.

"Nice choice."

"I thought so."

Suddenly, she's off her chair and standing beside the bar and dancing. And if that wasn't enough, she's singing too, and off-tune to boot. She sounds like a screeching bird. Her body sways with the music, and before long, she's gravitated to me. I'm not sure if she realizes it, but with her eyes closed, she is directly in front of me now.

Her body is so close that I can feel her move with each beat of the music.

The desire to reach out and touch her is all-consuming, and I wonder if she would welcome it. Needing to know, I move to touch her, and as I do, she opens her eyes.

The green of her irises is almost gone as she stares at me, a warm flush spreading across her face.

She does.

Equipped with that knowledge, I stand and then pull her toward me, moving my body with hers.

When that song ends, her next selection starts, and I let myself smile at this one. At least this one is not so bad.

"Come on . . . I know you know the words," she shouts above the familiar song.

"I have no idea what you're talking about."

That's a lie. I have traveled to the States enough to know the Holy Bible of songs. So with another lift of my glass and one more shot, I join in.

Belting out the lyrics I would never dare utter in anyone else's company. But I feel normal with this woman. I feel free. I feel like singing and making an arse of myself, and I love it.

With one arm swinging in the air, Addison sings into a pretend microphone with her other hand. I step in and grab my own "mic," singing along with her.

"Don't stop believin'!"

With each line of the song, I loosen up, immersing myself in the world this woman has cast around me. There's no work. No family business. There's no title and no family obligations.

I can just be me. Whoever that may be.

CHAPTER FOUR

Addison

"TIME TO GO HOME." I MOVE TO SIGNAL FOR MY BILL, BUT I feel Oliver's hand touch my shoulder.

"It's on me," he says as he nods to the bartender. "On my tab, Robin."

Normally, I would make a show of objecting, but in my current state of inebriation, I don't bother. Instead, I grab my purse and stand, but stumble instead, a full laugh escaping my mouth as I do. Lifting my hand, I try to stifle it, but that too is a lost cause.

"You are not driving, love." He reaches his hand out to steady me. His fingers wrap around my wrist, the rough pads of his fingers sending shivers up my spine and making me feel lightheaded from the heat radiating between us.

"Addison," I remind him. Not love. I am no one's love. "And you're not driving me," I respond, trying to remove his hand from my wrist. I need to break this connection. Just the touch of his hand makes me feel things, and I don't want to. Anything more will be bad.

"You're sauced."

I lift a challenging eyebrow, and then I nod. "I am."

Then the reality dawns on me. I am drunk. Very drunk. In a foreign country, unable to drive . . . *Shit*, I'm going to have to call someone to pick me up. I let out a groan.

"What's wrong?"

I don't answer right away, my mouth opening and closing like a drowning fish. Placing my head in my palm, I groan because I don't want to call Jasmine to pick me up.

"I can get you home."

"I'm sure you can, Romeo." I roll my eyes.

"Not like that . . ." His voice breaks midsentence as if in shock that I would assume that. But that's not what I meant, so I clarify.

"I'm not getting in a car. You're drunk, too."

"Not that drunk"—he shrugs—"but I have an idea."

"Oh, this I've got to hear." I sit motionless, waiting. He leans in closer, a smirk lining his perfect face.

"Let's get food," he says, and the corded muscles in my neck loosen. That was not what I was expecting, and he chuckles because he knows it. "That'd sober us up nice and well."

"This village is the size of my hand. Where are we going to get food?"

"At the inn."

I lift my hand to my forehead and then shake my head back and forth. "Jeez, do I have dumb American written on my face?" I say softly, but the edge in my voice is very apparent. "I'm not going to the inn with you."

He lifts his hand in surrender but never stops smiling. He's clearly having a good time riling me up.

"Not even if I promise to be a good lad?"

Yep. He is. And then, to make matters worse, he smiles. *Damn dimple.* When he smiles, I find it impossible to think. It's bad enough that I'm already drunk, but does he have to smile like that?

Why does he have to be so fun and make me forget? That's what he does . . . he smiles, and I forget.

His dimple should come with a warning label.

"You think?" His voice cuts through my inner ramble.

Shit.

Shit.

Shit.

"I just said that out loud?"

"Yep."

"That too?" My God, this man has me in knots. Not that the scotch helped matters. I'm not used to drinking like this. That's the reason and not his dimple or his smirk. And certainly not the way his blue eyes appraise me like I'm naked before him—a banquet—and he's going to eat me alive.

"Come on, Addy, what do you have to lose? In life, you can live, or you can exist. So how about we live a little . . . ?"

He reaches into his pocket and pulls out a coin, or I guess a pence. We are in England, after all. "Heads, you do something crazy. Heads, you come with me to the inn."

My eyes widen.

"For food," he clarifies. "For the best fish and chips in the village."

"Probably the only place that serves it in the village," I deadpan.

"Semantics." He smirks that sinful smirk and then proceeds to throw the coin in the air. I watch as it flips, and he catches it in his palm and then places it on the back of his hand.

When he shows it to me, the flare of excitement erupting in my belly is the complete opposite reaction I should be having to losing.

"Fine, let's go . . . Romeo."

"If I'm Romeo, does that make you Juliet?"

"Hardly. We aren't enemies and I'll never drink poison for you."

"Argh, hate to spoil it for you, but . . ."

"Yes, I know the story of Romeo and Juliet. Jeez. Plus, that would also require you to climb up my balcony and sprout sonnets to me."

His eyes gleam at my words. "Point me in the right direction."

"Har, har, har," I chide, and before I can say another word, he encases my hand in his.

"Your chariot awaits."

"I thought we were walking?" I allow him to hold my hand as I follow him toward the door.

"We are. I was just being clever."

"Kind of missed the mark."

"Clearly. Come on, let's go." He pulls me out through the doorway and into the summer air. The temperature has dropped, thankfully. What was once sweltering has cooled to what I would imagine is seventy degrees or less.

"Can you walk in those?" he asks, looking down at my shoes.

"Of course, I can." But as my heel hits the cobblestone, I tilt and angle to crash down. Instead, his hand shoots out, and he holds me up by the arm. When I right myself, I expect him to let go, but he grips me tighter, putting his other arm around my waist.

It feels good to be in his arms.

"Are you sober yet?" he asks, watching me not so delicately shove another piece of cod into my mouth.

"Nearly," I say around another bite.

"What did that poor fish do to deserve such torment?" He smothers a laugh, and I have the sudden urge to throw something at him.

"What?"

"You're an absolute glutton," he teases.

"Am not," I say, throwing a fry at his head.

He ducks, missing my attempt. "You might be." He laughs.

I narrow my eyes at him, pointing my fork in his direction. "You said it's the best fish in town, and you might have been accurate."

He grins, and our eyes lock on each other. At that moment, something shifts. Of course, he's good-looking, but up until this point, there was not a shot in hell that I'd let this go beyond a meaningless flirt, but if he looks at me like that one more time, I could be swayed. A man like him could convince a girl to lose herself—for at least *one* night.

"When you're done, let's take a walk."

"Where to?" I ask, suddenly nervous that this may go too far.

As if he senses my unease, he replies, "Just a walk, Addison. I won't take things further . . . unless you ask for it."

I believe him.

"Have you seen my shoes?"

He stands and grabs my hand. "You'll be fine."

"And how is it going to be okay?"

"Trust me."

And that's the crazy thing. I shouldn't, but I do, so I let him pull me up to standing. He keeps my hand in his, pulling my arm into his elbow, and escorts us out of the inn.

The moment we hit the cobblestone, the ground beneath me disappears as I'm lifted into the air.

"What are you doing?" I squeal.

"Keeping you safe like the gentleman I am." He continues to carry me. The small lights from the lamps on the street flicker, and soon, they fade away.

I probably should be concerned, but I'm not. Surprisingly, I actually feel safe in his arms.

Instead of wondering where we are going, I tilt my head up and stare at the night sky. It isn't often I have the time to appreciate it.

"It's beautiful," I whisper.

"It is," he responds.

I pull my gaze down and find him looking at me instead. Again, I should be worried by the way he looks at me, but I'm not. Instead, I find myself smiling. "Not me, silly." I lift my hand up. "The stars."

"They are rather bright tonight."

"I've never seen them so bright."

"Really? Do they not have stars where you're from?" he jests. "Where is this strange country that you hail from?"

"Of course, they do, but you can't see the stars in Manhattan that well."

Oliver stops walking, and I look up at him. I can't see the color of his eyes, but I know he's staring at me.

"Is that where you're from?" he asks as if I've given him a precious piece of information about myself.

"It is."

"And you're here for holiday . . . but there's something else, isn't there?"

The oxygen in my lungs starts to evaporate from the real reason I'm here, but I'm not sure what to say or even how to say it. So instead, I go for denial.

"I don't know what you mean." My voice comes out shaky, and I know even without looking into my eyes that he can hear the lies.

He takes a few more steps and then sets me down. Now sitting on a patch of land, God knows where, I lie back on the grass. It's dark, too dark to see anything but the night sky above. A part of me wonders if we're trespassing on private property, but another part, an even bigger part, doesn't care.

He lies beside me. He's close, so close. I can feel the way he inhales and then exhales. Neither of us speak as seconds, minutes, an hour might pass, but I have no idea because all I can think about is how his pinky touches mine, and I wonder if this will be the moment when he kisses me.

Do I want him to?

I don't even know.

With our heads facing the sky, my heart pounds in my chest. My breaths come faster than I want from his proximity. I can hear his breathing, and I'm sure he can hear mine.

He never does cross the divide. No matter how much I will his hand to touch mine, to take mine in his and go back on his promise, he doesn't. He keeps the promise, and while a part of me is thankful, a bigger part of me wishes he would.

When I can't take the tension, I open my mouth to speak. "Do you live near here?"

"No, I grew up here, but now I live in London," Oliver responds.

"It's so beautiful here. How can you leave?"

"Sometimes"—he pauses, and I wonder why—"sometimes you have to leave. Sometimes, the memories are too much . . ."

The air around us grows heavy with his confession as though the weight of the world rests on his shoulders. I don't know his pain, but I do understand pain.

"I don't know what you're running from, but you were right before. There is another reason I'm here," I admit on a sigh. Under the lights above, I decide to trust this stranger with a part of my heart I don't often show people. "This weekend . . . a door to my past closed, and like you, I'm running too."

"I'm sorry," he whispers back. "Do you want to talk about it?"

I know the sincerity I hear is real, and the thought comforts me. Knowing he wants to listen gives me peace and calms the sadness inside me.

"Not really. I'd rather enjoy the stars."

"So let's just have this one night when we don't have to be anything but Addison and Oliver. Let's pretend the rest doesn't exist."

Quiet descends again, and this time, I welcome it.

Our eyes lock, and although I can't see much beyond the moon reflected in his irises, I'm thankful we're pretending. I'm thankful we can spend this time together just being and not have to think about whatever's haunting us.

The pounding in my head is the only reason I know I haven't died. Although it's very possible I will. I haven't been this hungover in forever. Years, maybe.

I don't often drink, nor do I let loose. But last night was exactly what I needed. I needed to get away from New York because staying home and drinking away my sorrows wasn't an option.

If I had, my brothers would have known the news affected me, and I didn't want anyone to know. But how could it not when Spençer Lancaster's wedding was splashed on every magazine in the city?

So here I am now, going to see a property that has been in our family since the 1980s but not touched or developed because, as much as I pretend I'm here for business, I'm really here to nurse a broken heart.

As I'm still lying in bed, my phone starts to ring on the table beside me. Reaching across the mattress, I pull it toward me and look at the screen. It's my mother.

"Hey, Mom," I answer. "Are you okay?"

In my rush to leave New York, I never checked in with my mother. Ever since my father died, she hasn't been the same. She used to laugh and smile, but now she is raw and empty as if a shadow lingers above her. I miss my mother.

"I just wanted to know if you had dinner plans?"

The walls around my chest tighten as I realize she's lonely, and in my own selfishness, I hadn't thought of her.

"I'm so sorry. I'm actually not in New York . . . Do you want me to call—"

"I'll be fine, Addison," she responds. "Where are you?"

"I'm in England. Actually." I pause, wondering if now is a good time to ask, but since she's on the phone, I should. "I meant to call you and ask you something."

"What is it, dear?"

"Dad . . ." I hate talking about Dad, afraid that the mere mention of his name will set her off.

"I'm not made of glass. You can talk to me about your father." Her voice sounds stronger than normal, so I ask the question that's been bothering me the last few days.

"While researching some of the properties we own, I came across a property in England, one that Dad never mentioned. It's in Wiltshire. Do you happen to know anything about that?"

"Wiltshire," she repeats to herself, her voice lowering in thought. "I remember him not liking the place."

"Really? It's beautiful here."

"I remember him saying something about the previous landowner. Something about despising him. That he looked down on your father."

"Then why did he keep it?"

"I can't remember." I let out a sigh at her answer. Mom, forever eager to please, makes an effort for me.

"But I'll try to remember. I'm sure it'll come to me."

"Thanks," I respond.

"I'll let you go."

"If you need me—"

"I'll be fine. I love you, Addison."

"Love you too, Mom." I hang up, and with a stretch of my arms, I lift off the bed and pad into the bathroom to freshen up. I don't bother with clothes or makeup because Jasmine and Marcus have seen me at my worst.

The flight across the ocean to get here was not my finest hour. I never cry in front of anyone, but once the plane took off and New York was behind us, I couldn't hold back the tears.

Even though I normally stay at a luxury hotel when I travel for business, the house we rented has character. The home is spacious, but its thatched roof and stone facade resemble a cottage from the nineteenth century rather than a modern home.

I like it.

It makes me believe anything is possible.

A fairy-tale cottage where I can find the strength I need to go back to New York and be Addison Price again.

Because right now, I'm not her. Right now, I'm a version of myself I don't recognize. Last night, I was even more so, but this could be just what I need.

Telling that complete stranger about my life and admitting out loud that I ran, felt cathartic . . .

My brain starts to hurt from thinking this much after a night of drinking.

Lord, I am hungover. Plus, it's hot.

I fan my face as I walk down the narrow hallway and descend the stairs. The only issue I think I might have with this place is, apparently, air conditioners are not commonplace in the English countryside.

Once in the kitchen of the large property we've rented, I find Jasmine. "Morning," I grumble, that hangover intensifying by the minute.

She turns around at my voice and tracks my steps, amusement flickering in her stare. "Rough night?" she asks, her mouth twitching with the smile she's trying to hide.

"You could say that," I say as I take a seat at the kitchen table and do something I never do . . . I pull my legs up and sit cross-legged. I'm not at all acting like myself, but I'm too hungover to care.

"Coffee?" She lifts a mug up, and I nod.

"God, yes."

She chuckles as she walks to the counter. Jasmine is more than an assistant. She's like the little sister I never had. With two overprotective brothers, Jasmine is a breath of fresh air. Plus, I don't have many friends—only a few from college—so Jasmine fills that void too.

I see my other friends once a week, give or take, or at least when I'm in town. Sometimes, I go for a month without seeing them because I travel so much. I basically live out of my suitcase, but since Jasmine travels with me, she's taken on a lot of roles for me. And right now, the main one is the smell coming from the kitchen.

Coffee.

As I lift the mug to my mouth, my phone rings, so after I take a sip, I press the answer button. "Please tell me you didn't go to Europe to escape the Lancaster wedding when we need you most?"

"I-I . . . no," I whisper. My heart thumps in my chest rapidly at hearing that name.

"Addison," Grayson's stern voice scolds me over the phone.

"Don't Addison me," I say with defiance. *I have a right to a crushed heart.*

"Well, then don't make business decisions based on your heart," he retorts.

"I didn't leave because—"

"Addison," he snaps.

"Grayson," I respond back, daring him to start with me. After a deep breath, I continue, "Dear brother, if I was still hung up on Spencer, would I be here looking at a potential property for his next hotel?"

"Yes. You're a masochist when it comes to Spence. That's exactly what you would be doing on his wedding day. It's time to move on, Addison."

"I have," I shout into the phone a bit more aggressive than I mean to. But at least now I might get my point across.

"Mm-hmm." It's obvious he doesn't believe me.

"I met a man last night. Who's still hung up now?"

"*You.*"

Honest to God, I wish you could divorce your brother. Is

that a thing? *Divorcing one's brother?* "Yes," I repeat. He's quiet for a second. I can hear him take a deep breath over the line, and then he sighs.

"And how did that go?"

"Great!" Although, admittedly, maybe I shouldn't have shouted that.

"If it went so great, then why are you on the phone this morning talking to me?" the bastard responds. I love my brother, but he always sees through my bullshit, no matter how hard I try to keep it from him.

"Not everyone has one-night stands, Gray. Some people just like to talk."

"I'm aware. I believe they have a name: losers."

"You're gross, Gray. You can't say stuff like that to me. I'm your sister."

"Sure, I can. I'm your brother, and I love you." His voice is soft and sincere. "I want you to have fun. Move on."

"Didn't you hear me? I have . . ." I don't even buy my own lies, so no way does he believe me.

"If you say so."

"I've been saying so the entire conversation. I'm here for business, and then I'll be back."

"Whatever, Addison. Do what you've got to do." He sighs. "I'll speak to you later?"

"Yes. Oh, and Grayson, call Mom. Bye," I say and then abruptly hang up. *Why is it so hot in this damn house?*

I stand beside the table and pull my robe away from my body to cool down. The sound of the fabric echoes through the air as I frantically pull at it and sigh at the same time.

"Why is it so hot in here?" My voice or maybe my groans make Jasmine turn toward me. She places the frying pan on the stove.

"Are you okay?"

"Aren't you dying over there? I'm not even by the stove, and I'm dying. It's an inferno in this place." I wave my hands in my face.

"It's not that warm."

"Are you serious? I can barely breathe."

She walks over to the fridge and pulls out a bottle of water. I don't even bother drinking it. Instead, I place it on the back of my neck to feel the chill.

The condensation collecting on my exposed skin causes goose bumps to break out on my flesh. *God, it feels so good.*

"Better?" Jasmine asks.

I let out a sigh of contentment. "So much. Thank you."

Now that I'm cooler, I realize what a scene I made. I don't know what came over me. *Sure you do*, an incessant voice screams, *all the talk of Spencer, of working with him.*

Maybe Gray is right. Maybe I shouldn't. *Maybe I am making a big mistake.* I shake the thought away. I'm here now, in England, only miles from the property. I'm here to survey my land and see if I can build on it. I need to keep busy, and this is what I do best.

Regardless if I loved him once.

Regardless if it ended and broke my heart.

Regardless if he chose her.

This is my job. Nothing, not even a wounded soul, will stop me from work. Doing this and seeing if I can do this will prove I'm over him. It will prove I can keep my personal life separate from business.

Pulling the bottle away from my neck, I open it and take a swig. "I need to get dressed to go into town," I say over my shoulder, needing to get away from everyone, including myself and my own monsters.

"You're not going to eat breakfast?" Jasmine asks from the kitchen.

"No time," I mutter back, already walking away.

"What do you have to do this morning?" she shouts after me. "There's nothing on the books."

"Impromptu meeting with the surveyor," I lie. But as soon as I leave here, I'll change my appointment for today. I can't just sit around here doing nothing, or I'll go crazy.

"Your meeting is tomorrow." She knows I'm lying, but that doesn't stop her tiny voice from bellowing through the house.

"Hence the word impromptu," I respond, sarcasm dripping off my words.

She lets out a laugh. "Fine." She throws her hands up. "Go."

I know I'm being impulsive and impossible—the opposite of how I normally act—but truth be told, I don't care. I need air.

The English countryside can fix anything . . .

CHAPTER FIVE

Oliver

I'M BARELY AWAKE. I CAN'T EVEN OPEN MY EYES BECAUSE MY pounding headache feels like a freight train.

It was worth it, though, even if I hadn't expected it. Nor did I expect to meet her. But in the end, I wasn't me last night. I was just a normal bloke having a go at a gorgeous American.

Would it have been nice to bring her home? Sure. It would have been even better if we'd shagged. Even some heavy petting would have done the trick.

Alas, maybe in another time.

Another life.

And definitely another American.

Unfortunately, that means I'm waking up with a hard and unsatisfied cock, so I guess it will be a cold shower for me.

From across the room, I can hear my mobile going off, and the sound of it vibrating across the nightstand pulls me out of my thoughts. Who would call me this early in the bloody morning?

With great reluctance, I pull myself up. If I thought my headache was bad, it's even worse now as I hear the blaring sound of someone calling. Trudging forward, I reach for my phone.

Mum.

My mother always calls at the most inopportune time. Doesn't she realize I might be hungover?

Apparently not.

"Good morning, Mum," I groan, not at all happy to hear from her.

"Good afternoon, Oliver." It's obvious from her tone she's not impressed with me. It's also obvious from my tone that she woke me. "Don't you think you should be up and about?"

"Don't you think you should mind your own business?" I mutter back.

"And don't you think you should be taking care of business?"

"I was just about to," I answer from where I'm lying down. Thankfully, she can't see me, or she would know I'm full of shit.

"Funny, it sounds like you're just waking up," she clips.

"Well, that's debatable." I let out a long-drawn-out yawn, officially confirming that yes, I am, in fact, still in bed. I'm a wanker like that. "Mother, what can I do for you . . . ?" I trail off sarcastically for emphasis. I sit up in my bed, my back hitting the suede-tufted headboard as the sheet drops to my waist.

"Don't you think it's time you settle down and stop partying?"

"Jeez, Mum." I pull my mobile away from my ear and start shaking it in the air. *This woman.* "Just get to the point of this call."

"More pressing matters?"

"Mum . . ." I don't have time for her gripes today. I mean, maybe I do, but I just don't want to.

"Fine. The damn American is here."

Her voice is harsher than normal, but what did I really expect. She's hard-pressed to buy this property and can't see past her need, no matter how futile I find this endeavor.

"Already?" I ask, but I'm not very interested. The only American I'm interested in escaped me last night. Damn shame. Too bad her American isn't my American.

"Yes, but I was wrong. It's not him. It's his daughter."

Daughter? Did she say daughter? Could she mean Addison? No . . .

I drop the phone out of my hand.

What would be the odds? Addison said she's here on holiday. Did she lie?

With a shake of my head, I pick it back up from the bed. "Which American are you referring to?"

"As if it isn't bad enough that they have what's ours, now she's here surveying our land."

"*What*?" I really have no idea what she's talking about.

"The land. Her land. Our land." With each new sentence, her voice rises, and by the time she stops, she's practically seething. "The Prices must have finally decided to do something with it, and I need to know what," she hisses.

Regardless of her tone, I catch her intent. Her land. Our land. The American. It has to be Addison. The odds of it being another American are slim, especially around these parts. If we were in London at the family home there, it wouldn't be odd at all, but here in the country . . .

No one comes to these parts who doesn't belong. I was so intrigued by her because her presence was so odd. That was the reason she stuck out in our quaint village.

She has to be the same American my mum is going on about.

Needing to know more, I take a seat, phone in hand, and cross my right leg over my knee. "So, Mum, now you have me curious. Tell me everything you know about her."

"All I know is that Addison Price is as ruthless as her father."

After hearing what my mum had to say, I now know that my American is, in fact, the American my mum was going on about, and I know what I need to do—get close to her and convince her to sell the land.

Only . . . I can't reconcile the ruthlessness Mum accused Addison of with the woman who sang at the top of her lungs with me last night. I can betray someone ruthless, but the woman from last night . . .

I shake the thought away and remind myself of Mum's sacrifices. She isn't perfect, but choices define people, and if I considered all the sacrifices Mum made for me, I'd remember she's the best person I know.

No longer hungover, I get dressed and head out for the day. According to my information, Addison Price, as I now know her to be, has a meeting tomorrow with a land surveyor. Getting into my car, I head over to the property to look at what I'm dealing with.

It takes me fifteen minutes, down winding backroads, to find the barren strip of land. The grounds are damp from an early morning rain, and the sky is gray and cloudy.

Typical.

Looking out, I find the visibility to be low amidst all the hovering fog. I've often forgotten that once upon a time, this stretch of land was part of the entail.

Once upon a time, it belonged to my father, and before that, to my father's father, but it apparently belongs to someone else now. And from the sound of it, it belongs to Addy. Addison. Addison Price, to be exact.

I didn't recognize her yesterday. The name didn't ring any

bells. But then again, she didn't recognize me either. Now that I have spoken to my mother, nothing else makes as much sense.

The Prices are one of the largest independent property holders in the world. It never registered, though, and why would it. I don't travel to America often; I try my hardest to stay out of the media, and I don't pay attention.

As I'm pulling up to the land, tiny streams of sun push their way through the clouds. That's when I notice a car pulled over on the road in the distance.

A black Mercedes.

I stop and then get out of my car. Making my way to it, I see it's empty, so I set out to find the owner of said vehicle.

It doesn't take me long.

As I trudge through the grass, I see Addison all by herself. If I thought she was beautiful yesterday, she's even more lovely in the daylight. The way the early morning rays of light hit her face makes the red highlights of her brown locks glitter and bounce.

Raising her hand to cover her eyes from the glare, she looks in my direction. "Need help?" I ask.

"What?" she hollers as she keeps walking until she is directly in front of me.

"Do you need help?"

"No. I was just looking."

"At what?"

She shakes her head, obviously not willing to tell me more.

What a bloody shame.

Last night's missed opportunity to sink into her will now never happen. There is no way I can shag her now, knowing she owns the land my family wants. I would have liked to play with her a little, but now . . .

An idea slips through my head.

Why can't I? Maybe if I cozy up to her, she will be more apt to tell me her plans. "So you're here . . ." I pause. "For more fun?"

She stares at me blankly.

"What are you doing walking these grounds?" Maybe I'll get lucky, and she'll tell me what she's doing, and then I can skip right to the part about fucking her.

"Goddammit," she groans, and at first, I think she's talking to me. Then I notice her pulling on her pant leg.

"Everything okay over there?" I ask but don't move to help her. Instead, I watch, arms crossed in front of my chest as she struggles to dislodge her shoe from the mud.

"No," she responds, bending down and giving me a better view of her arse, a delectable one at that.

"Care to elaborate?"

"I'm stuck." I expect her to be angry, but once again, she surprises me.

She laughs.

With the knowledge I have of her now, seeing her like this and remembering her last night takes me completely off guard.

She's different from what I would expect of a Price.

From all the things I have heard over the years of the Prices, they are pretentious "new money" who treated my mother with complete disrespect.

But this goddess standing before me wearing stilettos is far from the stories I've heard of her family.

She might look the part of the stuck-up heiress, but the parts I see of her now, stuck in the mud with a smile on her face, don't reconcile.

"Aren't you going to help me?" She looks over her

shoulder while still trying to get her foot out of the mud. I step up beside her and grip her waist, pulling her toward me. When she becomes dislodged, her body presses flush with mine. Her chest rises and falls against my own, and the smell of her perfume drifts in through my nostrils. She smells divine, like a crisp, warm summer day and a bouquet of wildflowers.

What the hell is wrong with me? I shouldn't be smelling this woman, not when I know what I know. Damn pity she's the enemy now because I'd much rather lay her down right here on this property—*the property*—and fuck her.

Instead, I'm supposed to hunt for information on her intentions.

Bloody shame, all right.

"Why are you here?" I ask her again. I know the answer, but I need to steer my brain away from her body, so I step back and look down at her.

"I might have left a tiny bit of information out last night . . . This is actually my land. I'm not really here for vacation. I'm here for work," she responds, opening the forum for all the questions I want to ask her.

This is perfect.

I can ask her everything, and then I can report my findings, and once the conflict is out of the way . . .

I'll get into her pants. I'm a prick like that.

"Can I take you out to dinner?"

"I'm still hungover from last night. I can't even imagine ingesting alcohol again."

"Then we don't have to drink."

Her smile slips off her face. "I'm not sure . . ." She bites her lip.

Just as she says those words, another car pulls over on the side of the small dirt road. This time, it's a beat-up truck. The door swings open.

"Hello, Olly," Harry, the surveyor, says to me. The same surveyor who was passed out at the pub last night and never did get introduced to Addison.

I give him a tight smile as I widen my eyes. He gives me a small nod. He won't be saying my full name or title. He knows better. And I won't mention that the property surveyor is a tosser who likes to get pissed and also happens to be on my mum's payroll.

Addison looks from Harry and then back at me. "Do you know everyone?"

"It is a small village. Plus, we all drink at the pub." Harry tightens his lips, trying to hold back a chuckle.

"Ah, the pub," Addison mutters under her breath, her voice edged with sarcasm.

"Your favorite place on earth." I laugh.

"Are you ready, Ms. Price?" Harry says to Addison, and she pulls her gaze away and looks up at him.

"I should be going. Dinner tonight?" I ask again.

"I can't."

I look into her eyes.

"You know what . . ." She puffs out her cheeks and then blows out. "Okay."

"Brilliant."

Just. Fucking. Brilliant.

CHAPTER SIX

Addison

I DID THE ONE THING I SHOULDN'T, AND NOW I'M PAYING THE price, figuratively and literally. Because not only did it cost me money to have Marcus drive into town and buy me a pint of ice cream, but my body and dress size will suffer as well because I thoroughly intend to eat the whole thing.

Carnal rule #1: Never search TMZ when your ex is getting married.

Carnal rule #2: Never click on the link and scroll through the images.

Because the only solution to said problem is to eat a pint of ice cream, obviously and get drunk.

So that's where I am now. I'm sitting at my kitchen table with a spoon in one hand, deep in chocolate, while the other hand lifts a bottle of merlot to my mouth.

I'm a mess.

Not just a normal mess either. I'm a hot mess. My normally blown-out-to-perfection hair is in a sloppy bun on top of my head, and I've replaced my usual pantsuit with sweats and a tank.

Yep. I'm a mess.

"Are you really going to stay home and eat ice cream?" Jasmine asks as she steps into the kitchen.

"I am." I lift the spoon to my mouth and lick it before returning it to the carton. "And don't forget I'm going to drink this whole bottle of wine too."

She bites her lip while she bobs her head. I must look pathetic to her. Lucky for me, she won't judge me. "Sounds like a fun night," she deadpans.

"It does, right?" I reach my hand out toward her, offering the ice cream. "There's enough for two. Want to get drunk and eat this with me?"

She grimaces at the suggestion. "As appealing as that sounds"—her nose scrunches at the ice cream—"I'm going to have to—"

Her words are cut off by the sound of a knock on the door.

"I'll grab that."

I shrug her off and go back to my ice cream—priorities. A few moments later, I hear the sound of two sets of distinctive footsteps. With the spoon in my mouth, I lift my head, and what greets me makes the spoon drop to the table with a thud.

Oliver.

Oliver in my kitchen.

And I'm eating ice cream with a spoon from the carton.

"Now isn't this quite the sight," he remarks. The signature smirk and dimple included.

"What are you doing here?"

"We have a date." His voice is matter-of-fact as if this is public knowledge and everyone knows.

"I never—"

"You did." His voice is low and smooth, like warm chocolate sauce dripping over my ice cream. Decadent. *Delicious . . .*

And here.

"I never told you where I lived," I add. Sure, I told him I

would go out with him, but since I never gave him my address, I didn't think I'd see him. Drinking away my sorrows and eating until I was sick sounded like a better plan. "How did you even find me?"

"Love," he says as if that nickname is his answer. I place my spoon down and lift an eyebrow. "*Addison,* this is a small village. When an American rents a cottage, it's not hard to find out which one."

"So you're stalking me now?"

"Stalking is quite the accusation. I wouldn't commit to such a strong word."

"Yet, you're here." Looking toward Jasmine for help, I watch as her face bobs back and forth between us as if she's watching a tennis match. Her hand covers her mouth to hide her emotion.

"I'm just picking you up for our date," he retorts.

"A date I planned to ditch."

Cue the dimple. Cue the butterflies in my stomach. Damn smirk.

"Well, that isn't very polite, now is it?"

Jasmine laughs at that, and I want to call her a traitor. "It isn't very nice." She giggles.

"Traitor," I hiss at her, and that makes her laugh even more. "Just go."

"Yes, Addison . . . listen to . . . I'm sorry, I didn't catch your name, darling." At the nickname, the traitor, formally named Jasmine, blushes.

"Fine. I'll go." Without another word, I stalk off to my room to change because Lord knows I can't go out looking like this.

I'm dressed now, and believe it or not, I've brushed my hair and even put on some makeup. Nervously, I pace back and forth. I can't believe I agreed to dinner with Oliver. I don't even know him. He's some random guy I met at a pub, and then got drunk with and ate with, all while making an ass of myself. After he pulled me out of the muddy grass, he flung the question at me. Sure, he helped me today, but dinner? What was I thinking when I said yes?

Your dignity.

You were thinking of your dignity. I wanted him to leave, so I could finish with the surveyor and then take my mud-soaked pants and return to my solitude in the cottage, and the only way to get him to leave was to agree. Now, what do I do? What will we even talk about?

Looking down at my watch, I check the time once more. I've been up here for twenty-five minutes; how much longer until Jasmine sends the search party for me?

Why am I so nervous? It's not like I've never had dinner with a handsome man before or been on a date. Besides, this isn't a date. He knows I'm here alone, and he's just being friendly.

Yeah. Friendly. That's it.

Then why are you imagining your lips locked with his? And why did his large blue eyes seem to undress you with every glance he took today?

I'm on the fourth pass of my room when I hear the knock on the door. My heels clap against the wood as I take the few steps to open it and find Jasmine standing there. *Surprise, surprise.*

"He's waiting."

"I know." Taking the stairs down, I find him standing in the foyer.

"Hello," he greets, his smooth accent seductively rolling the word off his tongue. My cheeks warm at the thought, and I realize this man does something to me. I'm not sure what, but he makes me feel young and free. His lip tips up, and he gives me a smirk that could melt anyone, even me.

"Hi," I respond. "I'm ready now. Let me grab my coat." I step toward the closet, and when I walk back over, he takes my summer coat from my hand and helps me place it over my shoulder. When he does, his fingers skim my bare flesh.

"I didn't say so before, but this house is charming." He smiles as his eyes dart around the space, taking in the foyer, staircase, and parlor room all in view.

"Charming is one word I would use," I say back. He halts his perusal and looks back at me.

"And what other words would you use?" he asks.

"Hot," I deadpan all while lifting my hands and dramatically fanning myself.

"Hot?"

"Yes. Believe it or not, during the day, it's hot," I grumble.

"It has been a warm summer, but at least it cools at night." He touches my jacket.

"Yes, but not enough to keep it cool during the day."

"And most homes in England don't have central air." He shrugs as if it's a well-known fact.

"All things I would have loved to know before renting it."

"Us Brits, leaving all the important things out. Now let's go grab a bite, and I can fill you in on all the other things we leave out . . ."

"Such as?"

"Curious?"

"Always."

"I like that about you," he says, and it makes me smile.

Together, we walk to his car. We both get in, and a silence settles around us.

"So here's the thing," I say, breaking the silence. "Before we start this 'date,'" I air quote, "you should know, I don't really want to be here. To be honest, I'm only here so I don't have to hear Jasmine's lectures and have her harassing me all night."

"Wow. That's some honesty."

"Sorry. It's a fault of mine." I shrug.

"It's okay. I like it. Most women aren't so honest."

"It's a problem. I'm candid and don't mince words. I'm used to getting what I want, and I'm also a pain in the ass to deal with."

"You really are trying hard to sell yourself."

"No reason to sell myself. Just keeping it real," I add.

"Let's just have dinner. Maybe you'll enjoy yourself."

I nod and turn to look out the window as he pulls away from the cottage. We drive for some time, long enough that I know we are out of the small town and in the country.

Reds and pinks burst onto the horizon like an impressionist painting as the afternoon sun begins to set in the distance.

The farther we get, the more I loosen up.

Before long, we take windy roads into a new quaint village. Pulling over, we park, and we both get out. He's by my door with his hand outstretched before I can even take a step. His manners and chivalry cause me to blush.

Once inside the small restaurant, we are shown to our table and sit across from each other. For the first time in forever, I feel lighter. Being here with him helps me forget. Nothing will come of this, but it's a good distraction for the night. Besides, if I wasn't here, I would probably be sitting around and wallowing in self-pity. Instead, I'm drinking, laughing, and, surprisingly, having a great time.

Oliver leans forward, placing his forearms on the table, and cocks his head. "So now that I have you here, tell me something about yourself," he inquires.

"Not much to know," I answer fast and curt. I'm not one to talk about myself, and right now, I like the idea that this stranger doesn't know who I am.

"I find that hard to believe. I'm sure there are plenty of stories to tell."

"How do you figure?"

"To start, you're here in a foreign country," he says with an eyebrow raised.

"And . . . is traveling for work really that strange?"

"No, I guess it's not weird. Is it just you and Jasmine?"

"Yeah." I don't tell him about my driver because I like that this man likes me for me. Why ruin it by letting him know too much about me? It's not often I'm with a man who just wants to spend time with me without ulterior motives. It's only one night out, so why can't I enjoy myself?

"So what are you working on?" he asks.

I let out a sigh. "Do we have to ruin a perfectly good night by talking about work?"

He lifts his brow. "You think tonight's perfect?" He winks. If I thought the dimple was dangerous, it's got nothing on that damn wink. If he was sexy before, seeing him wink with that sexy smirk across his face just increased it tenfold.

"Well, maybe not perfect."

"Not up to snuff?" he jokes.

"Hardly," I respond back sarcastically, enjoying the playful banter.

"I'll remember that." He taps his temple with his finger as if he's storing it to memory.

"Promises, promises." I laugh.

"So back to work."

"Jesus. You're like a dog with a bone. I'm doing a tour to check out all my properties," I respond noncommittally. I can't really tell him the inner monologue screaming in my brain.

How do you say, "*I'm here because my ex got married?*" How do you say, *"I'm here avoiding the same ex I almost word vomited to you about when I was drunk,"* and when that's all said and done, how do you say, "*I'm here trying to prove I have moved on by surveying my property to see if it's a good location for his next hotel?*" Instead, I bite the inside of my cheek and don't say any of that. I smile and turn the tables on him.

"And what is it *you* do exactly?" It's my turn to lean forward, place my arms on the table, and incline my head.

"I thought we weren't talking about work?" he chides, shaking his head in mock disbelief.

"How come you're exempt?"

"Because I'm British." A smile spreads again across his face, lightening the mood.

"So what should we talk about then?" I say as my hand reaches out to the goblet of water in front of me, and I absent-mindedly start running my finger along the edge. "I don't really know how to do this," I admit on a sigh. "I don't do this often."

"Do what? Have dinner?"

"Stop being a smart-ass. Of course, I have dinner. I just don't do it often with a man," I say.

He stares at me, his blue eyes narrowing as he appraises me, and then he shakes his head. "I find that hard to believe."

"And why is that?"

A gravelly chuckle escapes his mouth, and it causes me to focus on his lips. Warmth spreads inside me.

"Fishing for compliments, are we?" He smirks, watching me watch him.

"What . . . no. I didn't—"

"I'm just having a go. But yes, you are lovely, so I can hardly imagine your dinner card is not always full."

"It's not actually. Most men . . ." I stop, my cheeks burning and my blood pounding in my veins when I remember all the men in my past who couldn't deal with my success.

"Most men what?" He leans forward, his voice heavy with curiosity.

I stiffen, but I allow the words to flow no matter how uncomfortable I am. "Are intimidated by me."

"Their loss is my gain. And, Addison, I don't get intimidated. So you have nothing to worry about."

Needing to change the subject, I ask him, "So now that you know what I do, what do you do for a living? Why don't you tell me about yourself?"

His eyes widen at my question. "I thought you didn't want to talk about work."

"I didn't. But I hardly think it's fair that I told you I'm in real estate, and you won't give me any information about yourself."

"That's not true. I'm happy to tell you about myself . . ." He winks, his voice dripping with innuendo.

"Okay, killer. What is it you do?"

"I do a little bit of this and a little bit of that," he answers.

"Vague much?" I deadpan, and it elicits a wicked laugh. One that makes my insides melt into a puddle of desire.

Shit.

I'm in trouble.

"I take beautiful Americans out to dinner." His words come out smooth like melted chocolate you want to dip your finger in and take a taste of. The type you know is bad for you, but you can't help but be tempted.

What's wrong with me? I don't go to dinner with handsome men and get reduced to a pile of melted hormones at a table. I am above this.

I try to right myself by straightening my back and trying to let the high-powered independent woman facade fall once more. That's my protection. My armor. I will not be reduced to a lusty nitwit at the table because this dashing Brit smirks.

Dammit. Referring to him as dashing isn't helping, so instead, I push all thoughts of his looks away and try again. "Do you even have a job?"

When he doesn't answer right away, I roll my eyes. "Got it. No job." I laugh.

"I never said I didn't have a job." He smirks, and now the goddamn dimple forms on his right cheek. The one that if I stare too long will certainly make me combust.

Lucky for me, I'm too busy trying to figure out what he does for a living to dwell on the divot in his scruffy cheek.

"Then what is it?" I smile and then lean forward onto the table, focusing my gaze on his, and then lift a pretend microphone up to my mouth as if I'm interviewing him. "So what is it you do for work, sir?" I say playfully. "What are you ambitious about?"

"I'm ambitious about you," he says with a straight face, and I can't help the groan that escapes.

"Wow. Does that line work over here?" I chide.

"Isn't it working now?" He grins.

"No."

Lies. Of course, it does. Because it doesn't matter what he says or, better yet, what I say if he keeps smirking at me from across the table like that. It wouldn't matter if he did nothing all day, every day, as long as he keeps looking at me.

It's official. I am not the woman who left America. No, I'm the woman who crossed the Atlantic and became a fool.

"Then why are your cheeks flushed?" he asks, but he doesn't even try to hide his amusement of this situation.

"Really?"

"Yes." He stops for a minute then lets out a deep breath.

"Fine. If you don't want to tell me what you do—" I throw my hands up in the air.

"It's more fun this way," he interrupts.

"Then tell me one thing you're ambitious about . . . other than me." At this point, I'm not above begging to find out more about him. To see what else makes him smile. *Lord, what happened to me?* I swear having this man stare and smile at me is like I had a lobotomy.

"I'm ambitious about cooking."

His answer surprises me. I tilt my head and let my gaze roam over him. "Seriously?"

"Yes. Is it so shocking?" he says before letting his mouth curve up.

"Are you a chef?"

He lifts his brow. "I thought you were dropping the whole career thing. Fine. I'm an M16 agent." He laughs. "See. More fun this way."

"You're impossible."

"I do financial investments. Manage property, like you. See, boring." His shoulders lift with indifference.

"Was that so hard?"

"Yes. Now back to cooking. Yes, I love to cook. No, I am not a chef."

"How did you pick up that trait?" I ask.

"Trait. Something tells me you aren't much of a cook?"

"I don't even know how to cook an egg," I admit on a sigh.

"So your future won't entail being barefoot in the kitchen."

"Har. Har. Har. Maybe I'll hire you since you don't have a job."

"I told you I have a job . . ."

"Fine, I'll hire another chef." I shrug, and he laughs at that. A full-body laugh. One that makes my stomach flutter with butterflies.

The rest of the meal continues much the same. The conversation remains light with nothing deep or meaningful, but it's fun, nonetheless.

As Oliver pays the bill, I take a final bite of my dessert and then lift my phone to check it. Bad mistake. The first headline on the mobile news is a picture. But not just any picture. It's a headline of the exclusive wedding images.

My heart starts to rattle in my chest. The oxygen that I breathed in easily only moments ago is now tight. My chest feels like it's in a vise, my heart constricting as I see Spencer smiling a smile he never gave me. I stand abruptly.

"Where are you going?"

"I need air." Without another word, I storm out toward the street. I can hear the sound of shoes behind me, chasing me, but I pay them no notice. I can't. The walls are closing in around me, and I need air.

As soon as I'm outside, I stop. The world starts to spin, and I fear I might get sick. My eyes close as the air from my lungs comes out in short gasps. With each pull of oxygen, the muscles surrounding my heart tighten, gripping me to the point of pain. In the distance, I can hear the hiss of cars, the sound of a horn, and see the lights flashing. But I'm too far gone in my own memories to notice until arms reach around me and pull me back.

Hot tears burn behind my eyelids as he starts to coo, rubbing my back. "You're okay," he states. But I'm not. How can I be? "You are." Each word comes out forceful as if he knows the doubts in my heart and is forcing me to believe.

"Look at me." I shake my head as reality sets in. I can't look at him, not with what just happened. "Come on, love. Open your eyes." Slowly, I do, and my body shivers. "You're okay. Just breathe."

He continues to stroke my back as I get my bearings back. The world around me comes back into focus—the fact that I'm in the street and that Oliver pulled me out—and I start to shake harder. I don't know what's wrong with me. How could I let this affect me so much?

A hand reaches out and tilts my jaw up, and I'm met with the familiar blue I've been staring at all night. I knew it was him behind me, but seeing his face brings a whole other emotion to the surface. My cheeks are red, and I try to lower my face because I don't want him to see me like this. The truth is, I don't want anyone to ever see me like this.

"Please don't look at me," I whisper.

"There is nothing to be embarrassed about. You can talk to me."

"I had a meltdown . . ."

"Happens to the best of us, love."

"Not me. Well, at least not normally. I'm not sure why I'm acting like this."

"These things happen. Even to me. Sometimes, it feels better to talk about it." He trails circles across my back, and I let him. I allow myself to take his comfort as I open my mouth to try to explain.

"My ex got married this weekend." He places a kiss on my forehead as I tell him this.

"I'm so sorry," he responds as he continues his ministrations on my back. I expect him to press for more information, but he doesn't.

"Aren't you going to ask me why I care . . . ?"

"It's your story to tell. If you want to tell me more, I'm here to listen, but if not, I'll just hold you."

"Okay," I utter back as I bury my head into his chest. I'm hiding from the world just as much as I'm hiding from myself.

He never rushes me; he never talks. He just holds me right there on the street corner. When I'm finally calm, I place my hands on his chest and look up at him.

"I should . . . you should take me home."

"Here's what I think. You have two choices. One: You go back to your cottage, you grab the what, the chocolate ice cream, and wallow in self-pity."

"Or?" I squeak out.

"Come with me and let me make you forget."

A part of me wants to go home and grab a spoon, but I can't. I've already let this go too far.

"Option two."

CHAPTER SEVEN

Oliver

Now that I know who she is and that I can't have her, she's even more enticing. She's now a forbidden fruit I don't just want to eat; no, now she's one I want to snatch from the tree and sink my teeth into.

"So where to now?" she asks timidly. The previously self-assured woman is gone and replaced with a version that seems delicate.

Real.

I like the tough exterior, but this softer version gets under my skin even more.

"We can go back to the pub?" I offer. I still need information, but also I have this intense desire to spend more time with her, so the pub is the perfect place to accomplish both.

I watch as her body tenses. She closes her eyes and then lets out a puff of air.

"Okay."

I take a step toward her. Then I place my hand on the small of her back and lead her toward my parked car.

It doesn't take long, but neither of us speaks. The earlier emotion she displayed still hovers around us, but I want to change the mood. I want her to relax, laugh, and have fun even though I shouldn't. I shouldn't want to see her smile.

I shouldn't want any more than to find out her reason for being here, but seeing her and watching her, I want it, nonetheless.

You're an awful son.

Or maybe you aren't.

Maybe this is exactly what I should be doing. Maybe this will bring me closer to her to see what she plans to do.

I shake my head.

"Everything okay?" she asks from across the seat, and I turn my head to her and make myself smile. It's not hard, though. Something about her makes me want her. But worse than that, something about her makes me want to make her smile and get to know her. I know I shouldn't, but I do, regardless of who she is. I'll deal with the consequences later because tonight, I'm going to have fun.

"Sorry, was just thinking," I mumble back, trying to right myself.

"Thinking about what?"

"About which song I'm going to get you to sing tonight."

"Sing?"

I look back at her, letting my lip lift into a smirk. "Oh, did I forget to mention . . . tonight is karaoke night."

Her mouth drops open, closes, then opens again as she tries to find words to say. "I'm not singing karaoke."

"Typical," I mutter under my breath and continue driving. Just because she laughed at herself in the mud doesn't mean she'll want to make a fool out of herself in public. Not many women in her position would.

Her hand reaches out. "What do you mean?" she asks softly. I expect anger at me calling her "typical," but I'm met with a completely different look. Confusion maybe?

"Do you want to live or exist?" I say as I pull the familiar coin out of my pocket and flip it. "Heads, it is."

"Not that shit again, and what the hell does living have to do with karaoke?" Now, her voice is more forceful. Confusion has made way to annoyance.

"Well, love, you haven't lived until you've had a pint of Guinness and sung your heart out."

I can see her glaring at me from where she sits, deciding that I wasn't insulting; rather, I was just having a playful go at her. So she crosses her arms in front of her chest and inclines her head.

"How come I have a hard time believing you would do something like that?"

"Because you don't know me. But I can assure you, once you do, you'll want to."

"Promises. Promises."

"Just speaking the truth."

With that, we fall into a comfortable silence again. Once we arrive, the pub is alive with people. Normally, I would be worried about my name or the paps finding me, but these are my people, and they don't speak about what I am. *Who* I am. The villages have known me all my life and respect me enough not to ask questions.

"Let's go," I say, stepping out of the car and walking to her side. I swing the door open when she still hasn't gotten out of the car.

She rolls her eyes. "Fine," she huffs out.

"Last time you were here, you sang."

"I was drunk."

"So let's get you pissed."

"I will not object to that." She laughs, cutting the tension in half.

I grab her hand in mine and pull her into the loud bar.

"Look who's here, Blac—" Walter, one of the frequent patrons of the pub, says.

I shake my head at him before he can finish.

"Black?" she asks.

"He likes to call me Blackbeard." I laugh.

"Oh, is that so?"

"It is." Walter quickly follows along. "He's a Blackbeard."

"And why is that?"

"Because my last name is Black." The lie slips off my tongue with ease. A simple lie, but if she knew my real name, Blackthorn, it could be traced back to the land. "And apparently, I always steal the attention of the most beautiful women in the room."

"Ahhh. A player, I see."

I shrug. A player is a better truth than the actual reality. "He's a bloody idiot." I laugh, and she laughs in return. I pull her away and look over her shoulder, nodding once.

He smirks back. He's used to this game. Normally, I don't want women to know who I am or how much money I have. There is a time and a place for those women, and that's in London, so this isn't new to him.

He doesn't see it as a deception. To him, it's for my peace of mind, but to me, it's more. I enjoy being just one of the villagers, and here, with these people, I can do that.

When we step up to the bar, Robin inclines his head to us.

"Same as before?" he asks as he wipes down the counter with a dirty rag.

"Same as always."

"And for the lady?"

I turn to Addison. "I'll have what you're having," she

responds before I can even answer for her. Back to being self-assured, I see.

"And then after the scotch, we'll each have a Guinness," I remind her.

"How could I forget?" she deadpans.

"And singing."

She rolls her eyes at my comment. Smart-arse too.

When the drinks are set in front of us, I push hers to her fingers. Our skin touches for a beat, and I watch as the glow that is present every time I touch her spreads. It makes me wonder what she will look like when I worship her whole body, when my fingers linger everywhere. Shaking the thought away, I motion to our libations.

When we both grab our drinks and drink them, I can tell she's trying to drink it fast to take the edge off. When we finish, I stand and reach out my hand to hers. She takes it, and with her tiny hand in mine, we walk to the stage. It's not really a stage. Actually, it's more of a makeshift stage because it wasn't here before. No, the last time I was here, there was no stage. Just an open floor plan, a few tables, and a few patrons. Nothing like the spectacle tonight. It's as if the entire village is here.

"Come on, time to sing."

CHAPTER EIGHT

Addison

I CAN'T BELIEVE WE'RE DOING THIS.

This is a far cry from my normal night out in New York. For one, I would have never been caught dead in a place like this. For two, singing in public is a hard no. In the city, everyone knows me, and being a successful woman in a man's world is hard enough without giving them ammunition to destroy you.

I would never allow myself to be vulnerable in New York. But here, with this complete stranger, I find myself wanting to be different. I want to pretend I don't have responsibilities, that I don't run a billion dollar empire, and most importantly, that I don't have a broken heart. That I can live.

"Are we really doing this?"

"Of course, we're bloody doing this."

"You. Are. Crazy." I laugh.

When he inclines his head, a piece of his hair falls over his brow. That with his dimple makes him look adorable. I'm not sure how it's possible, but he has this boyish charm I can't help but like. "How so?"

"Singing in public."

"It's just a spot of fun. Don't you want to have fun?" I should turn and run from the mischief sparkling in his eyes, but something tells me not to. Something inside me tells me to stay, let down my hair, and have fun.

He smirks and lifts an eyebrow. "Exist"—he shrugs—"or live." He motions to the microphone.

With a huff, I nod and allow him to take my hand in his and lead me. This isn't me.

But being me hasn't brought me much. Sure, I'm successful. Okay, more than successful. I'm one of the wealthiest women in the world, but other than a full calendar and email, what do I have to show for it? Maybe this is why I was never enough for Spence. Maybe Olivia let down her hair. Maybe she enjoyed life.

His warm hand engulfs mine,and the feeling sends tingles of pleasure up my arm.

"Stop thinking." He pushes me another step until I'm standing in front of the screen and a man beside it.

"Pick," he teases, and I do. It doesn't take long.

Standing with the microphone, I pick my song. Joan Jett. As the words scroll on the screen, I start singing, jumping in the air, and waving my hands.

As I'm belting out the lyrics *I love rock and roll*, I feel Oliver move next to me. His body presses close to mine, and his hands wrap around my hands as he shares my microphone. Together, we sing. *Let go. Live in the moment.*

Just as he asked me to. Just as he wanted.

And with him here with me, it's so easy.

It's invigorating. It breathes a new life into me. One I thought had been forever crushed. But instead, a new flame is rekindled from the ash of my own despair.

CHAPTER NINE

Oliver

After we sing, I offer to take her home. I would like to postpone the inevitable even though I know I shouldn't want to. I've been having fun with her, but there isn't anything else to do here.

"I'm ready," she says, heading out the door. I follow, and then we both slip into the car. My hand rests on the console not far from hers. I can feel the heat of her fingers dancing across my skin, begging me to place my hand on hers.

Something is different now. Something that wasn't there before we sang and let loose. It's like Addison was fighting a battle with herself and letting go helped pick the victor.

During the car ride, an energy courses between us. When I pull over, I look into her eyes. The green is gone, replaced by dark pupils glassy with want.

"Walk me to the door," she whispers, and I nod. Like the gentleman I am, I walk to her side and help her out, my palm flat against her spine.

When we pass through the arch of the front door, before she knows what's happening, I'm pushing her against the wall and stepping into her. I move so close that my chest touches hers before I bend my knees so my face is close to hers. Our lips aren't touching yet. I don't allow them to.

I want her needy. I want her desperate.

The proximity of my lips to hers allows my breath to tickle her. So close that almost no space separates us.

I exhale.

She inhales.

The desire coursing between us is palpable.

Lifting my hand, I run my fingers up her side. The material of her shirt lifts and bunches with the movement until I stop right below her breast.

Her body shakes beneath my ministrations, a whimper escaping her plump lips. Her pupils are dilated, her breathing shallow and heavy as her body trembles. It elicits a groan from my mouth. I can't take another minute of not kissing her, but to have her where I want her, I must. So instead, I hover close to her mouth.

Let her come to me.

It doesn't take her long to cross the imaginary divide, and her lips connect with mine.

Just a taste, I tell myself, before kissing her back and bracketing my arms around her waist.

The kiss is frenzied.

Heated.

Teasing.

I'm sure I'm leaving bruises from how tightly I hold her, from how passionately I kiss her, but I'm desperate. This moment might be fleeting, and I might not get another chance. So if this is my opportunity to play ignorant and be inside her, I'll take it.

Her breaths come out in shallow bursts as I move my hand and start to lift the hem of her skirt. The tip of my finger touches the lace of her thong and pulls it down.

"You want me to fuck you?" I ask. My voice is husky with desire.

"Yes," she moans against my lips.

Turning her so her hands are plastered against the wall, I kick her legs apart and bend her at the hips, tipping her chest forward. Once she's in the position I want, I unbutton my jeans and remove my cock, but I don't fuck her yet. No, I want her begging before I do. She must feel the anticipation because her body shivers and shakes as she waits for me. I trail my finger down her back, across her arse, and then between her legs, teasing my finger at her entrance.

With my other hand, I pull her hair back and allow my mouth to trail soft kisses all the way down to the crook of her neck.

Licking. Biting. Kissing.

"Is this what you need, love?"

She doesn't speak, just moans as she tugs me closer to her, rubbing her body against me. I know what she needs, so as she pants, I move my lips away from her skin and whisper in her ear.

"I'm going to fuck you. Right here. Because I can't fucking wait another minute. Do you understand?"

Still nothing, so I stop. "Talk to me. Tell me you want this," I growl while grabbing a condom from my pocket, sheathing myself, and then aligning my cock with her.

"Fuck me," she purrs back, and so I do. I push forward, thrusting inside her in one forceful move. Then I pull out slowly. So damn slow. But it feels like heaven.

Addison is heaven.

In.

Then out.

In . . .

Then out.

I continue to thrust, but as she pushes her arse back into me, I know we both need more, so I answer her moan by slamming inside her.

My pace and movements are frenzied and rushed. I'm teetering on the brink of an eruption, but she has to go first. Reaching around, I start to strum her until I feel her quiver and shake until she tightens and squeezes around me.

When I pull out, I instantly miss her warmth. Addison's legs give out when I release her, so I scoop her up and lead us to her bed.

"Where's your room?" I pull away and let my gaze slide down her body hungrily. She rights herself, takes my hand, and pulls me with her up the stairs, down a hall, and into the master suite. We keep walking until we reach the bed, and she turns around to face me.

I lean in, placing my nose in the crook of her neck, and then I move my mouth over the skin of her neck. My promise is there.

I'll have her, and once I have her, I'll find out everything I need to know.

I lift my head and slam my mouth to hers. With my free hand, I raise her jaw to deepen the kiss. Now with no space between us.

Our tongues collide. Time halts as I become lost in this woman.

It doesn't matter who she is. It doesn't matter why she's here. All that matters is the way she feels against me. The way she will feel around me.

Even though I just had her, I need her again.

I watch as she pulls off her clothes and stands in front of me in just her knickers. Black lace. "Take them off," I groan.

Her eyes widen in shock. "Again?"

"Again, and after that, all night. So get to it."

She does it slowly, torturing me until I ache. "You're lovely." A warm red flushes her face. I make quick work of removing my own shirt, and then with my right hand, I reach into my back pocket. Once I grab what I'm looking for, I remove my trousers and briefs.

Her breathing is erratic. My chest is heaving.

Gently, I push her back. Her knees hit the edge of the bed first, and then her elbows follow suit. Once she's lying before me, I spread her legs, opening her up to me.

Her eyes are wide as my mouth presses to her skin and kisses a path up to her knee. The movement makes her breath come out at a faster clip.

I continue my assault on her senses.

Teasing.

Torturing.

Until finally I have driven us both past the point of madness.

Moving up her body, I settle deeper between her legs, my hard length resting on her core.

"Please," she begs.

Finally, I push forward, breaching her with a force that takes her breath away and causes a primal moan to pour from her mouth. Once I'm fully seated, I let out the breath I was holding. It feels too good inside her warmth.

I thrust in slow strokes.

Letting her adjust.

When she loosens around me, I allow the force of my strokes to increase.

Hard.

Long.

Our hips rotate together. In. Out.

I drive in and out, picking up speed. Thrusting at a punishing clip, I feel mad, crazy with lust. I throw my head back, my eyes shutting as every muscle inside her clenches around me, and I fall, following her over the edge.

Once done, we catch our breaths together. My weight is heavy on her, so I lean up on my elbows. Her glowing skin and tousled hair make her look wanton in the bed.

Like the goddess Aphrodite.

We don't move. Instead, we stare at each other, both breathless, waiting for our hearts to return to their normal beat. A second later, I pull out.

She looks at me, her eyes fluttering shut. I need to get up. I need to leave. I've already taken this too far, the lies still bitter on my tongue, but I'm too tired and too sated from the pleasure still coursing through every synapse of my body. My eyes flutter of their own accord, and the most perfect, peaceful bliss engulfs me.

CHAPTER TEN

Addison

MY BODY IS SORE, AND MY EYES WON'T OPEN. I'M exhausted and apparently, once again, hungover. What happened last night?

My brain feels like it just went through the spin cycle of a washing machine.

Jumbled.

Fuzzy.

And . . .

What the hell?

I move my hand around in my bed and realize I'm touching someone.

What is going on? Painfully, I open my eyes and look across my bed at the body beside me.

Everything rushes back.

Every moment.

Every kiss.

Every thrust of his hips.

Shit.

My eyes shut fast. How do I leave without speaking to him? I can't. We're in my bed. I pretend to sleep, hoping to come up with a plan before he wakes.

"You'll pop a blood vessel with how hard you're trying to

pretend you're asleep." His husky voice drifts through the air, making my toes curl with flashbacks of the things he said to me last night.

I clench my eyes tighter, wishing and praying I could take a time machine back and . . .

Do what?

Would I change anything, really?

As much as I don't want him in my bed right now, last night was amazing. Would I really deny myself the memory?

Yes.

No. No, I wouldn't. Because even though my drunken, wanton behavior mortifies me, I want a repeat. A sober one. One I can catalog in my brain and remember forever.

"What's going on in that head of yours?" he asks as he places his fingers on my arms and starts to travel up my exposed skin, leaving a trail of goose bumps in their wake. "Nothing to be ashamed of, love."

"I'm not," I say behind my hands now covering my face. I'm acting like a timid child, not like the self-assured Addison I normally am.

The warm pads of his fingers trail over the exposed skin on my shoulders, along my collarbone, and up the hollow of my throat until it rests on my jaw. He tilts my head until I know I'm facing him.

"Open your eyes," he coos.

"No." Petulant child on aisle one.

"Please."

I reluctantly blink them open, meeting his gorgeous blues and a perfect five o'clock shadow that should be illegal at this time of day.

"Much better. Now tell me why you're hiding." His hand

frames my face.

"I'm not hiding." My words come out snippy, but by the way his lip tips up, he's well aware I was.

"Looks that way to me." His brow arches in challenge and I throw my hands in the air. My skin feels warm at the way he looks at me, and I suddenly feel even more naked than I already am.

Since I have nothing on, I'm not sure how that's possible, but I do.

"You're still here," I whisper. "I didn't expect you to be here when I woke up," I admit.

I have had trysts in the past, but typically, they don't spend the night.

He smirks at my comment. A gorgeous and dangerous smirk. One that would make my knees give out if I were standing. But lucky for me, I'm not. Or maybe unlucky because, instead, I'm naked in the bed with this insanely good-looking man.

"I'm not like most men."

"I'm not sure I agree."

"Really?" His words linger on my skin and now his fingers too. He trails them back down, this time catching the blanket and lowering it until I'm no longer covered.

The air licks at my exposed flesh, awakening every nerve ending until I'm hyper-aware of his fingers caressing me. "Are you sure about that?" He keeps up his ministrations, making me dizzy and breathless. Until I can't remember what he asked. "Are you?"

Lower.

"Sure." My nipples pebble at his touch, his fingers now pulling and teasing. "About." He stops, and I think he's finished, but he isn't. Instead, he trails his hand down. Cupping me. Teasing me. Dipping his index finger inside me. "That?" he finally says.

"Yes," I squeak.

"Yes to what?" A boyish grin grows on his face, and I'm lost in more than just his hands.

"I don't even know," I say and shake my head in disbelief.

He winks. "Okay."

Okay? *Okay?* What is he saying okay to?

He pulls away then, leaving me desperate and wanting. He stands, fully displaying his naked body, and I allow myself to enjoy the view. "Like what you see?" he asks.

"Hardly." I swallow hard as I lie through my teeth.

"Brilliant. Then I'll get dressed."

I want to beg him not to and to get back in the bed, but I don't. He laughs, leaning down and placing a chaste kiss on my lips. "To the toilet, love."

He leaves, and I try to fix my hair. When I realize it's a lost cause, I let out a huff. With him in the bathroom, there's not much I can do but wait.

Within a few minutes, he's back. Still naked. Still gorgeous.

"What are you doing today?" he asks, and I'm taken off guard.

"Nothing," I respond.

"Good."

"Good?"

"Yes. Now that I know you have no place to go, I plan on having my way with you all day."

He gets back on the bed, and it dips with the extra weight.

"But—"

"No buts, Addison. Actually, please object because doing so will have consequences." He smirks playfully. "Tell me you're busy, and I'll add on all night."

"But—"

"All night it is."

"Don't you have someplace you need to be? Someone you need to, I don't know . . . cook for?" I shrug.

"Just you, Addy."

I look at him for a beat. Just me? Should I?

I'm sure this has disaster written all over it, but as I watch him run his tongue over his lips, I realize I don't care.

"The only place I need to be is here. The only thing I need to eat is you."

"Okay . . ."

We spend the morning in bed. And when Oliver steps out to go to the bathroom again to clean up, I pick up the phone and see I've missed a call from Jasmine. I dial her back and whisper a hello.

"Addison, you okay?" she answers.

"Yes." My voice is so low I'm not even sure she can hear me.

"Why are you whispering? Oh my God, is he there still?"

I look toward the closed bathroom door and then cover my mouth for good measure so he won't be able to hear me speak. "Yes."

"Oh my God," she screams, and this time, I cover the phone completely with my hand. She's so loud I can actually hear her through the walls.

"Shh," I groan, still looking at the door. Jeez, this woman. Luckily, I hear the water on, so I know he's missed this whole exchange.

"Sorry," she mumbles back.

"You guys need to leave."

"I can't leave," she responds, her voice stern.

"J, as my friend, I need you to leave." I sigh.

"Ohhhhh." She starts to giggle over the line. I lean back in my bed, rolling my eyes at her even though she can't see me.

"Yes, oh," I mutter back.

"Um, should I . . .?"

"Go to London and take Marcus. I'll follow."

It's a good plan. It gives me a little more time with him but also an out if I need one.

"But how will you get there?"

"I'm a big girl."

She's quiet for a minute. Too quiet. "This isn't like you," she finally remarks. And she's right. It's not. But isn't that okay?

"I know."

"Just be careful."

"Always."

"Oh and, J, don't tell anyone."

She's quiet for a minute. "Fine. But if you need us, Marcus will come back." Once I hang up, Oliver is once again in front of me, and by the look in his eyes, I'm not getting out of bed anytime soon.

We spend the rest of the day in bed, and before I know it, the day has turned into night. Oliver has left the room to bring back supplies, and by supplies, I mean food. Apparently, in the need to ravage each other, we have forgotten to eat.

Now, lying in bed alone, naked beneath the sheet, I wait for him to return.

The door opens slowly, and in walks Oliver carrying a tray with an amused look on his face.

"Pickings were slim." He chuckles. "I did my best." He shrugs, but the smirk gives him away. I'm sure whatever he has will be decadent.

"What do you have there?" I lift my body up on to my

knees, and the blanket drops off me. Oliver's blue eyes glimmer with desire at the sight before him.

"Lie back, and I'll show you." His commanding voice warms my skin, and I do what he asks. I lie back onto the bed, the sheet pooling at my waist.

"Close your eyes."

I obey, and my skin pricks with anticipation.

It feels like hours pass. Each sound and smell magnified by the wait.

Then I feel it, or him for that matter. Soft fingers trailing over my collarbone, but then it's not fingers touching me anymore; it's something harder. He trails the food up my throat and across my lips, so I swipe my tongue out to taste.

"Open your mouth. Bite."

Strawberry. It tastes delicious in my mouth. Hard at first, then soft as the juices burst against my taste buds. I chew slowly and swallow, each bite more sinful than the one before. "Open," he commands again, and this time when I open, I'm met with his mouth. I'm met with his tongue sweeping alongside my own.

He deepens the kiss and moves on top of me, the hard ridge of his erection pressing against my skin.

Who needs food anyway?

The next morning comes before long, and a sinking feeling slithers through me. I don't want to leave. I've enjoyed the attention, the distraction, and—I won't even try to lie to myself—I enjoyed the way he played my body as if he knows me. As if he took a class on how to perfectly manipulate my body for pleasure. I'll miss it.

I barely slept last night, so I'm slow to get up. But apparently, Olly has other plans for me . . .

I'm not even sure how many rounds we've gone, but I get up from the bed and start to pack my bags.

"Where you off to?" he asks as he stands from the torn-up bed that holds the evidence of a crazy and impetuous tryst so out of character I can't believe I've done it.

"London," I say, turning back around to continue folding the shirt in my hand.

"Why?"

"Work." My answer is short, but I'm already running so late, I don't have time for idle chitchat.

"Have dinner with me?" He's standing by the foot of the bed now, tugging his shirt over his head. I drop the item of clothing in my hand and turn to face him again.

"Isn't that how we got into this trouble?" I mutter under my breath, and he laughs. "You'll be in London?"

"To see you . . ." He smirks. "So, yes."

"I can't," I say quickly. No. This can't happen again. This was a one-off. A complete one-off. I have too much to do. Leaning down, I move to grab another shirt.

"Why doesn't your answer surprise me?" He chuckles, making me stop what I'm doing to look at him, again. I'm met with unruly hair, a few days worth of scruff, and fully kissed lips. I let out a moan, and he smirks at me, causing me to growl.

"So why did you ask?" I say as I cross my arms over my chest and shoot him my coldest stare. It doesn't work. If anything, it has the opposite effect on him. Instead of getting annoyed by my hostility, he looks even more amused.

"Was hoping you'd be *living*, not merely existing." He winks.

"Well, as much as I hate to let you down"—I roll my eyes—"I am here to work." As much as I truly want to take him up on the offer, that's not me. Even though I wish it were, this person Olly met and spent time with isn't me.

I'm like Cinderella . . .

And the clock has just struck midnight.

CHAPTER ELEVEN

Oliver

HER BAG IS PACKED, AND I'M NOW DRESSED. I NEVER DID find out what I needed to know about the property. I was too distracted with her body to pry, but unfortunately, I still need to know, so I decide that we can't part, at least not yet.

I need more time.

"How are you getting to London?" I say once we are sitting in the kitchen. I lift the mug of freshly brewed coffee to my mouth and take a sip.

"Driving," she answers as she moves around the room, cleaning God knows what. This woman needs to relax.

"You're driving? Do you have a car here?"

She places the rag down. "Well, not exactly."

"It's a yes or no question, I'm afraid."

"I did have a car and a driver, but I sent him to London with my assistant, and . . ." She nibbles on her lower lip.

"Why did you do that?" By the way her eyes flash wider and her cheeks flush, I know *exactly* why she did that. And I appreciate it. "So if he's in London, how do you expect to get there?"

"I was going to call him."

I take another sip and then lower it. The sound of the mug hitting the table echoes in the kitchen.

"Well, that's foolish," I respond once I swallow.

"How so?"

"I'll take you. I'm headed that way myself."

I'm not. That's a lie. But I haven't found out what I need to know yet, so I'm not willing to let her go.

Lies.

That's not the real reason. The real reason is I still have her taste on my tongue, and I haven't gotten my fill of her yet. The thought is alarming, so I push it down. Tamp it.

You still need to find out about the land, I tell myself.

"Give me your bag. I'll take you." I move over to her, grab her bag, and head out the door.

"But—"

"No objections."

She follows me to the car, and we set off on our trip. For the first ten minutes, neither of us speaks, but not speaking isn't an option for me. The more comfortable she is, the better the chance she'll talk, so I reach toward my radio and lower the volume.

"Something wrong with that song?" she asks, and from my periphery, I can see her staring at me.

"No, I just figured we could talk," I respond.

"And what, pray tell, would you like to talk about?"

"Nothing in particular. Just figured since we are together in the car for a bit . . ."

"Don't you mean stuck together?"

"Yes, I'm sure it's quite the hardship to be stuck in a car with me," I tease. "But since we are, as you say . . . stuck, let's talk about something and get to know each other better."

"Okay . . ." She trails off. I can already tell she's reluctant to let me in, and that won't do at all.

"What about that game you Americans like to play?"

"And what game would that be?" she chides.

"Twenty questions."

"Wow. Stereotypical much? I feel like this is the beginning of every romance novel."

"Any other suggestions?" I glance over at her, and she groans.

"Nope."

"Then twenty questions it is. I'll start," I say, and she groans again. I try to think of a question but come up blank.

She starts laughing. "Not as easy as it seems to come up with a question, is it?" I shake my head at her, and then she reaches into her purse and pulls out her mobile.

"What are you doing?" I ask.

"Looking up questions, obviously. Since you are useless." From the corner of my eye, I can see her typing, and then I see her lips tip up. No chance this will be an easy question. "If you didn't have to sleep, what would you do with the extra time?" she asks.

"Be a vampire," I respond.

"Be serious . . ."

"I am." Swerving through traffic, I try to think of a better answer. "Read."

"Really?"

"Is that so shocking? I like to read, but I don't often find the time."

"What's your favorite type of book to read?" she asks.

"I like to read thrillers or the classics."

"Like *Romeo and Juliet*." She laughs.

"Yes. Like that and Oscar Wilde," I clarify.

"Ah. It all makes sense now, doesn't it . . ." She trails off as if my answer gives away all my secrets.

"What do you mean?"

"Living, existing . . . your motto is just ripping off a great." The humor in her voice is cute. I like hearing it.

"I'd hardly call it that," I say.

"Then what would you call it?"

"Stealing like an artist."

"Clever."

"Always."

"Modest too," she chides.

"Truly. The truth is, my headmaster when I was first shipped off to boarding school used that as his motto."

"That's an interesting motto." She doesn't sound convinced.

"I was a handful when I first got to school, barely existing . . ."

"Was there a reason?" she asks softly.

"Nope," I lie. "I was just a pain in the arse and he was trying to help me."

She doesn't say anything in response, so I turn my head to face her. Her smile is small, and her cheeks sucked in. As if she's sad for me. The quiet between us is oppressing, reminding me of how much everything I say to her is a calculated lie. So finally, when I feel like I can choke on it, I speak. "Should I ask you the same questions or make up my own?"

"Same. And my answer is rest."

"But doesn't that defeat the purpose of not sleeping . . . ?"

"Not really. Resting and sleeping are completely different things. I never allow myself to relax and rest, so if I didn't have to sleep, I would just rest. Next question," she says.

"Tell me about your family? Do you have siblings?"

"That's more than one question," she deadpans, "and will take a long time to answer." Her voice mocks, full of the sarcastic humor I have grown fond of.

"Take all the time in the world. We have a bit of a drive still. I just want to know something about you," I respond.

"I have two brothers and we're super close. I guess one would expect that when you work together, but I think we would still be close despite that." She sounds wistful as she thinks of her brothers, and from the corner of my eye, I can see she's smiling. "Grayson is the oldest. My parents got pregnant right away with him, apparently, and then it took them about five years to get pregnant with me."

"How old are you?" I ask, realizing just how little I know about her.

"Thirty-one."

"An older woman."

"Why? How old are you?" she responds.

"I'm thirty." I think about lying, but the truth is, this can't lead back to me, and after having so many lies between us, I'd like a bit of truth.

"I'm hardly that much older. So yeah, Grayson is older than me, and Jax is the oops baby. It took so long to have me that I guess they stopped being careful when I was four."

"Tell me about them. Are they like you?"

"By like me, you mean a brat?" She giggles, and I chuckle in response. "Gray is super serious, and Jax is trouble."

"Trouble how?"

"Between us, he's our resident hacker. He's a genius. Any info on anyone you need, he's the guy to call." That I didn't expect to hear. The new knowledge of her brother's talent makes me grip the steering wheel tighter.

I need to be careful. I can't have Addison asking her brother about me.

"Good to know."

"Grayson hates it." She laughs again.

"I can imagine." I hate it too but not for the same reasons.

"So what about you?" she asks, and my back goes stiff. Family is not a subject I can broach.

"Nothing to tell, love."

"I find that hard to believe."

"Only child raised in boarding school." And with that, I turn my attention back to the road.

Game over for me.

The rest of the ride continues in much the same manner, and when we are close to the destination, I realize in my attempt not to tell her about myself, I never did find out what I was meant to ask. I never did ask anything to do with the land.

As we pull outside the hotel, I turn to her. "Ever stayed at the Lancaster before?" I ask her.

Her nose scrunches. And then I remember while doing my research after my mother told me about her that she's been tied to the American tycoon in the past. I wonder if that's what Addison was running from that first night. Why she got drunk at a pub in the middle of nowhere? The thought angers me. If that's the case, why is she staying here?

"I always stay at the Lancaster."

"By the look on your face, I don't understand why you don't seem happy to be here."

"I own the property," she mumbles under her breath. "Where else would I stay?" She says it with disdain.

"You don't have to stay here," I say before I can stop myself, and as soon as the words pass through my lips, a stabbing pain of guilt ricochets through me.

I'm a horrible son. This woman's family hurt my mother, yet I still want to spend time with her. I still want to get to know her.

I still want to see her smile.

She lifts her brow. "And where else would I stay?"

"I do have a flat . . ."

"Okay there, Romeo." Her reference has me choking. This is the second time she's called me that. *How ironic*. She has no idea how close she is to the truth.

"Hardly," I respond, but deep down, I know that nickname isn't actually too far from the mark. Her family is my family's enemy. "I thought we already established no sonnets for me and no daggers for you. Prince Charming maybe . . ." I laugh, and she groans. "You could always—"

"Nope. Thank you very much, but I think I'll stay right here."

"Well, then give me your mobile number."

"For what?"

"Because I plan to see you again," I say matter-of-factly, not leaving much room for debate.

"I have to see a few properties. I'm busy." She swings the door open and steps out of the cover. Like the gentleman I am, I exit the automobile as well and grab her bag from the boot.

"Work, and then I'll pick you up after." My commanding voice leaves little room for objection.

"And if I say no?" She narrows her eyes.

"You won't." My voice is way too smug, but by the way her eyes widen, I think she likes it.

"Mighty sure of yourself." She huffs.

"Always." I halt my progress and watch her walk toward the entrance of the hotel.

"No."

"I'll see you at half past eight . . ."

"But . . ." she starts, but I've already started heading back to my car. I keep walking, but when she says, "Thank you for the ride." I turn over my shoulder and give her a smile.

"My pleasure."

As soon as I'm back in the car, I dial my mum. She's called over the past two days, but seeing as I had my hands full, literally, I've ignored her.

"Where are you?"

"Hello to you too, Mum," I respond as I pull my car out into traffic.

"I haven't seen you in days. Not since you told me you would check up on the American."

"And I have," I offer, hoping she doesn't press, but knowing my mother, I'll have no such luck.

"You have? What did you find out?"

"Not very much." Well, at least not what she's asking for. I know what makes Addison purr, but something tells me my mum's not interested in that information.

"Are you even trying?" she hisses through the line.

"Yes, Mum, I am. More than you know."

She must hear the innuendo in my voice because she tsks. "Don't fraternize with the enemy, Oliver."

"I would hardly call her the enemy," I respond.

"Oliver, remember your loyalties. Remember who you are."

Her accusation turns my blood cold. As if I could ever forget. The burden of it has been weighing me down for years.

"And who am I?"

"You are an earl." Her voice is hard and proud. "Thirty-first in line to the throne."

"As if I could ever forget. Plus, my cousin is about to have a kid—actually, two. So don't you mean thirty-third—"

"And this little American has something that's mine, that's ours. Find out."

"I will."

I hang up the phone abruptly, angry with myself for not having my head in the game. No. Instead, I let myself be distracted. Unfortunately, now that I'd had a taste, I'm not sure I won't be distracted again.

I do need to find out, nonetheless. But I guess I can do as the saying goes . . . kill two birds with one stone. Enjoy myself. Enjoy her. And find out what she's doing with my land. How hard can that be? And once I find out, then I can devise a plan to get it back.

I'm not sure why my mother is so adamant about this, but my mom is all I have.

Hours later, Addison is in my car again. I watch from my seat as she pulls on her seat belt, and once she's set, I drive toward our destination. I spent my day trying to figure out a game plan and then convincing myself I should even go through with it.

But now, taking in how beautiful she is, I'm happy I am. Because I'm not done with her yet.

Even if that makes me a prick . . .

"How long are you in town for?" I ask her, needing to gauge how much time I have.

"Not long." It's like pulling teeth with this one to find out anything, but I guess I can't judge. At least she's giving me answers, and I'm just telling lies.

With each day I spend with her, she gives me another piece of herself, and what do I give her in return?

Not even my real name.

"How were your meetings today?" I ask as I take my foot off the accelerator and stop at the light.

"Good."

"Anything of interest?" The light turns green, and I start to drive. From the corner of my eye, I can see she's looking out the window, lost in her own thoughts.

"Just work," she finally says.

"And tomorrow?"

Even though I'm driving, I continue to watch her. I watch as her chest rises and falls; I watch as she nibbles on her lower lip. Jeez. Will she give anything up? It would be a lot easier if she did. I'd find out the information I needed and then fuck her out of my system. But no, nothing is easy.

"Work."

"Come on. How about having a spot of fun with me?" Pulling my gaze from her, I turn back to the road.

"And why would I do that? What's in it for me?" she asks.

"A world-class tour of London?"

She chuckles. "I've seen London plenty."

"Not with me."

"I don't do tourist," she says, and I have to chuckle. No way could Addison ever be confused with a tourist.

"I would never think of it. I just want to show you the other parts of London. The parts an American would never see."

"Like your pub?" She grimaces.

"Exactly. Like my pub."

She lets out a breath. "Maybe," she answers. I remove the coin. "Jeez. No more of the coin. I'll go anywhere as long as you don't let a damn coin decide my fate."

"What do you have to lose?"

When she goes silent, I want to turn to her, but I don't. A part of me wants to pry, to ask Addison why she is the way she is, but if I do, I'm opening the door to something I have no business opening.

"Where to?" she asks, changing the subject, and I'm thankful.

"Dinner."

"Well, I must say I'm a bit disappointed."

I turn back to her while out of the corner of my eye, I watch the road for oncoming traffic. "How so?" I ask.

"I thought you would have a better plan."

"What makes you think I don't?" I muse.

"If you say dinner at your place, I'll have to beat you."

"Well, there goes that plan." I shrug.

"Oliver," she chides.

I flash her my pearly whites. "Relax, love."

It doesn't take long for us to arrive. She doesn't say a word. And it's actually quite cute. After I park, I walk around and help her out of the car, taking her hand.

"Where are we?" she asks as I escort her into the building. As soon as we enter, the lights and sounds assault us.

"What is this place?"

"It's spectacular, right?" I answer, knowing full well she's shocked by the location I chose.

"For a nine-year-old's birthday."

"Exactly."

"But we aren't nine."

"But isn't it fun to live like we are?"

She looks around, eyes wide.

"It's called Namco Funscape," I tell her as I lead her farther into the space.

"It's an inside playground." I can hear the awe in her voice. She wasn't expecting this. Good, because I'm full of surprises.

"It is."

"Are adults even allowed here?"

"Of course, they are," I answer, and she lifts her brow. "Why else would they sell booze? Obviously, it means it's for adults." She rolls her eyes at me, which makes me laugh. "Come on. Follow me, and I'll get us a drink."

Grabbing her hand yet again, we walk in. Lights flash and sounds explode around us. The arcade is alive, and despite what she says, I can see her amusement.

A small smile peeks out across her features, her full lips tipping up slightly to the right in what could be described as a smirk, but on her, I know it's her suppressed laugh. She doesn't want to enjoy herself, but like I thought, how could she not love it?

I'm not sure why I want her to enjoy herself so badly. I'm not sure why I want her to let her hair down and enjoy life, but I do. Something about the first time I saw her, her eyes sad and confused, lit something inside me. Then today, that ember ignited further. I still need to find out what her game plan is, but while I find out, I want to make her smile.

We walk over to the bar. Once there, I order us two Guinness beers and then lead her over to the attractions. We start by playing simple arcade games, but then an alley opens, so we head over to bowl.

Picking up a lighter ball, I hold it out to her, but she smiles broadly. "Do you know how to bowl?" I ask.

"Do you?" she responds.

"Do you really think I would take you anywhere where I haven't mastered the sport?"

"For some reason, I don't see you as the bowling type."

"And what type do I look like?"

"You look more regal."

I smile but turn to grab a ball of my own. If she only knew just how close she was to the truth.

"And no, I don't know how to bowl."

"I'll help you." I place my ball down and walk toward her. "Come on."

She walks with me to the marker on the floor. Holding the ball in both her hands, she bends her knees. She looks adorable.

"That's not how you do it." I shake my head. I step up behind her so close that her rear touches the front of my jeans. Reaching around, I take her right arm. "Let your left hand drop and pull back." I help her, stepping aside so she doesn't touch me. Our bodies are still close.

Every breath she takes makes my own body feel hyper-aware of the proximity. "Now let go," I whisper against her neck, and she lets out a small gasp just as she does. The ball flies forward, rolling straight down the middle of the lane, and knocks all the pins down but one.

"Holy crap." She pushes off me and jumps into the air.

"Beginner's luck." I smirk.

"Thank you," she says as she smiles. Her eyes sparkle with a softness I haven't seen before. She's exquisite when she smiles like this. Like a goddess come down to earth.

Shit.

This is bad.

CHAPTER TWELVE

Addison

ONCE WE FINISH BOWLING AND PLAYING ARCADE GAMES, we decide to eat. Sitting at a small table, I dip my french fry into the ketchup in front of me.

"I can't believe all the crap I've eaten since being in England," I mutter, but as I take a bite, I can't help but moan at the taste.

"But it's worth it, right?"

"Totally."

"So you don't eat like this in America?" he asks.

"I mean, I'm not on a diet or anything, but I'm just always on the go, so it's not often I sit down for fries."

"Chips," he corrects. "You're in England now. Chips it is. Or freedom fries."

I hold my hands up in mock apology. "Jeez. Chips, then."

"I'm just taking the piss." He chuckles.

Once I'm done with all my *chips*, I reach for a napkin to clean off the ketchup coating my fingers, but just as I do, our fingers touch. His hand is warm on mine, and he gives me a little squeeze. My cheeks flush from the contact, and within seconds, I'm imagining those hands, those fingers, touching me.

I look up at him through hooded lids. "Um, now where?" I ask, and he lifts his brow while a ghost of a sinful smile plays on his lips. "I'm not sure that's a good idea," I respond shyly. I'm not sure why I'm being shy because let's be honest, it's exactly what I want. Plus, it's not like we haven't done that already. Fantastically, actually. Mind-blowing, to be exact, but here in London, in this arcade, I'm a blushing virgin again.

"And why not?"

"I have work to do."

"Work. Work. Work," he drones on. "It's more fun to live."

"We can't always act like we're nine." Although sometimes I wish I can. "Don't you have work too?" I ask.

"Not right now. I'm taking some time off."

I wonder how he can take time off so easily. He's probably a self-made billionaire who barely works and mainly plays, leaving a trail of broken hearts across the globe.

Mental note: Have Jasmine research him. I could have Jax do it, but then my brothers would know, and I don't want that.

Nope. Not at all.

"Must be nice," I grumble back because as much as I would enjoy taking a vacation, that isn't in the cards for me.

"You should try it."

"I'll take a pass."

"I would invite you back to my flat, but seeing as you have a meeting and—" His voice is filled with innuendo, and I curse myself for telling him I had to work because I want nothing more than to go home with him right now.

"Well, I mean—"

"No," he cuts me off, and my mouth drops open.

"No?"

"Yes. No. You have work," he says, and suddenly, I hate the way I feel. I hate the rejection that slithers in my brain. The feeling of inadequacy.

"I'll pick you up at five tomorrow." He stops in front of the hotel, but I'm still staring at him in confusion.

"What?"

"You didn't really think I was done with you?" he asks.

I feel foolish and dumb, a combination I don't like to be, so I push my walls back up.

"I'm busy," I say, not because I actually have something to do, but because I'm being stubborn.

"No, you're not. You just want to be difficult."

My mouth drops open, and he reaches across the console to touch my lower lip.

"If you weren't working, I'd silence that brain of yours, love, but I know you are. So here's what we're going to do. You are going to get your delectable arse out of my car, and tomorrow, you're mine."

His fingers move back and forth, making goose bumps prick against my skin. "Okay," I squeak out.

"Brilliant." But first, he leans in, and his mouth meets mine. His tongue swipes against the seam of my lips until I open for him, and then he takes full advantage of the moment.

Our tongues collide, slowly at first, but the longer we kiss, the more frenzied it becomes until my heart's racing, beating fast against my breastbone, and my whole body is warm.

"Pity," he mumbles.

"What?" I say against his lips. But he just shakes his head as he pulls away, leaving me confused for the millionth time tonight. I move away and open the door.

"Addison . . ."

From across the car, I look at him over my shoulder. "Yes?"

He taps his fingers on the steering wheel and smiles. "Wear something comfortable tomorrow." The smile turns into a smirk.

"Comfortable?" I ask, still halfway inside the car.

"Yes. A jumper and trainers," he clarifies.

"Where are we going?"

He shakes his head at my question, but his blue eyes grow darker, almost mischievous. "Another surprise."

"I don't do surprises," I fire back.

"Sure, you do." He pulls out his coin, and I shake my head. "Heads says you do." He flips it in the air. "Heads." He shows me the coin. "See. Fate. Live a little." He winks.

Without anything else to say, I move to fully get out of the car and head inside. "Good evening, Ms. Price," the doorman says as I walk into the lobby. The staff knows me here. The property that this beautiful hotel sits on belongs to me. I always thought I would marry Spencer Lancaster, but apparently, that wasn't in the cards. That ship has sailed.

Now I need to come to terms with that.

At least, I have Oliver to distract me. He's the perfect diversion to take my mind off things. Especially when I'm here in Spencer's hotel while he's off on his honeymoon.

Bypassing the lobby, I head to the elevator that takes me to the penthouse. I don't bother checking my emails or my phone. There's no one I want to talk to. Instead, I wash my face, get in bed, and fall right to sleep.

The next day, I wake to a barrage of emails. Apparently, my meeting to talk about the property is canceled. Not that there's anything to talk about. Everyone knows Lancaster has first rights of refusal.

But why should I? Why do I allow him to walk over me?

So what if that's how it's always been? Just because I have always given Lancaster the first option to build doesn't mean I have to. I'm here a few more days. I can open it up for offers.

Spencer will be upset.

So?

So what if he's upset? He didn't think much of my feelings.

God, I sound pathetic. I'm everything I hate in the other members of my sex. I have become the pathetic, whiny ex-girlfriend I have always refused to be.

I pick up my phone and dial my brother. It might be midnight in New York, but Gray never sleeps.

"Where are you?" he barks. Big brother is pissed. Normally, I would care, but right now, I don't. I'm still in shock that a man has made me so weak.

Never again.

No. From now on, I'm going to enjoy sex, enjoy my time, but not allow myself to get attached.

"London."

"Still? Don't you need to go to Spain?"

"That's not for a while. For now, I'm here trying to figure out what to do with the estate in Wiltshire."

"That's a no-brainer."

"Not necessarily."

"How so? I thought you met with the surveyor and the developer, and we can lease it to be built."

"We can." Even though the idea of building something like that leaves a bad taste in my mouth. The land was so beautiful, the village . . .

"Then I don't understand the problem. Call Spence. I'm sure it would be perfect for his latest expansion. He wanted a countryside estate fit for a king. From the info you gave me and the pictures, it seems perfect."

"I'm going to entertain more offers."

"What's going on with you, Addy? Listen, I'm sure this is

hard. I honestly can't imagine what you're going through."

He knows nothing. I have not worked my ass off to be taken seriously just for everyone to question my motives and sanity. "No, you can't," I hiss. Because it's so much more than being left; it's the fact I let myself be weak. That I let myself believe in a future that was just in my imagination. I hate myself for being like that.

That's why this thing with Oliver has been so great. With Oliver, I can enjoy myself or as he so aptly says, "*Live*," without the fear of developing feelings. I'm back to America, and he's off to . . .

Where is he off to after I leave? He says he lives here but now I wonder where in London he lives? How do I not know this? *Because you don't need to know. He's only a warm body.*

"Fly home. Table Europe for now."

"I can't do that."

I'm not ready to leave.

I'm not ready to leave Ol—I stop the thought, not wanting to get ahead of myself.

"Yes, you can. What's the point of all this? Of working so damn hard if we can't take a break. Come home, and if not, take off. Take some alone time. Decompress. You aren't thinking clearly."

"I'm thinking more clearly than I have in years. This week, I'm entertaining competitors," I say before I can second-guess myself. I'm not sure what I'll do, but I can't go back to America, not yet.

"Jeez. I hope you know what you're doing."

"Did you ever think that maybe he won't want to work with us now? Maybe 'Olivia' won't want him to." It would make sense. I have a hard time working with Spencer, so I can't possibly understand why she would want him to work with me.

"Unlikely."

"Nothing is unlikely. We can't assume that just because the families have worked well together in the past, we still will."

"Fine, Addy. Speak to new developers. See if we can lease the property out for something else. Or better yet, what about selling?"

"I won't sell."

"Because?" he asks.

"It was Father's . . ." I trail off. "I want to find out why he kept it before I consider selling it. Maybe he had a plan?"

"If he wanted to develop it, he would have." As always, Grayson is the voice of reason. That's the thing about my older brother. He's level-headed, and he doesn't allow his emotions to control his decisions. Unlike me, apparently.

"True. I have to go. I need to speak to a few people, and I'm ending work early today."

"Hot date?"

"Actually . . ." I trail off, letting my meaning come across loud and clear.

"Really?"

"Believe it or not, I wasn't lying when I said I was over him, Gray. I am. Now let me go so I can work."

"Love you, sis," he says.

"Love you too."

I hang up the phone and call Jasmine's phone. It might be five a.m. London time, but it's time to work. She picks up after the first ring.

"You're alive."

"And you're up," I joke.

"This isn't my first rodeo with you." She laughs, and she's right. She's been my right-hand woman for years and is like a member of my family.

By the time five p.m. hits, I'm excited. Which says a lot because I'm never excited.

Ever.

When he meets me in the lobby, he's standing in the corner tucked away from the hustle and bustle of the city. His back, as well as his right foot, rests on the wall. Perched on his handsome face, covering his sapphire eyes, is a pair of aviators. It's an odd accessory to still have on. Honestly, it's an odd accessory due to the weather. It's not sunny and not rainy either, but since I've been in the country, they have experienced a revolving door of gray and fog. Not the type of weather that warrants shades.

I continue to stare as I walk closer. He reminds me of a young Hollywood heartthrob who's trying to stay incognito.

To be honest, I think I like that most about Olly, his lack of desire to be in the spotlight. Most of the men I date often do so just to get admittance into the best of the world. It's not like the average person knows who I am, but when I travel, when I dine . . . normally, my staff calls ahead. I can get in anywhere, go anywhere.

The anonymity I have had since being in England has been refreshing.

He hasn't seen me yet, but when my sneakers hit the floor, and I make my way over, he notices me.

A smile spreads across his cheek, and a small divot forms. The kind that makes me want to swoon like a wallflower in a regency romance.

"You listened," he says in greeting as his gaze sweeps over me.

"Were you worried?"

"Not in the slightest."

"Then why ask?"

"Conversation starter." He shrugs.

"Also known as you like to give me a hard time."

A larger smirk forms. *Head out of the gutter.* He nods as he steps forward, placing a kiss on my cheek, and then his hand finds the small of my back.

"What crazy location are you taking me to today? Let me guess, Madame Tussaud?"

"Come now, don't underestimate me. You are hardly a tourist, and I'm much too clever for that."

Passing through the streets, he weaves his way through traffic. As often as I come to Europe, driving on the wrong side of the road still has me closing my eyes.

There is a hollowing feeling in my stomach; I don't like to not be in control. Ever since I met Oliver, I haven't been, and although it's been worth it, it still goes beyond my comfort zone.

It takes us longer to drive to our destination today, and I'm not actually sure where we are. It's too dark to make out the sign in front of us, but I do notice an iron gate as we pass.

We pull through the entrance, and when we arrive at the "secret" destination, he parks, and we both exit the car. The first thing I notice about wherever we are is it's empty. We are the only car parked in the lot.

"Can we go in?" I ask as I step out of the car, and Oliver walks over to my side.

"Yes," he answers.

"But it's closed."

"I called in a few favors." He winks. "The last tour was an hour ago." He takes my hand in his and pulls me closer to the nondescript building. That's when I see the large wood door lined with limestone, and a blue sign directly next to it. Chislehurst Caves.

"And you got us in to see the caves after hours?"

"Apparently."

Once we're inside, an older man walks over.

"Mitchell, I presume?" Oliver asks, extending his hand.

"Yes, sir." He reaches out, and they shake.

"Pleasure to meet you. As you know, I'm Oliver, and this is Addison."

"I will be escorting you through the caves."

That makes me stop in my tracks. "We are actually going to see the caves?"

"Why else did you think we were here?" Oliver takes my hand in his and gives me a squeeze.

I look down at my feet. My feet not in heels. His request makes more sense now. "Um. That's why I'm in sneakers. A warning would have been nice."

"My apologies," he says, but I can tell by his tone he's not sorry at all.

Together, we walk through another wood door, and once we're through, it's basically pitch black. The tour guide uses the moment to light a lantern, illuminating the space. Gray stonewalls surround us, and the smell of earth and musk filters in through my nose.

As the tour begins, Mitchell talks about the history of the caves. But it's hard for me to listen over the pounding in my heart as we continue our descent farther under the ground.

"This is the home to the chalk caves." His voice echoes and bounces around us. "These caves were mined by hand. Do you know how long ago that was?"

I shake my head and turn to Olly. The light from the lantern is dim, but I can see a little smile tugging at his lips, so I know he knows the answer.

"The caves were mined in the thirteenth century. Hundreds of years ago." The blood in my veins flows harder with each step we take.

"What was it mined for?" Olly asks as we make our way farther into the enclosed space, but his voice sounds muted. All I can hear is the ringing in my ears as the oxygen begins to deplete in my lungs.

"The caves were mined for the use of flint and lime." His words ping-pong against the natural walls bouncing around us. "The mines were in use right up to the 1830s."

"Really?" I mutter, trying desperately not to freak out because that's what I feel like in this space. I feel like I'm not in control, and the thought has my heart beating rapidly and my lungs fighting for air. I try my hardest to concentrate on his story and his words.

"Yeah, they have been used both as a tourist attraction and even as an ammunitions depot during the First World War. More recently, the caves have been used for the telly." He laughs, shocking me.

"What shows?" His words have the result I hope for and momentarily distract me from my panic.

"*Doctor Who* is one example I can think of off the top of my head."

We all go silent again after his declaration and continue to walk. The darkness around us is staggering as we take in each dip in the earth, each divot, and each piece of flint hanging from the ceiling.

"How far in are we?" I rasp out, my back tightening. *Air.* I need air. "I can't breathe." I pull at the collar of my shirt. I need to take it off. "It's too tight."

I can't move; my hands feel stuck. Each pull of oxygen from my lungs burns as I try to breathe, and when I do get the air out, it comes out in ragged bursts.

Everything is closing in. The walls of the cave are closing in on me.

My chest constricts, and I feel faint.

What's happening to me?

That's when I can feel Olly's hand come across my waist to bracket me. He turns my face toward him, but he's blurry in the dim light. He speaks, but I can't hear him. His words sound jumbled to my ears.

"You're okay," he coos. "You're going to be okay." He pulls me closer against him, his familiar smell breaking through my panic. "Inhale, Addison." I take a gulp of air. "Exhale, love," he whispers close to my ear, and his words start to work as I follow his cues. I step into his warmth, place my own arm around him, and let him give me his strength. In his arms, I allow him to guide my body through the tour.

An hour later, we reemerge into the city air.

"Are you okay?" Olly asks, taking my hand in his and pulling me toward his car.

"I am now."

"I wouldn't let anything happen to you." He leans in and kisses me lightly on the lips. His voice is sincere, and although I haven't known him long, I know he's speaking the truth. I feel safe with him. When he held me in the cave and looked into my eyes, even against the void of light, I knew I could count on him. I knew I could trust him.

"I'm famished. Let's feed you," he says, breaking the tension.

"Sounds perfect. And I know just the place." I need to get lost in him right now. I'm not sure what's happening between us, but right now, after what just happened, I need to lose myself in Oliver.

"You know the place . . . ?"

"Yes."

"And where, pray tell, is this place?"

"My suite," I say seductively.

"Is that so?"

I stop walking and turn back to him. Placing my hands on his chest, I look into his lust-filled eyes. "My suite," I say again. He lets out a groan at my response and leans into me, brushing his lips against mine.

"Brilliant."

Together, hand in hand, we make it back to his car and then drive to the hotel. Once inside my suite, I walk over to the table in the living area and pull out the menu.

"Room service menu," I say as I hand him the book. "What are you in the mood for?"

He gives me a wicked smirk, and I feel my whole body go warm.

"Food," I deadpan.

He chuckles as he reaches for the menu and takes it from my hand. "I'll order a bunch of stuff, and then you can have a bit of everything."

"Sounds like a plan. Do they have a cheeseburger with fries?"

"I'm sure they do."

"Great. That's what I want." As he orders the food, I move over to tidy the room. Oliver sits on the little couch in the corner of the room.

"They said it would take about thirty minutes. Come sit with me," he says as he pats the spot next to him. I plop down in the seat next to him. "So while we wait . . . what do you want to do?" His eyes dance with mischief.

"Talk." I laugh back. His face drops like a long-lost puppy.

"There will be plenty of time for *that*." He nods and leans forward to rest his elbows on his knees.

"How about you tell me a little something about yourself?" he asks.

"Um, I thought—"

"I know what you thought. We don't have to talk about anything heavy. But you want to talk, so what do you want to know?"

CHAPTER THIRTEEN

Oliver

When a knock sounds on the door, I head that way and grab the food.

Once we finish eating, she goes to lean in, but instead, I grab her and pull her onto my lap. Our lips collide, and she melts into me. We are all tongue and teeth until she starts to grind against me with reckless abandon. I pause to pull away and stare into her eyes.

"Naked. Bedroom."

She doesn't move. Her chest just rises and falls with her frantic breathing.

"Now," I order. Shaking from her lust-filled haze, she finally obeys. She walks to the room and I follow. Once inside, she starts to undress.

First, her jumper. Next, her jeans. She shimmies out of her knickers and stands before me naked with her clothes discarded haphazardly on the floor somewhere behind her.

My hungry eyes trail over her bare body, and I can't help but lick my lips, ready to claim her.

She places a hand on my chest and lightly pushes me back onto the bed. I widen my eyes.

"Taking charge, I see."

"Yes."

Sliding up the bed until my back rests against the headboard, I watch through hooded lids as she crawls up the bed like a cat stalking prey. Her fingers glide up my calves, then my thighs until her mouth kisses my skin. She's so close that the urge to lift her head and place my cock in her mouth is all-consuming.

When her tongue juts out and swipes away the moisture collecting on the tip, I think I might die. When she then swirls it around the head, I can't help the groan of pleasure that escapes. Before I know it or can comprehend, she is fucking me with her mouth.

Up.

Down.

Up.

Down.

My hips lift in succession with her moves, pushing my cock to the back of her throat. "Up," I grit out as my dick twitches in her mouth.

My hand runs down the length of her breast until I reach her nipple. I pull and pinch it until it becomes erect and hard, then I lean over and swipe my tongue over the peak. She lets out a primal moan.

"I need to taste you." I throw her down so she's on the bed now, and I'm the one hovering, the one stalking. "Legs open."

She does.

"Lean back," I command, and she obeys that too.

Reaching my hand out, I spread her legs and cup her. I start to devour her with my mouth. My tongue laps at her like a starved man. She's fucking perfect. When I start to suck rougher, her whole body gyrates against my face.

"You taste amazing," I mumble, and the vibration of my

mouth causes her to let out a gasp of pleasure as my tongue continues its assault. "Delicious," I mutter through my licks.

As I start to tease her again, her body quivers and shakes against me. Allowing her to catch her breath for a second, I gently suck her into my mouth. When the tremors subside, I thrust two digits inside her.

"Do you want me to fuck you?" I ask. "Tell me what you want."

"Yes," she begs.

"Yes, what?"

"Fuck me."

"Say please."

"Fuck—"

I cut her off with my mouth, sliding my tongue in and feasting on her. She softens against me.

"Please," she finally begs.

So because she begs, I reach into my discarded pants, pull out a condom, roll it on, and then I'm lowering to hover over her. I align my cock and push forward, fully seating myself in her.

I start to fuck her in earnest. A groan of pleasure escapes as I become fully enveloped in her heat, thrusting in and out at a painful rhythm. Her body quivers around me, and I know she's about to come.

Then she does, her inside walls gripping me tightly as she lets go.

Slowly, I flip our bodies until she's on top, and then I pull her above me. With my hands on her waist, I push her down on my shaft and start to move her up and down, helping her keep the rhythm I want.

"Fuck . . ." I groan.

She begins to move faster. Our rhythm is torturous and absolutely divine. She leans forward, her breasts hovering close to my mouth. It's the perfect angle, allowing me to taste her as she rides me.

My head falls back, and I shudder inside her. "You're making me crazy. Fuuuuccckkkk," I grunt.

Once I finish, my body goes lax, and she falls forward on me. Our breaths intermingle as we both try desperately to calm our racing hearts and process everything.

Addison's eyes flutter shut in peace. I imagine what it would be like to actually be with her. For this to be real. Do I want that? A feeling spreads through my chest.

No. I shake my head. This isn't real. This is a means to an end with the added benefit of scratching an itch. I move to lift her off me, but I feel her head shake on my chest.

"Stay," she whispers. And I do the one thing I know I shouldn't. I stay.

"Okay."

I lie with her for another minute, but then eventually, I move her over. "Where are you going?" she asks, her voice laced with sleep.

"To tidy up." I stand from the bed and make my way into the bathroom. I need a breather. To get away for a minute to calm the racing of my heart.

CHAPTER FOURTEEN

Addison

As cliché as it sounds, I have never experienced this before.

No, I'm not dumb enough to think this is anything more than it is, but I have never felt this type of passion.

Not even with Spencer.

I shake the thought off. He has no place in my head or heart anymore.

Once Oliver returns, I follow suit and make my way into the bathroom. I grab my toothbrush and get ready for bed. When I finish brushing my teeth, I make my way back into the room.

Oliver has reclined back on the bed to wait under the sheets. A warm flush spreads across my skin. It's not often I sleep with a man. It's less often that I spend the night. Being with Oliver is almost a first of sorts.

"Stop thinking"—he pats the bed, the empty spot waiting for me—"and come to bed."

I'm still naked, so I search the room for PJs. When I don't find anything right away, I walk over to the dresser.

"Stop."

My hand is now holding a shirt. "I'm putting this on," I respond.

"No need."

I lift a brow.

"We'll sleep naked," he says.

"Oh, is that so?"

"Yes, love, it is. Now get in the bed."

I roll my eyes, but even so, I find myself following his orders. I'm not sure what it is about him—the arrogance or the way he speaks—but I find myself doing all sorts of things I'd never do before him. Like sleeping in my bed naked.

"Do you have a meeting tomorrow?" he asks.

"No."

"Good."

I turn my head and stare at him.

"We have plans."

"You made plans that fast?" I deadpan. "You only just found out I was free. And you haven't used your phone to make plans. Did you send a carrier pigeon?"

"You're an arse." He laughs. "Good thing it's so delectable."

"Har. Har. Har."

I lie back, trying to get comfortable, but the sound of my restless legs echoes in the quiet of the night. I try to silence my brain and the endless barrage of thoughts.

What is this?

What am I doing?

Everything is happening too quickly. Especially how free and alive I feel when I'm with him. This isn't good. I need to pull back. I can't allow myself to fall for him. Where will I be when he leaves? Because eventually, they all do . . .

"Addison." His voice cuts through the night.

I turn toward him. I can't really see him in the dark, but I can feel him. His hands find me, pulling me against his chest, and I rest my head on his bicep. "Sleep."

And with that . . .

I do.

Before I know it, I wake the next morning encased in the warmth of his arms. I can't remember the last time I slept so well. Maybe months. Maybe years. But I can't allow my brain to go there because I'm only here for a few more days, and then I'm off to more meetings. Back to my life. Back to my work. Back to my solitude. The thought is sobering.

"Are you hungry?" I didn't even know he was up.

"Not yet," I say.

My stomach chooses that moment to make itself known.

"I think your stomach objects."

"My stomach knows nothing." Again, it gargles. And with that, I can't help but laugh. More like a snort. *How embarrassing.*

"Let's get up and order breakfast and then go out."

"What's on the agenda?" I ask.

"I know this sounds hard to believe, but nothing."

I sit up and pull the blanket to cover my chest. His eyes follow my movement, lingering on my chest. I shake my head at him.

"Eyes up here." I laugh. "And what do you mean nothing?"

"We are going to go out with no plan." He shrugs, now looking into my eyes.

"Really? That doesn't sound like you."

"I know. Isn't it brilliant? When was the last time you went out without a plan? I guess never." He smirks, and the dimple on his cheek pops up.

"That is not true," I mutter, and he waits for me to say something, and then it comes to me. "The night at the pub."

"So you see, the plan is brilliant. That night worked out well for you."

"How do you figure?"

"You met me."

I stay silent, not really knowing what to say. On the one hand, he's right. But on the other . . .

I can't let myself think about that. As much fun as this has been, this too shall run its course.

"I'm going to shower." I stand, letting the sheet fall back on the bed.

"What should I order you?" he asks.

"Waffles. Big, fluffy, delicious waffles."

Stepping away from the bed, I head to the shower and turn it on. The water washes away the remnants of last night, but I know the memories will stay with me well after the suds disappear down the drain.

When I exit the shower, Oliver hands me a towel, then takes my place.

It doesn't take us long to eat, and before I know it, we're both dressed and out the door.

We decide to walk the streets and see where it takes us. Eventually, by foot, we head down to the tube stop and make it to Portobello Road Market. Despite it still being early, it's already awake and alive.

We meander hand in hand, looking in shops and perusing small alleys. It's nothing like I have done before. It's not often I travel without my team. But here, with my sunglasses on, tucked away in Oliver's arms, I know I'm safe.

CHAPTER FIFTEEN

Oliver

WE SPEND THE DAY WALKING AND PICKING UP SMALL trinkets. Nothing of value, but by the way her eyes light up at each location, you would think every piece was worth a fortune. I'm not supposed to enjoy my time with Addison as much as I am, but regardless of what I want . . . I do.

She's different from what I thought. She's different from what my mother thinks. I assumed once I got to know her, she would be cold and ruthless. And maybe she is in business, but here with me, I see a different, softer side.

It's refreshing to be with someone who just enjoys me and isn't looking for what I can give them or bring them. Maybe it's because her net worth rivals my own. She doesn't need anything from me, and I like it.

The more I get to know her, the more I doubt my plan. Doubt how I can find out the information and leave her unscathed. She doesn't deserve it. At first, I didn't care, but now I find myself caring very much about what happens to her.

Think of the land.

Think of the desperation in your mum's voice.

My mother might be a lot of things, but she's not one to become attached to something unless it's important.

Something about the land is important enough for me to continue down this road.

I have to stop thinking this thing with Addison can be more.

This is temporary.

She'll be leaving soon, and as much as I want to stay in this bubble and play ignorant, I have a goal to achieve, and tonight I'll know more.

"Let's go in this shop," I hear her say, pulling me from my thoughts. I turn my head in the direction she's pointing. From the outside, it looks to be antiques, and when I step inside, I see I'm correct.

Along the walls are vases and bowls. On the tables, items cover all the surfaces. The shelf underneath the table isn't visible under the clutter.

"Look." Addison holds up a book, and I squint as I walk closer to see the writing. "It's a *Romeo and Juliet*." Her lips tip up into a huge smile, a smile so bright it makes my heart lurch in my chest.

"It's a vintage 1969 *Romeo and Juliet*," the shopkeeper says. I can see the image on the book is from the movie.

"We'll take it."

"Aren't you going to see how much they want for it first?" Addison lifts a brow.

"Nope."

Her nose scrunches at my comment. I know it's not because of the money. Addison is a billionaire, but I think it's because I'm buying her something, and maybe she's not used to it. "You don't need to buy me anything." She moves to hand back the book, but I take it out of her hand and place it on the register to purchase.

"I know I don't have to."

"Then why?" she whispers.

"Because I want to."

She stares at me for a minute, and I watch her throat as she swallows the emotion building inside her. "Thank you." Her voice is quieter than normal, so I walk over and place a kiss on her head.

"My pleasure."

After we leave the shop hand in hand, we make our way back to her hotel. I don't like the fact I keep coming and going because of the chances I'll run into someone who knows me. I hate bumping into people on a normal day, but to add fuel to my dilemma are the lies upon lies I have spun.

She doesn't know who I am.

She doesn't even know my real name.

The lies are bitter on my tongue.

They make me feel like a right prick, but every time I hear my mother's voice, therein lies the problem. I'm not a mum's boy by no means, but this piece of land means something to her—more than she's letting on—and for that reason alone, I need to give her peace of mind. Even though we've had our differences, she's the only family I have.

She raised me the best she could and took the brunt of my drunk father's anger for me. I have to do this.

There are so many unspoken questions I want to ask her. She had said she tried to acquire the land, but that Addison's father had refused to sell. Now that Addison's in charge, maybe the offer would be accepted.

"Penny for your thoughts?" Addison asks me, and I shake my head and give her a tight smile.

"Nothing."

"Doesn't look like nothing."

"Just thinking about what we should do next."

Her lips part into a smirk.

"I need to feed you first." I wink, and she flushes red.

"Well, then hurry up because I'm hungry."

Thirty minutes later, we're at a small pub ordering fish and chips, again.

"When do you go home?" I ask.

She stops mid-bite and places the fork down. "I'm supposed to go home Friday."

"As in two days?"

"Yes."

"Don't," I blurt out before I can stop myself. *I need more time.*

"I can't stay."

"Why not?" I need to stop this insanity. Why am I saying this? The more I spend time with her, the more likely she'll find out the truth.

You're not willing to end this yet because maybe you can find out more information.

Or maybe it's because . . .

No. I'm not doing this for me. *I'm doing this for the property*, I say to myself in my head. But it feels fake.

"I have work to do."

"You can't go on a holiday?"

"I mean, I can."

"So take one . . . with me."

Her mouth drops open at my suggestion, and her eyes grow wide. She looks at me as if I spoke another language.

"I have known you for a week. How can I take a vacation with you? I don't know anything about you."

"People have done crazier things."

I take out the familiar coin and she shakes her head.

"I'm not leaving this to chance."

"You sure?" I move to flip it, and she places her hand over mine to stop it.

She shakes her head. "I'm sure. Some people may leave it to chance and go off on a whim because a coin said to, but I'm not that person," she responds honestly.

"Sure, you are. Live . . . Let me show you how."

CHAPTER SIXTEEN

Addison

HIS WORDS LINGER BETWEEN US, AND THEN A DISTURBING thought plays in my mind. This is how Spencer met Olivia, and they ended up together. I have no idea what comes over me—spite, anger, or the desire to live and not just exist—but I find my mouth opening, nonetheless.

"Yes. Okay. I'll go," I say before I can second-guess my decision.

"I would say cheers, but our glasses are empty." He lifts his hand in the air to get the bartender's attention.

"Another round, mate?" the bartender asks.

Oliver nods before turning back to me. "Where should we go?"

I shrug. "I know where I don't want to go," I mutter while looking into my fresh glass in front of me.

"And where is that?" He lifts his glass to his mouth and takes a sip as he waits for me to answer.

"Anywhere I own the property." My words rush out fast. What I really should say is anyplace that reminds me of Spencer because right now, I'm staying at the Lancaster Hotel, and his presence is everywhere. I will not make that mistake again.

"So no London . . ."

"And no country," I add.

"So England is out. Where else do you own property?"

"England isn't necessarily out; we would just have to be creative." I laugh. "And as for where do I own property, the answer is *everywhere.*"

"So then what shall we do? You can't ban all countries."

"Fine, fine," I huff out.

"Are there any stipulations I should know about? Now that we ruled out any property you own."

"I also don't want any that have a hotel built on them . . ." I answer lamely.

"So no property and no hotels. Got it. So we will sleep where . . . a tent?" He's quiet for a second, and then he inclines his head. "Is that what you do? Do you build hotels?"

"Oh God, no."

"Oh . . ."

"Most of the time, I lease the land out." I take another sip of my drink. Just thinking about this has left my throat parched.

"And who leases the land?" His brows knit together, and he stares deeply into my eyes.

"It varies."

"Go on . . ." He rolls his hands.

"Sometimes we turn the property over to large developers to build malls in America."

"And the other times?" He leans forward on his elbows as if he's waiting with bated breath for my response. It's odd. I'm not used to someone paying this much attention to me. Sure, people in business care but never a man like this. Usually, they are out for something from me, so they want to talk about themselves. It's not often the other way around. So I lean back in my chair and let out a breath.

"Well, most of the times in exotic locations, we do business with the Lancasters, as I mentioned I think," I admit. Because even though I don't want to talk about Spencer, I want to talk to Oliver and tell him things.

"Oh, that's right. Hotels."

"Yes. Do you know the Lancasters?"

Please say no, please say no. I don't think I could handle it if he does.

"No," he responds, and the muscles I didn't know were tight in my back loosen. "Is that why you are here?"

"Somewhat," I answer. His face looks sunken all of a sudden, and I wonder why. "Everything okay?"

"Yes." I cock my head at his one-word answer. "I just remembered something I need to do later."

"Oh." I don't know what that was all about, and I wonder if maybe it's because I'm working with Spencer.

He takes a sip of his water and then clears his throat. "Now what?"

"Anything."

"Good. I was hoping you'd say that."

A sense of excitement courses through me at our possibilities.

"I can't believe I'm doing this. Oh my God, I can't believe I'm doing this," I say.

"To be honest, I can't believe you're doing this either," Jasmine says, standing across from where I'm sitting in my suite in London.

"Jasmine, you're not helping."

"Sorry, boss." Her voice drops in volume, and she grimaces as if she's afraid she offended me.

"It's okay. It's pretty out of character." I smile reassuringly, and she lets out a sigh of relief.

"It's really out of character. I don't think you've ever done anything like this in all the years I've worked for you."

"I don't know what's gotten into me."

"Must be the crazy British sex you're having."

I bury my face in my hands. "Jesus."

"Just keeping it real, boss."

It feels good to be here with Jasmine. Traveling around, I've missed this. I miss being with my friends and hanging out with the girls, but Jasmine gets me—not often but enough. Right now, she's helping me pack my bag for an impromptu trip with a man I barely know. It's exactly what I need.

"Are you packing this?" she says, lifting her eyebrow. I look down to where she's holding a piece of something.

"What is that?"

"How would I know? You packed it to come to London."

"Let me see that." She hands me a scrap of material that, at a quick glance, looks like a bathing suit. I probably packed it thinking it was a bathing suit because no way would I have packed this for any other reason but to go swimming. Except it's not a bathing suit. Nope, not at all. This thing couldn't even be called lingerie. It's like dental floss.

"I am not packing it," I say, shaking my head at her, and she grins in return.

"I'm packing for you." She snatches it out of my hand and walks over to my open suitcase.

"You can't do that."

"Sure, I can." She folds it up and places it in. With a smug look on her face, she smiles. "See?"

"You're impossible," I groan.

"One, you love me. Two, you'd be lost without me." She shrugs, walking over to the drawer and pulling out more of my clothes.

I look at her for a minute, and she's right. "I would be," I say, and my words stop her movement. She turns to face me, now holding one of my half-folded shirts in her hand.

"What?" Her eyes are wide, and she's staring at me.

"I would be lost without you. I know I don't say it often enough, but thank you." My voice is soft and sincere. It's not often that I open myself up, especially about my feelings, but after everything she did for me to get me here, I needed to tell her.

"You don't need to thank me," she whispers, nibbling on her bottom lip.

"No, I do. You don't have to be here with me. I know I pay you, but I don't pay you for this, and you're still here. You're like family, Jasmine."

Jasmine smiles, and I smile back. At this moment, as Jasmine and I pack my bags together, I feel free. Like anything is possible.

Is this what Oliver meant? Is this what it feels like to live?

Not long after, Olly sends a text that he's here. He was pretty secretive about our trip, which piqued my interest at the same time as it made me nervous. Butterflies bounce frantically in my stomach as I head to the elevator. My descent feels like it takes forever, but before long, my sandals are clicking on the marble floors of the lobby.

My small bag clanks behind me as I roll it out the door. Jasmine wanted to help me bring my luggage down, and Marcus insisted. However, I rejected them both because this is my trip and my chance to step outside my comfort zone and be self-reliant.

When I step outside, I see the familiar Range Rover parked on the street. I'm not even three steps on the pavement before Olly gets out of the car and heads toward me. Taking the bag, he escorts me into the car with barely a hello, then deposits my bag in the trunk. The driver side door then opens, and before I know it, I'm being kissed.

Not just any kiss. No. This is a hungry kiss filled with promises I'm sure he'll fulfill shortly.

"Are you ready?" he asks.

"Ready? I have a suitcase; what more do I need?"

"Nothing. Just you," he answers.

"So, Mr. Mysterious, where are we off to?"

"Wouldn't you like to know?"

"That's kind of why I asked the question," I quip.

"Where we are going is close enough to drive." His attention focuses on the road ahead of us, and I try to ponder where we could be going.

"Wow. That certainly gives a lot away."

"How about we play a game? You make guesses—"

"I'm too old for games."

"One is never too old for games." Innuendo is clear in what he means and what type of games he's talking about.

I swat at his arm. "Im"—I drag it out—"possible."

"Who, me?" He lifts his hand, pointing at himself.

"Are we leaving the country?" I ask.

"No."

"Are we going to the country?"

"No."

"Can you say anything other than nope?"

He shakes his head, but says, "Yes."

"Grrrrr."

"Let me guess." He lets out a chuckle. "Im . . ." He pauses, puckers his lips, and in his best American female accent, he says, "Possible."

"Well, you are."

"I promise you, Addison, you will like the surprise."

"Fine. I give up." I lean back into my seat and try to get comfy. I'm not sure how long this will be, but despite the scowl on my face, I'm excited. I'm excited to be stepping out of my comfort zone and doing something that makes me feel alive. It might not be like me, but I like this person I am around Olly.

CHAPTER SEVENTEEN

Oliver

WE PULL UP TO MY HOLIDAY COTTAGE SOMETIME LATER. I haven't been here for years, but like all my properties, it was easily readied. No staff will be here this week, which is unusual but necessary. I didn't need any red flags raised if they referred to me by my name, *title,* or whatever they needed to bloody call me.

I had missed this place, but until pulling in the drive up the windy path that leads to a bluff, I didn't realize just how much. I pull over the car, turn the ignition off, and glance over at Addison.

I know from my research she's been everywhere and seen everything. I know her wealth rivals mine, but you can't fake the excitement and wonder in her eyes. The green dancing as she takes in her surroundings.

"This is beautiful," she breathes out. "Wh-what is this place?"

"This, love, is my beach home."

"This is hardly a beach home," she responds.

"Come." I pop open the driver's door. "I'll show you around."

I open her door for her and take her hand. When she steps out, the breeze catches her hair, and it makes her free locks float like the tide.

"Sorry about that," I say as her strays whip around her face.

"Oh God, don't apologize. I love the fresh salt air." She reaches her arms above, to stretch maybe, but it looks like she can fly.

I stare at her as she stretches with her eyes closed and arms outstretched. She looks like a goddess.

"Let me show you inside," I say, my voice low with need.

She opens her eyes, and the way the light reflects off the green makes them look like a clear ocean. There is a depth far beyond the surface in her gaze. If I'm not careful, I'll fall for this woman.

Who are you kidding? You already are.

Which makes you the biggest prick in the world. You are hurting her every day.

With every lie, you hurt her. But it's too late to tell the truth.

"What about our bags?" she asks, pointing at the boot of the car.

"I'll get them later," I mutter. Getting inside her is my first priority, and this is taking far too long.

"Later?"

"Yes, Addison, later. Right now, I have other plans." Now her eyes go wide, but I'm too far gone to laugh at the look there. Instead, I turn from her and make my way to the door.

"Such as?"

Once unlocked, I grab her and pull her inside. "You talk too much." And then I silence her with my mouth.

After having my way with Addison, I make my way to the car and grab the bags. Once inside, I see my staff stocked the cabinets and pantry just as I asked.

Addison walks up from behind, and I hear her laugh. "We could survive the alien apocalypse here."

"We most certainly could." I chuckle.

"That's a lot of food." She starts to browse through it, stopping every now and then to pull out a bag and look to see what's there.

"It is," I respond as she lifts a bag of biscuits up and turns it around to read the label.

"Are you hungry?" she asks.

"Yes. I'll prepare lunch."

I take the bag from her hand and place it back on the shelf of the pantry before closing the door.

"I can do it. Although I hope you have PB and J. I'm not much of a cook."

"Only marmite," I respond, and her eyes go wide, obviously not having any clue what I'm saying. "Forget it. You're lucky I'm your company for the trip. I'm a fantastic chef."

She rolls her eyes at my comment. "Yeah, I've heard that rumor once or twice."

"Now you get to see it in person."

"I'd like to help," she says softly.

"And you will but not right now. Let me do this for you. Later, we can prepare dinner together . . ." As the words leave my mouth, I realize how much I want to do this for her, and how bad an idea this trip really is.

Bile collects in my throat from all the lies, but as long as I have her sequestered in my humble abode, I won't dwell. Time is limited, like grains of sand, and I don't want to waste them by thinking about the inevitable.

"Not sure how much I can help, but I'd love to try."

"Then I'll teach you." I walk up to her. "Would you like that?"

She smiles broadly. "I would."

"Good. Then that's what we'll do." I lean down and place a kiss on her lips. They're still puffy from our previous romp, and if I don't move away, not only will we go for round two, but she'll probably also pass out from hunger.

"Go rest, and I'll make us something."

"I'm not going to rest while you make . . . what are you making?"

"Sandwiches."

"That's easy. I can—"

"Addison, set the table."

She rolls her eyes and lifts her hand to her forehead to salute me. "Where are the plates?"

"Bathroom," I deadpan. "In the cupboard."

"Oh, yeah."

It's obvious she has never set the table before.

When I walk in with two chicken cutlet sandwiches, it looks off. Ironically, as fancy as she is, the table looks a fright.

"I'm bad at this domestic shit." She shrugs.

"No matter. Come sit," I say.

When she takes a bite and actually groans, the sound goes straight to my cock. "This is not a sandwich." Her mouth is still full of food when she says this, and while I usually find this display uncouth, it's adorable on her.

"Two slices of bread do, in fact, make a sandwich," I respond matter-of-factly, lifting the sandwich for good measure.

"No, this is heaven."

"Wait for dinner. Or, better yet, dessert." I smirk.

She shakes her head and takes another bite. I watch as she chews; I watch as she swallows, and then I watch as she licks her lips. I might have dessert now.

"Not sure how you can top this."

"Oh, I can top this."

The mood changes as the room fires up with sexual innuendo. But since we do have to eat, I lift my own sandwich to my mouth.

We sit in silence, both of us enjoying the food, and then together we clear the table. Despite what Addison says, she's not horrible at being domestic at all. She is actually getting the hang of it.

Shame that it can't last.

CHAPTER EIGHTEEN

Addison

THE AFTERNOON SUN HAS BEGUN TO DIP LOW INTO THE sky, making way for the night. From where I'm reclined, I enjoy the colors streaking across the tiled floor.

The light glimmers, creating a rainbow. Today was a good day, and right now, it's even better. I'm relaxed—really and truly relaxed—and able to enjoy a sunset. I'd never be able to enjoy one if I were in New York.

"So are you gonna help me or what?" I hear from across the room. Turning my head to the sound, I find Olly staring at me. I can't tell if he's joking or not because his eyes give nothing away. His face holds no emotion whatsoever.

"Help you?" I ask, and he nods, and now I can see the corner of his lip tipping up slightly. I also notice a tic in his jaw. He must want to smile or laugh. "Are you serious? Are you making fun of me?" I narrow my eyes and assess him.

Still nothing. Then his mouth opens, showcasing the heart-melting smile I have grown accustomed to. "Of course, I was serious. I want you in this kitchen."

"Nah. I think I'll just stay here and watch you." I smirk, lifting my brows suggestively. I lean farther back into the couch and take a sip of the rosé we have been enjoying.

"So you're just going to sit there"—he licks his freaking

lips—"and watch me?"

"That sounds about right. Oh, and don't forget drink." I take another sip, still sitting in my spot.

He moves across the island to grab something in the drawer, and once it's in his hand, he answers, "Nope."

I stare at him, wondering what my retort should be, but my tongue becomes tied as I take in the sight before me.

There he stands with no shirt on, a spatula in his hand, and his sweats slung low on his hips. His perfect V showcased as he moves around the kitchen with ease.

He is divine.

Each chiseled ab . . . an eight-pack, to be exact.

Dear Lord.

This man is no mortal.

He is a god amongst men, and in the kitchen . . . let's just say, nothing has ever been sexier than this image.

Ever.

"But watching you cook with no shirt on is much more fun." I laugh.

"And imagine how fun it will be when I have you bent over the counter," he remarks. My mouth drops open, and if possible, drool collects on the floor beneath me.

Damn. Now that's an image I'll never be able to stop from thinking about. The need to fan myself is present as the room grows considerably warmer. I watch as his upper lip pulls into his signature smirk, and my face grows warmer and warmer until I finally can't stop myself from pulling my shirt away from my heated skin and trying to cool myself off.

"Come on." He chuckles, and I groan.

"Fine."

I stand from the couch and head over to the open floor plan

of the kitchen where Olly is standing. He's now got his hands full of mixing bowls, which he places on the island, and then he's off again to grab more provisions for this dinner.

"Where do you want me?" I ask, and as the words leave my mouth and his smirk widens, I realize my mistake. "To cook."

"Right over here." He gestures beside him, and I watch as his tongue slides along his lower lip.

I pull my gaze back up. "So what are we making?"

"We're going to make risotto."

"Risotto?" My eyes widen. "Isn't that a lot of work?" No way can we make risotto. Well, maybe Olly can, but I can't even boil an egg.

"Yes, but aren't the things we work for the best?"

He pulls me toward him and places me in front of the counter. I can feel the warmth of his front touching my back, and then he places a soft kiss on the back of my head before he walks away and starts to dig into the cupboard.

The heat from his body is missed instantly.

I watch as he grabs knives, measuring spoons, and measuring cups and places them in front of me, and then he pads off toward the fridge. When he returns, his arms are full of fresh produce.

"Okay, so what do you want me to do?" I ask, staring at the pile, the confusion evident in my voice.

"We're making lobster risotto." He shrugs as if this is no big deal. It's a huge deal. Who makes lobster risotto . . . at home? And in a small beach cottage, at that? Without a chef.

"Do we have the ingredients?" His eyebrow rises, and he looks at me as if I just said the dumbest thing in the world. "We have lobster?" I ask, trying to be cute, and Oliver actually rolls his eyes at my ridiculous question.

"Yes," he deadpans.

"Let me see."

He laughs as he hands me a Tupperware bowl, flips the top open, and places it in front of me. Inside the plastic are pieces of fresh lobster meat in a yellow sauce.

"I never said it was alive," he responds to my question and then places the open container on the counter.

"Ahh. Touché."

"The lobster is butter poached." The cooking knowledge and terminology this man possesses has me dumbfounded. It's like he's talking in another language. "It means the lobster has been taking a bath in butter for hours."

"Holy crap. That sounds delicious."

"You have no idea," he answers wistfully.

Now that I know we are making this dish, and that, apparently, Oliver is a professional, I need to know more. "And what are we doing with the risotto?"

"Well, that's where you come in," he responds. He walks up behind me and places an apron in front of me, tying it around my neck. I look down to see it's a rather cute black and white one with little flowers on it.

"Why do you have an apron in your kitchen?" I ask, wondering who this belongs to. A part of me internally cringes, hoping he doesn't say it's an ex's.

"My mother," he answers before stepping aside to stand next to me.

"Okay. So what do you need me to do?" I wait for him to give me instructions.

"I'm going to sauté the veggies, but I need your help chopping them first."

"What vegetables are we adding?"

“Butternut squash, peas . . .”

“Well, I don’t have to chop the peas,” I deadpan.

“But you do have to chop the onions,” he retorts.

I grimace at the notion.

He hands me the onions and butternut squash and heads over to the gas stove. It flickers, then flares to life as he places a large skillet on top of it.

“Doesn’t it need spray oil or something?”

“First of all, no.” He shakes his head and rolls his eyes. “You really don’t know anything about cooking, do you?” He chuckles.

“Duh. Hence the lesson,” I retort.

“The first thing you need to know is that you always heat the pan.” He reaches around and shows me a circular flat object, then he points at the top of it for me to see. “This is a pan thermometer. Once the pan is three hundred seventy-five degrees, we will add the oil we need. Only then do we start to cook.”

“Who would’ve thought it was so technical,” I mumble under my breath.

He shakes his head. “Everyone except people who can’t boil an egg.”

I spend the next few minutes chopping an onion. My eyes are watering as if I’m crying.

“Here,” I say, and Oliver turns around and looks at me. With one hand, he reaches for the container I have filled full of chopped onions, and with the other hand, he swipes my cheek, removing the stray tear that must have fallen. We stare at each other for a beat, locked in each other’s gaze before he leans down and kisses my forehead. When his lips move away, I finally shake myself from the trance.

The moment is too much with us staring at each other while we chop vegetables. It feels too much to be real, too domestic, too much like we are a couple, cooking dinner together.

Which we are not.

So I take a step back, turn to the counter, grab my knife, and start to cut up the butternut squash.

"Cubed?"

"Yes."

I chop away. When I've finished all the vegetables, I step up next to Oliver at the stove. "What are you doing now?"

"I was browning the rice. That's the secret to good risotto. That and constantly stirring. What we're going to do now is we're going to sauté the vegetables. Then we will cook the rice and chicken broth slowly, stirring it constantly."

Oliver hands me the spoon, and I'm shocked. However, I'm not so shocked when he stands behind me, his front to my back, with his arms wrapped around me, and we both begin to stir.

Time stands still as we're pressed against each other. It's like we're moving as one in the kitchen, and this feeling is even more hedonistic than making love.

The teasing of his heat.

The torture of his touch.

The creating something with him.

It's a togetherness that I like. That I want. I can't remember feeling this way in a long time.

Eventually, my arms grow tired, so Oliver puts in more strength. I can feel the beating of his heart against my back, and then he bends his knees behind me, and he's kissing my neck, all while stirring the pot. I swear my breath comes out choppy, and it's like we are in a heated dance of foreplay.

I move my ass back to swirl against him, and he groans.

"It's done," he mutters, but I don't hear what he says, or maybe I don't understand, or maybe my brain is just so filled with lust that I don't comprehend anything. Before I know it, I'm being lightly pushed away from the stove, and then it's turned off, and the dish is done.

Together, we sit at the table. It's nice in a way I'm not used to at all.

First, I'm staring at a plate of food I helped create. That in and of itself is special. Second, being here is relaxing. I haven't thought about anything other than Olly. Not work. Not New York. Nothing.

I'm living in the moment, enjoying the present, and it's fantastic. I wonder if his life is always like this.

"This looks delicious," I say while licking my lips. Olly doesn't respond. Instead, he stares at my mouth and watches the movement of my tongue. "The food, Olly."

"Hmm," he says, still staring.

"Let's eat," I press.

With that, he chuckles, lifts his fork, and dips it into his bowl. I follow suit and fully groan as I place the warm food in my mouth. It's not just delicious, it's divine.

Heavenly, really.

"Wow," I groan.

"It's good, right?"

"Good? This is restaurant quality."

"I told you I could cook." He shrugs.

"This is more than cooking. How did you learn how to cook like this?"

He places the fork back in the bowl but doesn't pick up another bite.

"Growing up, I had a cook. She taught me everything."

"Didn't you want to play?"

"I—" He pauses, and his forehead scrunches up. "When I was home . . . I didn't have any friends to play with," he finally says.

"And you have no siblings?"

"No."

A heavy feeling starts to spread in my chest. I can't imagine not having my siblings. Sure, Gray might drive me insane, and Jax is a pain in my ass, but I've always had them, and when my father died . . .

They are my everything.

I don't know a lot about Olly, but the thought of him growing up alone makes me sad for him. "So when you were home, you learned how to cook?" I ask, interested in his childhood. "Weren't there any kids for you to play with?"

"Where I lived, there weren't any children or, at least, none that I spent time with."

"That must have been lonely."

He sits back in his chair and nibbles on his lower lip. "I wasn't home often." His voice is so sad. I want to hold him in my arms; I want to go back and find the little boy who was all alone and be there for him.

"Boarding school?" I ask.

"Yeah."

The idea of boarding school is so foreign to me. No matter how much money I grew up with, my parents were always around. For everything.

"I can't imagine that. Did you like it?"

"Well, I never knew any different. I started going when I was a child."

"What was it like?"

"Honestly, it's the only thing I know. It was good times, though. I liked to live away more than I liked to live at home."

I lean forward on the table. "Why?"

"I never got along with my dad," he says as he lifts the fork to his mouth and takes a bite.

"And now?"

He places the fork down, the sound of the metal hitting the table echoing in the space. "He passed away."

A feeling of sadness works its way through me. "We have that in common. But where you never got along, my father was my everything," I whisper, unshed tears filling my eyes. One falls, and I swipe it away.

"Sorry."

"It's okay."

"When did you lose him?" he asks, his voice low. I almost don't hear him.

"Only a few years ago. Two, to be exact. Heart attack. It was very sudden. He taught me all I know. Everything I have is because of him."

I love my father and miss him every day.

His brow furrows, a strange look passing over his features, and then he shakes his head. "Boarding school was fun," he says, changing the subject.

"What did you like best?" I ask, allowing him to steer the conversation away from an obviously sore topic.

"I made some great friends. We got into all kinds of trouble. Still do." He laughs.

"Tell me about them."

"I'm not very close to many of them anymore. Just my best mate, Nathaniel."

"What's he like?"

"An arse." He chuckles. "But the best kind of an arse. Always up for a good time."

"Is he married?"

"Heavens no. That bloke will never get married. All he does is party."

"Sounds delightful." I roll my eyes. That sounds like someone I have no desire to meet.

"He really isn't that bad."

"And any other friends?"

"For a while, we hung out with one other bloke, but that faded fast."

"What happened?"

"Nathaniel found him in bed with his girlfriend."

Suddenly, I feel ill. I might have told Olly a little about my relationship with Spencer, but I left certain details out. Awful things I had done that I can never take back and will always regret.

The dumb mistake I made in my early twenties had dictated my life for too long. People change. I changed. Shaking the memory of indiscretion out of my mind, I turn back to Olly.

"Are they still together?"

"Yes. Cecile got married to the tosser."

"Sucks." I should know.

"It does," he agrees.

I know what it's like to lose the one you think you love. It's awful.

"Let's drink," he says, lifting his glass filled with wine.

I lift my own.

We lean forward so our glasses collide. "To moving on," he says, and I smile.

"To moving on. Letting go," I add.

"And living," he finishes.

"To living."

Once we finish, we both take long sips. As the wine works its way through my body, I let it melt any resistance I still harbor inside me. There isn't much. Most of it has been obliterated already, but the last remainders are gone now.

I want what he spoke of. I want to live and not just exist. I want to open myself up to the possibilities even if it might not be with Olly.

The possibilities of this developing into more are slim, but I can't regret it even if it ends tomorrow because he's opened my eyes to what I'm missing. And now, sitting here across from him, enjoying his company and laughing and being, I realize I won't go back to New York the same woman when our time is up.

Olly has changed me.

CHAPTER NINETEEN

Oliver

SHE LIES BESIDE ME, HER BODY WARM AND TUCKED INTO mine. I want to stare at her, admire her beauty, but instead, I force myself to get up. I can't let myself go there.

In the end, being with Addison is two things—a fantastic distraction from my life and a means to an end—and I have to remember that. No matter how lovely she looks and feels beside me.

She's more than that, and you know it, a voice hisses in my head, but I shoo it away.

She's not. Not really. She's a one-night stand, turned into a weekend fling, turned into a little bit longer, but there is no future here. Just fun and a bit of information.

Then why do I feel like a bloody wanker right now? And why do I feel like I can't face her?

I climb out of bed, swinging my legs over the side to place my feet on the wood floors. The soft tapping of my feet as I pad into the bathroom isn't loud enough to wake her, yet I still find myself tiptoeing.

On the way out of the room, I snatch my mobile off the counter and head to brush my teeth. I close the door slowly, the sound of the hinges echoing loudly in the silence of the morning. As soon as it's closed, I swipe the screen open and see my mother rang.

Shit.

Knowing she'll keep calling, I ring her back.

"Hello, Oliver," she answers, annoyance evident in her voice. Apparently, she's not happy I haven't answered her last five attempts.

"Mum," I respond.

"Is that all you have to say to me?"

"Well, Mother, seeing as I just woke up, what more could I have to tell?"

"I hear you're away."

My fists tighten. Who is she speaking to? Why can't she mind her own business?

"I am."

"And where are you?"

From behind me, I hear the door open, and the soft thud of feet hitting the marble tile. "I have to go," I say and abruptly hang up the phone before she can object. In the mirror's reflection, I see Addison. Her face is contorted in confusion.

"Who was that?"

"Just a mate of mine," I respond. I turn to face her, and I notice an uptick in her cheek and a line forming between her brows.

"A mate?" she asks, not believing me, and she shouldn't. Our relationship is a house of cards these days—built on lies and sure to fall to the ground soon.

"My friend, Nathaniel." There's no reason to lie to her, but at this point, I'm going to hell anyway, so I might as well light a bigger flame.

"I'm sorry." She looks guilty, and I feel somewhat bad. The truth is, we were talking about her, and now I'm lying to her. I'm the bastard, not her.

She has every right to be suspicious, but she doesn't know that. I take three steps toward her and lower myself to meet her gaze.

"There's nothing to be sorry for, love." I lean in and place a kiss on her lips. I expect the kiss to deepen, but she pulls back. A question lingers in her eyes, but I smile and pretend it's not there.

"We're going into town today."

"We are? What do I need to wear? Are we jumping off a cliff, maybe climbing some mountain?" She laughs, and the sound helps evaporate any residual anger from speaking to my mum.

"None of those adventures. I thought we could check out the village."

"That sounds great," she says. Walking past me, she sets off to get ready.

An hour later, we're in the seaside village that I remember from my youth. I haven't been here in years. Although I keep staff here year-round, it's not a place I come often.

This was merely a holiday cottage my mother's family had owned for years. London keeps me busy, so I never get out here. Being here with Addison feels different. I could see myself—

I stop the thought right in its tracks. Instead, I turn to her. "Are you hungry?" I ask her.

"I could kill for coffee."

"So let's get that for you."

I pull her with me, her arm resting in my elbow. We weave through the narrow alleys until we stop in front of a weathered building. The rusty old sign hanging from the doorframe reads Ms. Maddox Bake Shop. What it lacks in appearance, it makes up for in character.

When I push in the old oak door, a small chime rings

through the air. It's just the same as in my memories with mismatched furniture and knickknacks everywhere. I hope everything is the same.

When a woman I have never seen walks to the counter, I'm disappointed because I was hoping to see Ms. Maddox. I've known her since I was a lad, and she always brings a smile to my face. "Do you still have the blueberry scones?"

"Of course, we do."

"Blueberry scones?" Addison scrunches her nose. "Is it good? I don't really like blueberries," she whispers to me.

"You've never had a blueberry or a scone until you've had a blueberry scone from here."

"Sold. Let's get scones."

With scones and coffees in hand, we leave the bakery. Although there was seating, I know the perfect place to sit outside a bit up the road on the park benches that face the water. It's terribly warm today, but the fresh breeze and the warm coffee make for a perfect breakfast.

"This is amazing. Oh, my God . . . I have never tasted anything like this."

"It's brilliant, right?" I say with a mouth full of food.

"It really is. I'm not much of a dessert person, but wow."

"Not much of a dessert person?"

"Nah."

"I thought everyone loved dessert." I speak casually with a bit of jest in my tone, but she catches my meaning, and her cheeks flush in response. I love how affected she is by me.

"I mean, don't get me wrong, I do like sweet things, but typically, I don't eat them." She lifts the scone to her mouth, and I watch as her lips wrap around it, and she closes her eyes and groans.

Bloody hell.

That sound out of her mouth should be illegal. My jeans start to grow tighter as I try to figure out a way to drag her back to the cottage and have my way with her.

"Well, now that I know you love scones, I might have to make sure you have a stash before you leave."

"To take home with me?" she whispers.

Something about her voice has me on edge. I'm sure she's under no illusions that this means more. She's made it quite clear she wants nothing more than this from me, and there is the little matter that we really can't have a future.

If she ever finds out my lie . . .

CHAPTER TWENTY

Addison

WE SIT IN PEACE FOR A WHILE, AND I CAN'T EVEN comprehend how relaxed I am. I can't believe I have to leave soon. I'm not ready.

Reality is a bitter pill to swallow. Something I don't want to do. On the one hand, I need to get back to work. I need to go back to New York and then finalize my travel plans again. Also, I can't hide from Lancaster any longer. It's not like I'm officially hiding, but I need to meet with him and tell him about the land.

"What's on your mind?"

I keep staring at the ocean in front of me, lost in the way the waves crash against the rocks. The way they smash like broken crystals is mesmerizing. "I'm just thinking about work," I answer honestly with a sigh.

"I thought we decided no work. No reality. Just here. Living."

"We did."

I feel his hands touch my jaw until my eyes are meeting his.

"What's going on?"

"Are you sure?" His lip tips up. "Wouldn't it be breaking our promise?"

"I'm sure. Talk to me."

"I have a piece of property . . ." I inhale, and he stiffens. It's an odd move, but then again, he must think I'm on the verge of a nervous breakdown.

"Go on," he says.

"It's actually the one where you saw me. When I got my heel stuck in the mud." He looks at me intently. His eyes not blinking.

"What's the problem?" His voice sounds gritty and gravelly. Like there are rocks in his throat. Or maybe he's choking on his words.

"See, the thing is, I came to look at it for the Lancasters." Continuing to stare at me, he doesn't speak. His jaw is firm, and I know I'm taking far too long to tell this story, but every time I think of him, I feel broken. "Remember that ex . . . ?"

That's when he finally blinks. "Your ex is—"

"Spencer Lancaster," I interject. "It was a long time ago, but he was . . . he meant a lot to me."

"What happened?"

"I cheated on him," I whisper, the words hurting even now. "I was young, and he was my older brother's friend. I was so insecure when we dated, and I never thought I was good enough or worthy of him. One day, I heard a girl talking about how she had a drink with him, and rather than ask him, I let my insecurities win . . ." I trail off.

"I understand. You don't have to say anything more."

"The pain has lingered for years. I thought maybe one day he'd forgive me, and he did but only so much. The day I left was the weekend of his wedding. I came to England to get away. I surveyed the land because he had mentioned building in the country. I thought—I thought if I did it, if I found him the property on the heel of his impending marriage, it would look like . . ."

He nods with understanding. “It would look like you were over him.” He sighs.

“It was dumb. The best way I could have shown I was over him would have been to attend his wedding,” I admit and then let out the breath I didn’t even know I was holding. It’s so easy to speak to Oliver. Easier than speaking to my brothers. He understands.

“So now what will you do?” he asks.

“I don’t know. What’s the point? I told my brother I was going to put my foot down and make a statement instead.”

“What does that mean?” His Adam’s apple bobs as he speaks.

“I was going to open negotiations with other developers.”

“And the point being? Because, from what I see, if you do that, you’ll look like a woman scorned.”

“I don’t know what to do,” I whine.

“So why do anything?”

My eyebrow lifts at his question. “What do you mean?”

“Why develop it at all? It seems to me you are doing it for the wrong reasons. Maybe you shouldn’t.”

“I have to.”

“Why?”

“I-I don’t know.” I lift my hands and cover my face. When I remove my hands, his face is stern, and his jaw clenched. “Let’s stop talking about this.” I smile. “I feel like I made this day too heavy. Forget I said anything.”

“I can’t, Addison.” He sighs, and he looks sad for a moment.

“Please. I have a lot to think about, but I don’t want to ruin these last few days.”

“Okay,” he whispers, and I move closer to him and place my lips on his. At first, he doesn’t kiss me back, but then he melts against my mouth. Falling into the kiss, he erases the last few moments and creates new ones.

Luckily, the day got better. It took a little bit, but eventually, we faded back into the easy, comfortable relationship I had grown to crave.

We spent the afternoon walking through the town, and then we walked back to the cottage. We were out for hours, and my cheeks were rosy from being sun-kissed all day. Today was warmer compared to the past few days. The sun had peeked out from behind the clouds throughout the day, but as it happened, it must have been stronger than I thought.

"What are we cooking today?" I ask.

"I've decided we cooked too much yesterday, so tonight I'll take you out."

"Oh, big fancy dinner in town." I wink, knowing full well there are no fancy restaurants in the village.

"Something like that."

"Interesting."

He surprises me when we walk to the back instead of walking to the front door. He surprises me, even more, when he starts to pull me down a small path through the back garden and then down a hill. We take a turn, and that's when I realize the path leads to a secluded area adjacent to the water. Grass leads to sand or more like pebbles. It feels jagged under my shoes, but a little bit over toward the cove is a flat patch.

On the ground are a blanket and a basket. "I-I don't understand," I say, gesturing to the objects.

"While you were showering"—his smile touches his eyes—"I set this up."

I shake my head in disbelief as he helps me down and sits beside me on the large blanket now spread across the ground.

"The sun will be setting soon. But the full moon will illuminate the sky." He leans forward and opens the picnic basket, grabbing a bottle of wine.

"You've thought of everything."

"Indeed, I have." He grins.

And I know he must have because, with just a peek, I know this night is perfect.

Unfortunately, the next day comes before I know it. And even though I want to stay, my time has come to go back to the real world. I don't want to leave the bubble Olly and I have created for ourselves. I want to pretend a little longer and be ignorant of the world around me. But seeing as I have missed calls, voice messages, and texts, I know I have to surface and head home.

"So this is it?" I whisper.

"It is." He's crossed his arms over his chest, and his shoulders are tight as if, like me, he doesn't want this to end. Standing in the foyer, we stare at each other, but we don't speak for a minute. The weight of the silence is heavy.

Suffocating us with unspoken words and promises.

But what can we say?

What is there to say?

We always knew what this was.

He leans forward, bending until his face is level with mine. I should walk away, but I don't.

I let him kiss me, and despite knowing what I shouldn't do, I kiss him back. I allow myself to fall into the kiss, the illusion, and the hope for a future even knowing this trip is about to be over, and I have to return to reality. Olly lifts me into his arms and walks me to the bedroom. Through deep and passionate kisses, he undresses me. He pulls my panties down my thighs and removes his clothes next.

I lie back with him hovering over me, but the look in his eyes is almost too much. He looks like he wants to consume me, as if he is memorizing the moment. I know I am.

He widens my legs and positions himself at my entrance. With a tilt of my hips, I meet the warmth of his caress. He doesn't enter me, though. Instead, soft fingers tease my sensitive skin. They dip inside me and find the sensitive spot buried deep within.

My body starts to quiver as he pushes upward with his fingers and massages me, bringing me so close I'm teetering on the brink of eruption. Just as I'm about to explode, he pulls back, leaving me vacant and greedy for more as he aligns himself against my core.

Finally, our bodies come together, and then and only then do his lips find mine again, pressing firmly to kiss me deeply. There are unspoken words. He doesn't want this to end and neither do I, but we both have lives, and our own future, and we made it clear from the beginning that it couldn't be more.

His grip tightens around me as his control wavers. He's holding back to let me adjust to him. I push forward, taking him deeper, and again our bodies meet as he enters me fully.

I exhale, relaxing into him and letting him claim me completely. He thrusts in and out, each stroke lighting a fire. The bond between us grows with each move he makes. My heartbeat pounds as he throbs within me. The surge of release tingles as a shiver claims my whole body until I soar higher than I ever thought possible.

When we finish, we lie in bed to catch our breath. I look over at the clock on the wall.

It's time.

The car will be here now, waiting for me.

Reluctantly, I rise, and he groans. The type of groan that makes my heart hurt. Standing, I walk to the bathroom, and he follows. We both dress in silence.

Once I have my clothes back on, I go to walk toward my suitcase, but he shakes his head.

"I have it." He pads across the room and grabs my rolling suitcase. With the handle now in his hand, he stares down at it and then back at me. "This doesn't have to be goodbye," he finally says.

"Then what should it be?" I whisper.

"Until we meet again?" he responds, his voice tight with emotions.

I nod, but the words stick on my tongue because even that false promise hurts.

It feels like a lie because I know we won't meet again. I can't run the risk of falling for him. That's not in the cards for me right now. I gave my heart away once, and it was stomped on, so I won't make that mistake again.

No matter how amazing Olly is. No matter how much fun I have with him and how, when I'm with him, I forget about everything but us, I can't risk it.

Oliver stands, watching me, his forehead scrunched. "Are you sure I can't drive you to the airport?"

"No. Thank you. The car is enough."

"I don't mind," he says, his voice sincere.

The walls around my heart tighten and ache, but I give him a tight-lipped smile and turn away quickly.

As much as my heart breaks, I have to leave.

He walks me to the door without saying anything. He doesn't object to me leaving or to him not driving me. I fear he will, but I'm thankful he doesn't because right now, my emotions are all over the place. I don't know what I would say if he told me not to leave. If he asked me to stay longer.

I would.

And that thought alone has me climbing into the waiting car without a goodbye or a farewell kiss.

The door closes behind me, and for a brief instant, I want to open the window as I go. Like those scenes in the old World War Two movies where the train starts to move, and the heroine runs down the platform as it leaves.

But I don't.

Instead, I slump in the air-conditioned car, relaxing into the crisp leather seats, and close my heavy eyes.

I don't dare open them. I know what's behind the heavy lids.

I won't cry.

I can't.

The ride is silent, and I'm happy I don't have a long drive to the small private airport I had Grayson send the plane to. We pull up directly beside the plane, and once my door is open, I walk up the tiny metal ladder and take a seat.

It's one of our smaller planes, and we only have one flight attendant on board today. Jasmine and Marcus flew back last week, so it's just me by myself. She offers me a drink, and behind my sunglasses, I nod.

A moment later, she brings me a glass of wine, but oddly enough as I swirl the glass, lift it to my mouth, and take a sip, it's not my favorite cab that I want. No, what I crave now is something different.

A dark stout.

The thought so preposterous it makes me laugh.

Monday morning.

Which means I have a long week ahead of me.

I've postponed the inevitable, and now it's time to face Lancaster and my brothers. I know Jasmine will expect a full update, but I wonder if I can sneak into the office. Doubtful.

When we pull up to the building on Park Avenue, a heavy feeling weighs on my chest. My driver pulls up, walks around, and opens the door for me. It's warm today. I changed on the plane into slacks and a blazer, but my snug pants cling to my body in the oppressing heat. Either that or I'm nervous and I'm sweating. I'd like to believe it's the former. I don't open the door to the building. It's opened for me, and everybody welcomes me back.

Walking toward the private elevator, I hit the button to the penthouse and head up. Lucky for me, there's no elevator music, and no one is with me. I'm not ready. I need to drop my facade. I need to pretend the past two weeks have not happened. I need to believe I have everything under control.

Because I do.

The elevator door opens, and I take a step out. My heels clank on the marble floor, and all eyes rise. I'm not even halfway to my office before Jasmine approaches me. Her eyes are wide, her smile hidden, but I know she's dying to ask.

"Morning."

"Hey, J," I respond.

"So we have things to discuss," she leads, and I roll my eyes, knowing what she's getting at. She wants gossip, lots and lots of gossip, including positions and locations. This girl has a hard time remembering I'm not just her friend, but I'm also her boss.

"I guess."

"I cannot wait to hear," she squeals.

"We're in the office, so you won't be hearing very much." Together, we walk through the glass doors of my office, and she shuts them.

"Now that we're alone, tell me everything."

"Jasmine, just because we're in my office doesn't mean I'm gonna tell you details."

Her eyebrow rises. "So there are details?" she teases.

"You know there are."

"Just give me one."

"This is highly unprofessional." I laugh. "It's a good thing I have never been professional with you."

"Go on . . ." She laughs.

"It was amazing."

"When are you going to see him again?"

That feeling starts to spread, tightening the muscles in my back. I lift my hand and try to rub at the knot that has formed on my shoulders.

"I'm not."

"I don't understand. Why wouldn't you see him again?"

I let out a sigh. "Our lives are too different. Mine is here, and his is there."

"What the hell does that have to do with anything?" she asks.

"I just want to leave it as the perfect memory."

"That's the dumbest thing I've ever heard."

"What do you mean? Wouldn't you rather have a perfect memory than have it all go to shit?"

"How do you know it will all go to shit?"

"Everything goes to shit eventually."

She shakes her head and sighs. "Addison—" she starts, but I lift my hand to stop her.

"We have a lot of work to do."

She nods, understanding I've ended the conversation. I sit behind my desk, and she takes a seat in one of the chairs facing me.

"So why don't you get me up to date."

"Have you decided if you're going to entertain other offers?"

"Actually, I am."

She nods in understanding.

"Gray will not be happy," I add. Even after Spencer and I broke up, Grayson felt a sense of loyalty. It's not that I don't, but now I don't see the need to bend over backward for him. His family has been taking us for granted for far too long.

Maybe I sound jaded, or maybe I sound hostile. Maybe I sound like a woman scorned, but I'm not. I'm just a shrewd businesswoman. A part of me remembers Oliver's words. Maybe I should do nothing. The property has sat undeveloped for years. Maybe I should leave it like that. Father never built on it.

I'm about to pick up the phone when my door flies open.

"You're back," Grayson states.

"I am."

He lifts a curious brow. "And how was your . . . vacation?"

"Just what I needed."

"And now you're ready to work?"

"I am."

He inclines his head and studies me. But he won't find anything because my walls are up. I might miss Oliver, but

I barely know him, so how much can I miss? And as for Lancaster . . .

Spencer is a thing of the past. The time away did wonders for me. There was a time I never thought I would meet someone I could connect with in the same way as I did Spencer—not just in the boardroom but also in the bedroom. But going away and meeting Oliver helped remedy that.

Not only is it possible for me to meet someone who can challenge me, who can make me think, but now I know someone out there can fulfill all of what I need. It's just a shame that someone won't be Olly. But sometimes, I think people come into your life for a reason. You might not know what it is at the time, but eventually, their intent becomes clear.

I might not have a future with him, and I might never see him again, but he came into my life exactly when I needed him. He showed me there was a future out there for me, and I deserved to be happy.

For that, I will always be grateful to Oliver Black.

CHAPTER TWENTY-ONE

Oliver

With Addison gone, nothing's keeping me on the coast or in the country. I don't even bother heading back to my estate before I go straight to my flat in London.

Keeping a flat there is imperative, not only for my seat in the House of Lords but also for work. Originally a solicitor, I no longer practice. Instead, I manage the property and the investments. And apparently, I manage my mum. Or at least I try.

Normally, she's rather easy. After my father died, she remained secluded in the country. She doesn't talk about the times before, but I know she was terribly unhappy.

I don't remember much other than the fighting and the drinking. When things got bad, I hid, and then, luckily for me, I was sent to boarding school.

Unlucky for her, she was stuck. Not often are people happy when a husband or a father dies. From what I could tell of Addison, she was devastated, but that was not the case for me. In my life, it was almost cause for celebration.

The mean old earl. The drunk. The village idiot.

His legacy in the village is quite the opposite of mine. People respect me. I don't get in anyone's way, and I mind my own business. I certainly am not showing up at the pub drunk, belligerent, and angry. But that was then, and this is now, and now I'm ready to have a drink with a friend.

Reaching across the console, I grab my mobile and dial. "Olly . . ."

"Nathaniel."

"Are you in London, mate?" he asks.

"I am," I respond. "Fancy a cocktail?"

"That would be brilliant," he says.

"I'm surprised you're in town," I add.

"You know summer in the city is my favorite time." He chuckles.

"How could I forget? I assume, though, you are avoiding your family?"

"Yes, well, Grandfather isn't in town, and Eddie is being a wanker." He really hates his cousin, but Nathaniel isn't wrong. He is a complete tosser, and I would hate to call him family. "Anyplace, in particular, you want to go?" he asks.

I think long and hard. I could say out to a club or maybe the posh new lounge that opened, but after spending the past few weeks with Addison, the idea of being with a woman other than her holds no merit. I prefer a glass of scotch with my best mate, so that's how I answer.

"I was thinking Blacks." We both belong to Blacks, a private gentlemen's club. Nathaniel and I belong to a lot of private clubs, but this establishment has been around for hundreds of years, and only the elite are members.

Every time we are both in town, we go. That's not to say we don't frequent other spots, but typically, we go there to catch up.

With Nathaniel recently out of the relationship with Cecile and single, he's always jet-setting, so we aren't often in the same location at the same time.

"Half past nine work for you?"

I park my car and head into my flat. I'm not even inside more than a minute before my mobile rings. "Hello, Mother. It seems you feel the need to harass me on a daily basis."

"Well, you haven't spoken to me. You haven't told me what you found out."

"There is nothing to tell, Mother."

"Not acceptable." She scoffs.

"What in the bloody hell do you expect me to do?"

"I expect you to be a good son and tell me what you found out."

My hands clench, and I watch as the knuckles turn white from my frustration and anger. "I found out nothing, Mother. There, are you happy?"

"Hardly. I'm actually disappointed."

I run my hands through my hair, tugging forcefully at the root. I don't know what it is about this piece of land, nor do I want to at this point, but it's apparent I have no choice.

"From what I can tell, she's planning to lease the land to the Lancaster family." A part of me feels like I'm betraying Addison's trust. The other part just wants my mother off my back.

I did what I said I would and found out what she wanted to know. Maybe I don't have the answers, but I tried. Now I have to try to forget about the woman who haunts my dreams. It's going to be a hard task, but there's no future there. It all started as a lie.

"The Lancasters?" She pauses for a minute, thinking, and then it comes to her with a groan.

"A groan? Really, Mother? Not acting very ladylike, are we?"

"Sh-she's leasing our land to be developed into hotels?" Her voice trembles.

"Apparently. Or maybe not."

"What do you mean maybe not?"

"I tried to persuade her to consider other options," I admit, knowing this train of thought might calm her.

"And were you successful?"

"There's really no way of knowing."

"Can you find out?"

I let out a sigh. "No."

"Please." Her voice is short, and it's the last straw. Even though she's polite, there's an edge I don't like.

"Goddammit. The answer is no."

I'm done toying with this girl. Even I know what a wanker I've been.

"Think about it, please." This time, she lowers her voice, and it's almost like she's pleading with me to reconsider.

"Tell me what's so goddamn important about this land, and maybe I'll think about it."

She's quiet.

"Mum?"

"Come home."

"I'm not bloody coming home. If you have something so important to say, tell me now."

"Very well, I'll come to London."

"To London?"

"Yes."

Shit, this is bad.

"Hey, mate," I say as I walk into the room and find Nathaniel sitting at our table. Well, not necessarily our table as much as it's the table we always occupy when we come to Blacks. Ever since we joined the club right out of university, this is where we meet. Nathaniel is ready for me. The hundred-year-old scotch sits in a glass tumbler. Neat. Three fingers. Just the way I like it.

He stands, walking up to me, and gives me the signature back hug. One tap. I give one back, and then we both sit.

"What brings you to town, Nathaniel?"

"The usual." He laughs. That means women and booze. If I thought I needed to grow up, he needs to grow up faster. He's always out and about, flaunting his latest flame to the paps. Basically, he's the opposite of me.

"What about you?"

"A spot of business."

"Oh, bloody hell, working! That's awful," he exclaims dramatically and loud enough for a few members to turn in our direction.

"It's not that bad." I chuckle.

He shakes his head.

"Nathaniel, we're thirty. It isn't that bad."

"Speak for yourself. I haven't turned thirty yet, but the dreaded day is fast approaching."

"Any plans?" I lean forward, placing my elbows on the table. I could use a trip. I know I just took one, but I could use one even more after Addison.

"Ibiza."

"Rough life."

"The roughest."

"When are you heading out? Maybe I'll accompany you."

"Probably in a week, maybe two. I plan to celebrate the big day drunk on the beach."

"I'll see what I have going on."

"So what's going on with you?"

"Not very much," I answer, but my brain doesn't get the

memo. Instead, the image of long, lean legs and flowing brown hair pops into my thoughts.

"By the look on your face, it doesn't seem that way."

"You know I don't kiss and tell." I chuckle.

Nathaniel leans forward, a smirk lining his face. "So there's something to tell?"

"No."

"You said that way too quickly for me to believe you."

"Nothing worth talking about."

"Very well. So then what do we have to discuss? We certainly aren't going to talk about work. Or this girl, apparently, either. What else is there? How's your mum?" he asks.

"Driving me insane."

"Now this I need to hear."

"There isn't much of a story. She basically became obsessed with this plot of land. One that was once in the entail."

"What's so special about this property?"

I shrug. "That I do not know."

"Another round?"

"Always."

It's been two days since Nathaniel and I had drinks, and I'm still in my flat in London. There's no allure to going back home to my estate. It's not like I brought Addison there, but when I think of going, I think of her. I can still imagine her touching the sticky countertop at the pub. I can't help but laugh when I hear a knock on the door. I'm under no illusion of who it is because I've been waiting for this for two days. My mother is in town.

I fling the door open, and she strides in as if she owns the place. In her mind, she probably does, but ever since the death of my father, I own the place. And not just this place but all of them. Every last one. Well, that's not true. There's one piece of property I don't own. Nor do I care to.

However, I am curious what the fascination is. I move aside to let her pass. When she does, she walks over and takes a seat on my couch. I, on the other hand, walk over and grab a tumbler.

"Would you like a drink, Mother?" I ask her.

"It's a bit early to drink now, Oliver."

"It's five o'clock somewhere." I shrug. "In Japan, we could be at happy hour right now."

"Since we are, in fact, not in Japan, I shall have to pass on that drink and so should you." She gives me a disappointed look, but I pay her no mind.

"Very well. Your loss. It's a fabulous scotch."

With my scotch in hand, I take a seat adjacent to my mother. "Since you won't have a cocktail with me, why don't you tell me what this is all about."

"If I must."

"You must," I say sternly. "Enough of these riddles, enough mystery, just tell me about the land." I watch as her posture grows tight, her face pales, and suddenly, I wonder if I should take back my request, but I can't.

"What do you know about the land?"

"That's the problem. I know nothing. All I know is that Addison's father became the owner of the land."

"As you know, the land was once part of the entail. What you probably don't know is that this land and this family have had a horrid time at keeping finances straight. During World War Two, your grandfather was forced to break apart pieces of the property that belonged to the title in order to keep the estate.

"As time went on, the land became a bargaining chip. All my father wanted was a title. Back then, our money was new money, not old and not titled, and my father was desperate for a title."

"So what happened?"

"He sold me."

"He sold you!" I shout, not really understanding what she is saying. How can that be? How could Grandpapa have sold my mother?

"Maybe the word sold is harsh, but I was forced into a marriage with a man I didn't love . . ."

Shit.

I can't imagine being forced to do anything. I don't even like what I felt pressured to do with Addison even though I enjoyed myself immensely the whole time.

"What happened?"

"Things were okay at first. But then your grandfather died, the earl. That's when it all went bad."

"What did Father do?"

"With a new title, he was arrogant. I brought a hefty amount of money and land into the marriage, but no amount of money matters if it's mismanaged." She sighs.

"And Father mismanaged the money?"

"Yes. It didn't take long for him to crack under the stress. He approached my father for more money, but Father already had what he wanted, a countess as a daughter. All the doors had already opened to him. There was nothing more that he needed, so when your father approached him for financial help . . ."

"The bank was closed."

"Precisely. He started to drink . . . He was out of control. H-he . . ." Her voice cracks, and it's a jarring and startling sound in the quiet of my flat. My own heart starts to race at what she's getting at. At what I fear she might tell me.

I move off my chair and sit beside her. Her head is now down. Long black strands cover her face as her body shakes. I place my hand on her back, encouraging her to continue. As much as I don't want to hear more, I know I need to. This is as much her story as I fear it is mine, so she must tell me no matter how painful it is.

"He started to have affairs. Around that time was when I fell pregnant with you. I had hoped . . ."

"That having me would make him happy?" I whisper. How many women have been in this position, hoping the love of a child would help? But even I know it would never have made a difference with my father. He was a cruel and selfish man, and the thought of my mother grasping at straws breaks a part of me I didn't think could break.

My soul.

She nods. "It got worse." She sniffles, and I reach across the couch and grab a tissue for her. Once she collects herself, she places the tissue in her hand, balling it up with anger. "He was bleeding money . . ." She starts back up. "Selling property. There wasn't very much left. The entail had once again been broken apart. There were only two plots left . . . the one the estate sits on and . . ."

She doesn't have to finish for me to know what she's talking about. "That piece of land was meant to be our salvation. If farmed properly, it was the only piece that could sustain the lifestyle we were accustomed to. The rest of the land wasn't suitable for farming. It was our last hope."

She stops, and I touch her again. “Please, Mum. Go on.” She shakes and shudders at the movement but continues.

“By this point, your father had become an angry drunk with a penchant for debauchery and gambling. One night, despite my pleas, he went out. There was a card game with a wealthy American who was supposed to be a horrible card player . . .” Her words hang in the air, and the last piece of the puzzle falls into place.

A wealthy American.

A card game.

A wager.

“Price?” I hiss.

She bites her lip to stifle a sob, but it doesn’t help, and her whole body is shaking now. “Price.” She looks down at the floor, and I know it was Price.

“That was the night our fate was forever changed.”

“What did he do?”

“You know what he did,” she cries.

“I need to hear it,” I implore. I need to know what the bastard did. I want to know what it was all for. I need to know that my happiness, my lack of a childhood, and my future were all about a greedy man’s card game.

“He lost everything. All but the estate. To this day, I don’t know how we’ve maintained it. That was the first night he beat me. I never thought it was possible, but I married a man no better than my father. He was worse. For years, we hung on but just barely. You were so young, and I’m thankful you don’t remember what it was like. He took on wealthy mistresses, and he kept up appearances. But when he was home . . .”

I don’t think I can hear more, but through the pain lancing my chest, I listen to my mother tell me the things I was too young to notice but always knew were true.

"Then he died. He drank himself to death. When he died, our lives didn't change. Your first few years were hard, but then my father died. I made a promise that by the time you were able to govern the estate, there would be an estate to manage."

"But why then . . . ?"

"Because all this is for nothing without that land. Every scar, every broken piece of my body and mind, and all the years I endured pain was for this, to get your legacy back. The legacy that ruined me."

"We have the legacy. We have the bloody title. Why do we need the land?"

She shakes her head.

"Then I'm done. I did my part. I don't care about the land and neither should you."

"Yo-you don't understand."

"Then make me."

And then she does. She tells me the one thing that changes my life . . .

"I'll get it back."

No matter the consequences.

CHAPTER TWENTY-TWO

Addison

For the past week, I've been throwing myself into work and forgetting all about the three weeks in Europe. With my gaze fixed on the number dancing across my computer screen, I barely register the sound of my phone ringing in the distance.

On the third ring, I realize it's my cell phone, and no one's going to answer it. The number isn't registering, and it's from overseas.

It's not him.

Don't get excited.

I almost don't answer it, but in the end, I do because it could be about the land. The land I still haven't made my decision on.

"Addison Price," I answer.

"Well, hello, Miss Price," he coos. I would know that voice anywhere. Goose bumps break out across my skin at the memories that flood my brain.

"Oliver." My own voice sounds breathier than I want, but hearing him on the phone does wicked things to my body.

"At your service," he says, and I can't help but laugh. *Typical Oliver.*

Now that the haze of surprise has lifted, I lean back in my chair. "I didn't expect you to call," I answer honestly.

"I didn't expect to."

"So why did you?"

I can hear him breathing into the phone. "I missed hearing your voice," he admits on a sigh. I'm not sure why he sighs, but he does, and I'm not sure if I should be bothered by it or happy he couldn't stop thinking about me either.

"You did?"

"I did." Hearing him say that makes butterflies swarm in my stomach.

I smile to myself as the door opens.

"Addison, do you have the specs for the property in Barcelona? Lancaster is meeting with the architect—"

"Grayson, can you give me a moment?" I eye him and then the phone. He furrows his brow and opens his mouth to speak, but I lift my finger, silencing him.

"Can I call you back?" I mumble into the line.

"Bad time?" Oliver asks. I let out a puff of breath, and he chuckles into the phone.

"You can say that."

"Okay, but Addison . . ." He trails off, his voice husky with intent, and it makes me want to moan into my cell. But seeing as I'm not alone—as my brother is in my office—groaning or moaning or even looking like I could potentially do either is not in the cards.

"Yeah."

"Ring me back."

"I will," I promise before hanging up the phone.

"Who was that?" Grayson asks me, pulling me out of the haze created by hearing Oliver's voice. Damn Grayson for butting his head in my business yet again.

"None of your business," I answer forcefully.

"Touchy much?" He's too clever. Too smart. I've basically set off red flags in his mind by the way I answered.

"Jeez, leave me alone."

He lifts one brow and then squints his eyes, trying to figure me out. After a tiny nod as though he's solved the puzzle, he lifts out his hand toward me. "Then give me the figures."

"God." I groan now but not in a good way. "I'm busy."

"And I need them."

"Why don't you get Jax to hack into my computer? That would be easier."

"But would it be as fun?" He smirks.

I roll my eyes and turn my attention back to my screen. "I'll email it over by the end of the day, and if that's not soon enough, I give you permission to tell Jax my computer is his—but no snooping."

"You're just asking for trouble now."

"That I am."

The day can't end soon enough, and before long, I'm at my penthouse apartment facing Central Park. Before I can even think about calling him back, I head over to my wine fridge and set out to open a cab. From across the room, I spot a bottle of Glenlivet, and suddenly, it's not wine I want. I want to close my eyes and pretend I'm in England. Pretend I'm at the cottage on the coast drinking with him. I pour myself a glass and then head into my room to slip out of my work clothes.

Once I've donned silk shorts and a matching button-down, I pick up my phone. What time is it in London?

One a.m.

Should I call?

He told me to. Practically ordered me to. Yes.

I dial the number and close my eyes as I wait. I'm not sure

why I shut them. Maybe in fear. Maybe in prayer? I picture him in my mind. He's so gorgeous.

"Hello, love." His voice pulls me out of my daydream. "Do you miss me?" he asks, and I swear my whole body shivers with need and anticipation.

"I do," I whisper into the phone, but by the way he breathes, I know he heard me.

"Good. I miss you too."

The line goes quiet for a second, and I wonder what to say. "How was your day?" I ask lamely.

"It would be better if you were here."

"Mine too . . ." I sigh.

"How so? What would we be doing now if I were there?" His voice drips with innuendo.

"Olly," I chide, my skin warming.

"I can almost see you now. Your skin turning that shade of pink it does every time you're turned on."

"Oliver," I repeat because I don't want to admit he's right. My skin feels hot and heady as though a flame is dancing across it.

"Don't Oliver me. Tell me, Addison. Are you hot?"

"Yes," I say so low, but even I can tell my voice sounds strained with unsuppressed desire.

"Close your eyes."

Instead of them shutting, they do the opposite. His words have them popping wide open.

"I know you're not listening," he coos. "I miss you. I miss kissing you, I miss touching you, and I miss hearing you come."

"I-I—"

"Shhh. Just give me what I want."

"I'm not sure I can."

"You can." His gruff voice makes my insides warm like an inferno building inside me.

"But it's not enough," I groan to myself, and he chuckles on the line.

"Then Facetime."

"What?" I say too loudly. "No."

There is no way I can do that.

"Yes."

"I can't."

"Sure you can, love." When I don't say anything, he continues, "I promise you, you will never feel more alive . . .. Now hang up the phone, and I'm going to ring you back. I want to see your face when you come."

Warm heat spreads across my cheeks as I think about what he's saying to me.

"I'm waiting . . ." He trails off, but I still don't do anything.

All of a sudden, I hear a call waiting in my ear. "Can you hold?" I ask, pulling the phone from my ear to see who's calling. My heart starts to race as I look at the name.

"Aren't you going to answer that?" he coos. *Oliver is Facetiming you.*

Shit.

Shit.

"Answer."

So I do.

"Hello," he says through the phone, his piercing blue eyes locking onto mine. "So you are blushing."

"No," I say too quickly, and he lets out a throaty laugh.

"I think the red looks lovely on you. I missed speaking to you, but I missed your blush even more. Touch yourself," he commands, and my eyes go wide. "It's okay, love." He smiles at me. "You can do it. It would make me very happy to know you're thinking of me and touching yourself."

"I don't think I can . . ."

"There's no place for thought right now. Stop. Live. Touch yourself."

"But—"

"Just imagine I'm there with you. What would I be doing to you right now?"

"Touching me?"

"Yes, love. That's right. I would be touching you. Now, close your eyes, and I want you to pretend your hand is my hand. Can you do that?"

"Yes," I squeak out. I'm not sure what it is about this man, but no matter what he says, I find I don't want to say no to him.

Closing my eyes like he asked, I slide my free hand down my chest, down my stomach, and between my thighs.

I raise my lids for direction, and he smiles back at me. "Open your legs, Addison." My eyes open wider. How did he know I hadn't done that?

Following his cue, I do. I part my legs and then caress my heated skin. I find myself wet and needing. I didn't know how desperate I was for release until Oliver mentioned touching me.

"Now imagine my fingers there. Pressing against you."

I lift my hand until my fingers circle my entrance, but I don't breach myself. Instead, with pleading eyes, I ask him to guide me the rest of the way.

"Close your eyes again." I do. "Pretend it's me."

I nod. "Fuck yourself," he orders, and I do. I start to fuck myself with my own hand, and it feels so fucking good. My thumb presses down, as my two middle fingers are now inside me.

"Harder, Addison." His words urge me on, so I do what he says. Pressing harder, I imagine it's his fingers inside me. "Can you feel me?" he groans, and I open my eyes to see him looking back. There is heat in his stare, and I know from his breaths that I'm not the only one getting pleasure from this call. Knowing he's touching himself has me rubbing harder.

I rub, touching myself the way he's instructing. "More," I moan.

"Put your fingers inside you."

I slip my finger inside, then nod, letting him know I did.

"Show me." His husky tone forces me to comply.

I angle the phone down, and he does the same. I watch as he strokes himself from root to tip, and I match his pace. Once my breathing regulates, I look back at him through the screen, and he smiles.

"I can't wait to see you." He winks.

Wait, what?

Before I can ask what he's talking about, he's already gone. I drop the phone on the bed and throw my hands over my face. Did I really just do that? Who is this person I am when Olly is around? I'm not sure.

But if this is living, I like it.

The next few days pass at a turtle's pace. I'm giddy with excitement by the time Friday rolls around. On Wednesday, Olly called and told me of his travel plans to come visit me today. I can't believe he's actually going to be here. I can't believe I'm this excited.

Before I know it, the end of the day comes and with that also comes a very excited Jasmine.

"You know what time it is."

I roll my eyes. "Yes, J. I know exactly what time it is."

"It's four fifty-nine."

"I don't really need you to tell me what time it is."

"Are you sure? Because I can do a play-by-play. It's in my job description."

"That's funny. I'm pretty sure that wasn't in the job description." I scoff.

"It was added later," she chides back.

"And who added this?"

"Why me, silly."

I open my mouth, feigning shock.

"Pretty sure calling your boss names is frowned upon."

"Well, I guess it's a good thing you're a cool boss." She smiles.

"Oh, am I?" I joke.

"Yep." She lifts her watch and starts jumping. "It's five o'clock."

"Jasmine," I playfully scold.

"Why is Jasmine jumping in your office?" Jax says, popping his head into my office.

"Little brother," I greet him. "I haven't seen you in forever."

"I've been working."

"Also known as locked in your home office probably hacking into the Pentagon," Jasmine mutters under her breath.

"Nope. Just doing Grayson a favor."

"Anything I should know about?"

"You know Grayson . . . he uses my skills for whatever suits him."

"What about me?" Grayson steps into my office.

"Great, the gang's all here," I deadpan.

"On that note, I'll be leaving. Have fun tonight," she says before realizing the can of worms she just opened. Her hand lifts to her mouth as she grimaces. I shake my head, and she mouths, "Sorry."

Once she's out of the office, the inquisition begins. "What's tonight?" Grayson asks, crossing his arms over his chest and narrowing his eyes.

"Mind your own business." I scoff.

My brother's eyes widen as he cocks his head and smiles. But I know Gray, and this isn't a nice smile. The way only one side lifts up on the left makes it a calculated one . . .

"Mind my own business? Now I'm intrigued."

Shit. Just as I thought. Now, he'll never let me be, not until he knows all my secrets. He's always been this way. The protective older brother who needed to know everything I was doing. Nothing has changed over the years. Only now, he's found a partner in crime with Jax as his sidekick in the "drive Addison insane" game.

"It's really nothing, Gray. Can't you just leave it at that?" I plead.

"No. First, you go away with God knows who. And now, you have a date."

"It's hardly a date," I say before I can think better of it, but once the words leave my mouth, I realize my mistake. If Grayson wasn't chomping at the bit to get information before now, I have basically dangled a huge piece of steak in front of not one but two hungry lions.

A look passes between my brothers, and I groan as I lift my hand to my face and cover my eyes. "So, Addison . . ." I move my hand and look at my eldest brother. "Who is this mystery man?" Grayson asks, shooting a look at Jax and nodding. I shake my head adamantly at the exchange.

"No, no. None of that covert code. There is no snooping into my personal life."

"You let me hack into your computer all the time."

"Only 'cause I'm too lazy to tell you the information you need. This is different."

"It's not different."

"Sure it is, and if you can't see the difference, we might have to sit down and have a little discussion about your extracurricular activities . . . maybe with the FBI . . ." I trail off for impact.

My brother laughs at that, a full belly laugh. "You wouldn't dare."

"Try me." I narrow my eyes.

"Now I really need to know," Grayson exclaims. "Adds, you've never been so secretive about a guy before."

"Oh my God, will you both please leave me alone? I'm already late."

"To your date . . . ?" he leads.

"Yes. To my date. Happy?"

"Not yet, but it's a step in the right direction." Grayson's lip tips up and makes me want to march over to my brother and hit him upside the head. But since that is not in the cards, being a mature adult and all, I settle for a scowl.

"Relax, sis," Jax says. "We're just playing."

"No, you're not. You're not playing," I chide. "You know it, I know it, and by the time I'm out of this office, I give you two minutes before you're delving deep in the dark web to find all my secrets."

"Well, if you know I'm going to do it, why don't you just give me a name? That way, it won't take so long." He shrugs.

"Oliver. If you must know, his name is Oliver," I hiss.

"Last name?"

"Nope. I am one hundred percent not making it any easier for you."

He doesn't respond, just nods a knowing smile.

"Well, if that's all you boys want, I'm late. Don't bother looking in my calendar. I didn't add it," I say to Grayson. "And you . . ." I point my finger at Jax. "I'm not bringing my cell, so there will be no pinging."

"She's good." He gestures to Gray, who nods proudly.

"Bye." They're both belly laughing by the time I make it to the elevator.

I take my cell out of my purse and call Olly. "Change of plans. Meet me at Central Park. Corner of sixtieth and Fifth. I won't have my phone, so just be there at six thirty."

"Everything okay?" he asks as the doors open, and I step inside and press the button.

"Just a couple of thorns in my side." The elevator doors close, and it starts to descend.

"Do I even want to know?"

"Brothers. Very annoying brothers. I might lose you. I'm in the elevator."

"Got it." His voice cuts in and out as I make it to the ground level. "See you soon."

I go straight home before heading across the street to Central Park. I picked the park for a reason. I haven't seen Olly in a few weeks, and I don't want it to be a given that he's coming over. I know maybe the lines blurred the other night on the phone, but for all I know, the attraction won't be there for either of us now that we're in New York. Maybe the appeal was that it was a vacation fling. Maybe seeing him on my home turf will make the luster fade.

Who are you trying to kid?

I'm so desperate to see him that I doubt that will ever happen.

I make my way into my closet first. I pull off my fitted A-line dress and grab a pair of faded skinny jeans, ballet flats, and a white T-shirt. If I know anything about Oliver, he's not into the pretentious nature of the Upper East Side.

It's refreshing.

I'm used to men with too much money who only care to show their wealth, so it's a welcome change to be with someone more humble. Sure, Oliver obviously has the funds to own that cottage, but the wealth I'm used to, well, that's a whole different story.

I wonder what he will say when he sees my apartment.

If he comes back with you.

The thought of his lips on my skin has my skin prickling with excitement.

Before leaving, I check myself in the mirror one final time and then make my way to the private elevator that leads me out the back entrance.

New York City is still bright, despite the time. This is my favorite season in the city. The sky is a brilliant shade of pink as it ducks behind the buildings. The lush and green park just begs for a long, leisurely day of picnicking out on the lawn. Maybe we should do that tomorrow.

Don't get ahead of yourself, Addison.

As I cross the street, I see him. He's standing beside the streetlight on the corner, just as I instructed. He's furiously typing on his phone, and my eyebrows pinch in.

Who is he texting?

He looks up from his phone, places it in his pocket, and spots me. He doesn't wave, but I wouldn't expect that of him. Instead, his lips tip up into a smirk, and my own lips part when I see his.

My feet move faster, desperate to be with him again, and finally, after quick steps, I'm standing before him. He's even better looking than I remember. His presence seems so large and vibrant even against the Manhattan backdrop.

"Hi," I say, and he raises his arms and pulls me to him.

"Hello, Addison." Once he engulfs me in his tight embrace, I relax into him. He leans down and places a kiss on my lips. "I missed this," he says against my mouth.

"Me too."

He moves his mouth against mine, and there, on the sidewalk of Fifth Avenue, he kisses me like he hasn't seen me in years instead of it only being a matter of weeks.

Catcalls ring out beside us, and I pull back, warming at the thought that I just kissed him in the middle of the city with an audience.

After the claps end and Olly's laughter subsides, I look around. "Where to?" I ask.

"I want to take you to my favorite spot to eat. And then, I want to make love to you all night long."

"Okay," I squeak. I'm shocked how the moment I'm in front of Oliver again, all my previous personality is gone, replacing the cutthroat businesswoman with a blushing schoolgirl.

He takes my hand in his and guides us about a block and a half. The street directly in front of Central Park has nothing except a few vending carts and a place to grab a horse.

"Are we taking a horse?" I ask, still not understanding.

Maybe we just haven't gotten there, and we still have to walk some more. Thankfully, I changed out of my heels, so walking isn't a problem.

"Right here," he says.

"Right here?" I ask back. Because clearly, I'm missing something. "This is your favorite place to eat?"

"Yes. Right here." He steps up to the cart. "Two hot dogs," he says to the attendant.

He hands him a few bills, and the next thing I know, my mouth hangs open as Olly gives me a dirty water hot dog. One I would never be caught dead eating; one I have never tasted in my whole life.

"The best food in New York."

"Clearly, you're from England and just don't know good food."

"Or you're just sheltered." He laughs. "Go ahead. Take a bite, love." He takes a bite, and I swear he closes his eyes to savor the food in his mouth. I have to hold back my gag reflex. No way am I eating a hot dog that's been sitting in water all day.

"No. Nope." I shake my head dramatically, making him chuckle.

"Oh, come on, Addison. You only live once."

"Yes, but a stomach bug could last forever."

He takes another bite. "Look, I'm fine." And then in front of my face, he clutches his chest, starts to make a strange sound, and bends his knees, hunching over. Oh my God. Oliver is fake dying in the middle of Fifth Avenue. Are you kidding me? I try to hold back the laughter threatening to erupt.

"Save me . . ." he groans. "You will only save me if you die with me. Take a bite of your hot dog."

I'm so embarrassed, but at the same time, I can't help

the euphoric feeling of laughter bubbling out of me. I haven't laughed this hard in so long. All because he is making a huge scene in Central Park.

"Be my Juliet. Die with me."

The crowd is cheering around us. "Take a bite."

"Take a bite."

"Bite!"

"Bite!"

I want to die of embarrassment as the crowd cheers for me to eat this disgusting hot dog.

"Okay. Okay. Stop it. Fine." I take the bite.

"Swallow the hot dog," someone yells, and I do.

Everyone cheers, and as the surprisingly good hot dog travels down my throat, Oliver stands, grabs me, and kisses me full on the mouth.

"You suck."

"I know." He winks. "Now take me home. Because I have a promise to uphold."

Olly keeps his word and fulfills his promise. He makes love to me all through the night. In the middle of the night, he wakes me up to soft kisses and sweltering touches.

This morning, I wake to him beside me. I can't remember the last time I slept this well. Probably at the beach cottage. I never thought I'd be that woman—you know, the one who can't sleep without a man—and I'm not.

When we were away, I was wrapped up in the moment, feeling as though my mind was playing tricks on me, but now that we're here, at my apartment, in my city, I know it could be more. But I haven't opened my heart to another since Spencer Lancaster.

I had put my heart on the line with him, and I wasn't enough for him. I realize now that we were just not a good fit, and that what we had was an adolescent crush. He was best friends with my older brother, and I had fallen in love, but now seeing how I am with Oliver, I realize what I felt for Spencer was a mere childhood infatuation.

That's not to say I love Oliver—I know it's way too soon for that—but I know this feeling is different, and I know it could turn into more. And while that thought usually scares me, with him, it doesn't. I'm not scared. I'm excited.

I want more.

His words dance in my brain, and I now understand existing versus living. When I'm with him, I appreciate the small things, like laughing on Fifth Avenue while eating a hot dog. Most Manhattan socialites wouldn't do that. They would have never been able to enjoy throwing their head back with the sun hitting their face as the crowd cheered them on to swallow a piece of disgusting meat.

I might have joked that it was disgusting but as gross as it was, it really wasn't *that* gross, and the truth is I will never regret that moment.

I feel an arm snake around my waist, then a sleepy Oliver nuzzles the crook of my neck. "What are we doing today?" he asks in a husky voice.

"Eating," I reply.

"I can do that," he responds, crawling under the sheets, parting my legs, and making me forget my own name.

It takes us a full hour to roll out of bed. And once we do, we shower; he washes me, and I wash him. I can fully see showering together might be a problem seeing as I'm lost in his kiss as he lathers my body with soap.

I pull away. "Food. Real food. I'm starving."

"Very well. I'll feed you."

"Food, not your penis," I respond, lifting an eyebrow. He shrugs, and I step back under the water to rinse off.

Once we're both dressed, we set off to start our day.

The first day of our time together was amazing. I wonder if he'll spend another night, and when he does, I can't even pretend I'm not ecstatic.

Finally, on day three, my alarm goes off, and I groan. I don't want to go to work. I don't want to leave him.

"Don't go," he says against my skin, parting my legs and teasing me with his fingers and tongue.

"I have to," I mumble. Not wanting to at all.

"Take a holiday." His breath touches my skin and makes me dizzy.

"I already took one."

"Take another one." He circles my skin, teasing me until I'm breathless.

After I come undone from the wicked things he can do with his mouth, he crawls up my body, and I spread my legs to cradle him in the apex of my legs.

I lift my hips, and the tip enters me. He pushes a bit farther before pulling out. He moves his arm across the bed to reach for the condom.

"I get the shot," I say before I can stop myself.

"Are you sure?"

I nod, and he steals the air from my lungs and my sanity all in one thrust.

After our morning romp, Oliver sits beside me at the kitchen island. How can one man be so handsome? His hair is disheveled, and he's shirtless. His perfectly formed forearms rest on the counter as he inclines his head and just stares at me. He looks at me like a starved man, a man who didn't just have all types of crazy sex with me and is still ready for more.

He'll be the death of me, that's for sure. His sexual appetite is unlike anything I have ever seen. I have never met a man who can touch me or kiss me as he does. As though he can never get enough. He smirks as I appraise him, obviously knowing where my brain is, so I pull my thoughts to today.

"What will you do while I work?" I ask, trying desperately to distract myself from my fantasies.

"Check into my hotel, I suppose." His shoulders shrug as if it were the simplest answer in the world. I didn't even know he had a hotel to stay in.

Lord, this man distracts me to the point of oblivion. "Have you had a hotel this whole time?"

"I have." He leans back and grabs the mug in front of him.

"And you're paying for it?"

"I am." He lifts and takes a sip, his eyes locked on mine the whole time.

"You can . . . you can cancel it if you'd like." I nibble my lip, and he stands from the counter, stalking over until he stops directly in front of me. He moves closer, his lips hovering over mine.

"Would you like that?"

"I would."

I walk into the office late—much later than normal—and I'm greeted by a smiling Jasmine or more like a smirking Jasmine.

"So . . ."

I just smile, and then Jasmine, being Jasmine, starts to cheer in the office. If I was going for discreet, this is not the right play. My eyes widen, and she stops. I walk up to her. "If there was a chance my brothers didn't know I was here, they do now."

She bites her lip. "Sorry about that."

I shake my head, but I'm not really mad. I just like to give her shit sometimes. "Don't worry about it." I laugh.

"Must've been some weekend."

"And then some . . ." I trail off, allowing the innuendo to be obvious.

"Stop it." She covers her eyes and laughs before peeking out from behind her hands, her cheeks red now. "You're going to see him again," she whispers now.

"Actually, he's staying with me," I say, trying my hardest to keep my composure when, in truth, I can already feel my face warming at the idea of Oliver in my bed.

"He's staying with you?" she whisper-shouts, her brown eyes widening considerably with the new information.

"Yes, but don't tell my brothers." I lift my fingers to my mouth, and she goes to say something but is cut off.

"Don't tell your brothers what?" Grayson says.

"Jeez, don't you people have a life?" I fling my arms up in the air dramatically.

"Not particularly. Unlike you, we work." He smirks.

"Unbearable."

"We have a meeting in fifteen minutes. That's what I'm doing here."

That has me lowering my hands and then leaning forward to place them on my desk. "A meeting? About what?" I ask.

"Lancaster is here. It seems he and Grant want to open another chain of hotels. Exclusive residences all over the world.

They will be renting and selling the units. This might be the perfect time to pitch them the land in Wiltshire."

"No," I say before I can think.

"No? What do you mean no?" he asks.

"That's what I said. No, I'm not prepared to discuss that piece of land."

"Are you not prepared to discuss any plans with him or just that piece of land?"

I think about it, and I'm not sure what my answer should be. On the one hand, we have a history. On the other hand, he's my brother's best friend, and they're like family. Can I really be this petty?

"I'm ready to discuss land, but to be honest, I saw the property." I think back to the quaint village with the cobblestone streets and the dodgy pub. And most importantly, I think of Oliver. And as much as I don't want to base this decision on him, I can't imagine him living in a town with a one-billion-dollar hotel development. I imagine that would tarnish the pub where I sang, where we danced, where we drank, and where we met.

"Well, you should think about what you're going to do with that land, and you should think about it sooner rather than later."

"I promise I will. Just give me some time. Trust me to make the right decision."

"Trust has never been a problem for us," my brother says, and I smile because it's true. No matter what I decide, my brothers will have my back.

Once I'm alone, I pick up my phone and dial my mom. With Spencer coming to the office for a meeting about the property, I realize I never did see if she figured out what was so special about the one in Wiltshire.

"Hello, dear," she answers. She sounds tired, and I wonder if I woke her from one of her many naps. She tends to sleep a lot. Her doctor told me it was a side effect of her depression. I hope that's not the case.

"Did I wake you?"

"Oh, no. I was just resting." She pauses to take a breath. "I promise I'm okay," she says when I don't respond.

"If you're sure?"

"I am." Her voice is stronger now, and I know she's trying hard to convince me I shouldn't be worried. "Is there a reason you're calling, Addison?"

"Actually, there is. Did you ever remember anything about the land?"

"I did. I remember your father acquired it on a trip abroad. He never got into the details of the purchase, but I remember him going on and on about what a pompous man the owner was. Apparently, the previous owner turned his nose up at your father and his new money. I remember the owner tried to buy the land back at some point, but he refused. Your father was a stubborn man." My mother's comment makes me laugh. My father hated to be judged for his money, but what he hated more was the disrespect he received from people who viewed him as beneath them. He worked hard to become the man he was, and if you wronged him, he would never forgive you.

"So then why didn't he build on it? Or lease it, or honestly do anything with it?"

"Well, that's the part I remember, and it made me laugh at the time. Your father was so put off by the British aristocracy that surprisingly enough, he started to read up on it. You know how your father was."

That I did.

"In his readings, he came across an interesting article about Shakespeare. Apparently, and there were some speculation and contradictions to the story, he had bequeathed his land to his daughter's husband with a bunch of stipulations. Your father became fascinated and decided that one day, he would do the same thing for your husband."

"So what you're telling me is that Dad never built on the land on the off chance I would get married?"

"Yes."

"Well, that's the most ridiculous thing I have ever heard. I don't need a damn dowry."

"He meant well."

I shake my head and laugh; only my father would come up with such a backward plan. That's why I loved him so much. The good news, though, was now the land was free game to do with whatever I pleased because Lord knows I'm not saving it for any husband of mine.

An hour later, I find myself in the glass conference room with Spencer and Grant Lancaster. Pierce, the youngest Lancaster, is missing from the table. But then again, as an artist, why would he be here? Jax is not here either. It's just me and Gray.

"No Olivia?" Fuck. I hate when I say shit like this without thinking. I cringe at my words.

Damn, this was the wrong way to start this meeting. His eyes go soft, and he inclines his head.

"Addison."

I shake mine back and forth. "No. No. I'm just playing. No hard feelings." When I say the words, I'm actually shocked by how true they are. Looking at him from across the table, I realize all the feelings I've had for Spencer have evaporated, and it's a good feeling. I have no animosity, and I have no regrets. Actually, I just want to be happy.

"No hard feelings," he responds. "Not after everything you've done for us." After he says that, the room's quiet. It's a bit awkward with the implication of everything the Lancaster family and my family have gone through.

Secrets, betrayals, and unrequited love.

Finally, Grayson breaks the silence when he puts down a portfolio. "These are the properties we have pulled for your new venture."

"I think the one in Malaga would be perfect," I say.

"Malaga? Interesting."

"Have you been?"

"I can't say that I have. I have been to Spain, of course. The usual locations such as Barcelona and Madrid. But never Malaga."

"A few areas in the States could be promising. For one, the Great Smoky Mountains would be perfect for your needs."

He leans forward, looking interested, and I spend the next hour discussing everything from the properties to the zoning laws in each region. By the time the meeting is over, I'm excited to get home to Olly. It's funny how things can change so fast. Only a few weeks ago, I wouldn't have been able to sit across from Spencer after he just got married, but Oliver helped me.

Never once during the meeting did I think of Spencer in that way. Never once did my heart hurt, and the whole time, I thought of Olly.

Unfortunately, I have to work first. Walking down the hall, I pull out my phone and dial Olly as my heels clatter against the marble.

"Hey, love," he answers.

"Hi." I can't help the smile that forms on my face from just hearing his voice on the line and knowing he's waiting for me.

"How's work?" he asks.

"Work."

"That bad?"

As I walk back into my office and sit behind my desk, I think about his question. "Actually, no."

"What happened?"

"It's a long story. Spencer Lancaster was here."

The line goes silent, and I wonder if he's upset. Or maybe even jealous. "Okay . . ." His voice still sounds odd, and it makes me feel on edge.

"Do you . . . want to meet for lunch?"

"Can you get away?" he asks.

"Well, I usually have lunch at Townsend Café once a week with my friends, but they canceled, so my calendar is wide open. Want to join me?"

"I'd love that," he responds, but his voice doesn't match his comment. Something is up.

Olly is already at the restaurant when I get there. He smiles when he sees me, but it doesn't touch his eyes. Is he worried about Spencer? He has nothing to worry about. Regardless of Olivia, I'm over him.

"Hi," I say as I lean down and give him a chaste kiss. I take a seat, and it's rather quiet until after we order.

"So this long story . . ." he says. "Are you going to tell me?"

I incline my head, and for a moment, I want to say no and tell him to lose the attitude, but then I think about how confused I am over us. I can't imagine what he's thinking.

"To be honest, it went a lot better than I thought."

"How so?" he grits out.

"Just business as usual. We talked about the next project, and I think we found the perfect plot."

"Is that so?" His jaw tightens. Why is he so tense? Maybe something happened to him while I was at work.

"It is."

"Care to share?"

I lift my brow. "Is everything okay?" I ask, and he takes a sip of water.

"Yes, of course. I'm just curious about your day." His Adam's apple bobs as he swallows, and it feels like he's holding something back.

"Oh, okay. Well, as I was saying, I think we found the perfect spot. I think they are going to build on a plot in Malaga."

"I thought . . ." He stops himself mid-sentence.

"You thought what?" I ask.

"Never mind." He shakes his head and then rights himself.

"You thought I was going to lease him the property in Wiltshire," I respond, starting to put things together.

"I did."

"Is that what this attitude is about?" I lean forward in my chair and stare at him.

"I don't have an attitude."

"Oh, yes, you're perfectly wonderful company." There is no missing the sarcastic bite to my tone.

"Don't be cheeky."

"Cheeky? You have been a bastard this whole lunch."

"I'm sorry. I just—"

"I heard what you said, Olly, and you're right. To sell it to him won't prove anything. I'm over him regardless of the property."

"You are?"

"I am."

He takes my hand in his and kisses my knuckles. "Any reason?" His lips brush against my knuckles.

"I met someone else."

Kiss.

"You did?"

I nod.

Kiss.

"And who is this cheeky bastard? Do I need to challenge him to a duel?"

"Probably. But you should be careful. He's quite cunning."

"Is that all?" He continues to pepper my skin with kisses, his tongue softly trailing in its wake up my arm.

"He's also dashing, and he taught me how to live."

"And how did he do that?"

"Made me sing karaoke at some pub." I laugh.

"Brilliant." His blue eyes lock on mine, and we stare at each other. Eventually, he clears his throat. "So what are you going to do with the property now that Lancaster isn't going to use it?" he asks, and the comment breaks the haze of emotions swirling inside me.

I right myself and smile. "Well, I won't allow it to be developed into a hotel. I can't imagine tourists in the pub."

He lets out a throaty chuckle. "No. That would be bloody awful. One tourist is enough."

"I might consider selling it, but it would have to be the right offer." He nods and lifts my hand again to his lip. "Or," I say, and his movements halt. "We could also consider building something else . . . something more on par with the village. I'll have Jasmine look into our options."

When I walk back into the office, I walk over to Jasmine's desk. "J, put some feelers out. I'm considering selling the land in Wiltshire. Also, look into other companies that would be interested in building. But something other than hotels."

"Really?" She sets down the paper she was working on and looks up at me, eyebrow lifted.

"Yeah, I was thinking about it. For the right person, I could sell, but I'm not developing hotels there."

Olly had gotten to me, but I wasn't going to admit it.

CHAPTER TWENTY-THREE

Oliver

ADDISON IS AT WORK. THE PAST WEEK HAS BEEN different from what I expected. I've enjoyed spending time with her, but the deceit lingers.

She mentioned the other day she might sell the property. And if she does, she doesn't want it to be built on. This is exactly what we need. It's imperative for this deal to go through and my estate to buy the property from her. I think about making an offer myself, but I can't think of a way to do it that won't uncover my lie.

I can't make an offer for the property because she will know I lied about everything. Not just my title, or my name, she will know that since the beginning, this has been my goal.

It shouldn't bother me as much as it does. If I was smart, I wouldn't have formed feelings for her, but Addison is a hard woman not to care about.

No. I'll have to have my solicitor make the offer.

There's only one hitch. The problem is still there. How do I go about this without Addison finding out? My lies and deception hover over me like a black cloud, like dark, smoggy air choking me and making it hard to breathe.

"What am I doing?" I groan as I thread my fingers through my hair, scratching at my scalp like a jackhammer is in there, and maybe if I scrape hard enough, it will come out.

God.

Tell her. You have to come clean.

You're an arse.

I can't silence the voices telling me to confess the truth. They scream so loud I can't think of anything else, but I can't do it.

I just need to let my solicitor deal with my mess.

As I've convinced Addison not to build, my job here is done. Plus, she'll probably sell now. If my solicitor makes an offer on my behalf, it won't trace back to me.

From here on out, this is not my problem. In good conscience, I know no hotel or strip mall or housing complex will be on our property. Addison wants what I want. Yes, I planted the seed, but I didn't make her fall in love with the village, and with my pub.

She fell in love on her own, and now I need to end it. After so many lies, I know she won't forgive me if she finds out the truth. So I just need to break all ties before that happens.

Now, I'm thinking about how I can make this as painless as possible.

We haven't issued any false promises. We haven't spoken of any future. If I go, she won't expect to see me again. The seeds were planted, and she'll make the right decision.

As if conjured from my thoughts, she rings. "Hey, Olly," she says.

"Love," I respond. "To what do I owe this pleasure?"

"I was thinking of you," she whispers into the phone as if she doesn't want anyone to hear.

"Is that so? And why, pray tell, were you thinking of me?"

"Well, actually, I was thinking of the village and my property, and that made me think of you."

My back stiffens. This is my moment. The moment I can convince her.

The moment that will ruin us.

Do what you need to do. "Addison," I utter.

"Yes," she responds, and I can hear the concern in her voice.

"I would never presume to interfere with your business." *Lies.* "But in this case, I feel I need to."

"Okay . . ." she answers softly, allowing me to continue.

"I think it would be in the best interest of the village if you sell the property. I'm sure a local resident would be interested in farming the land."

When she doesn't speak, I go on. "I know it's not my business, but maintaining the land without growth hurts the village, and selling the land to build on can hurt us more. The land should be farmed on. The jobs that farming would bring—"

"Is that what you want? Would it give you peace of mind?" Her voice is so sincere it makes bile collect in my throat.

"Yes."

"Okay, Olly. I'll see if a local would want to buy it."

I hate myself.

It takes me a full thirty minutes to collect my thoughts enough to ring my solicitor, and then another thirty to devise a plan for my mother to make the bid on the property in the name of the estate. By the time I get off the phone, I have drunk three fingers of scotch, but it's not enough to drown out the voices, so I add another three.

Maybe that will kill the guilt spreading within me.

Two weeks have passed since I set off a chain of events that I can now no longer stop. My mobile rings and I step over and answer it. It's my mother. Surprise, surprise.

"Hello, Mother," I grit, not wanting to hear from her now.

"Where are you?" she asks, and a normal question like that irks me today because I know it's a loaded question. I know I won't like where she's going with this inquisition.

"I'm still in New York." I wait for the other shoe to drop and her to put two and two together.

"Why?"

"Well, Mother, you told me to settle it, to fix this, so I did."

"By sleeping with her." Her curt tone makes my fist clench.

"Not that it's any of your business, but yes. What did you expect me to do? How did you think I was going to handle this?"

"Well, I'm ringing to tell you the deal is done. They accepted our offer. So now that you've done what you set out to do, don't you think it's time to come home? It's time for it to end."

"I know."

I shouldn't allow my mother to dictate my life, but I feel partly to blame for the abuse she suffered at my dad's hands. Maybe it's because his tainted blood runs through me, but I feel like I have to make amends.

"It needs to end, Oliver. Break it off."

"I am."

"End it now."

"It's nothing serious."

"I don't care. End it. We have what we want. I'll fly to New York to sign the papers—"

"You're coming here?"

"Yes, and you better end this with her before I get there, or I will tell her everything once the ink is dry."

I go to speak, but every time I open my mouth, my mind flashes. The way she laughs. The way her cheeks flush. Her hair fanned across the pillow.

I would rather end it on my terms than let my mother hurt her with the truth of my deception.

"Oliver," her voice cuts through the moment.

"I'm going to end it."

"Oliver," I hear, but the voice is different. It's not my mum. It's not coming from the phone. It's coming from . . . I turn to see Addison standing by the door. Keys dangling from her fingers. Her jaw tight.

I hang up the phone and turn to her.

"What's going on?"

"It's not what you think."

"Then what is it, Olly?"

"Addison. I—" I need to tell her. I have to tell her. But the words are stuck in my throat. There is no way to say this and for her not to hate me.

But I can't find the words.

I'll wait. If the contract goes through, then I can tell her. But right now, too much is at stake. If I wait, I can fix it. If I wait . . . I can deal with the consequences. The fallout.

But I can't tell her now, that much is certain. I haven't come up with a plausible story.

"Who was that?"

"It was my mum." Not a lie.

"Enough bullshit, Oliver. What are you hiding? I know there's something. Are you . . . ?" She pauses and inhales deeply. "Are you married?"

I storm toward her. My hands reach out, grabbing her face and then kissing her fiercely on the lips. "I am not married." Her body trembles beneath my touch. "Do you understand me?"

"Yes." Her voice is low, unsure.

"Do you believe me?" I ask again, but this time, my voice has more bite, imploring.

"Yes." Her words tickle my lips, and I pull back to look at her. The smile she gives me knocks the breath out of my lungs. She looks at me like I am more than a title, more than my family name, and more than my place in society.

In her eyes, I am more than the son of a drunk who fell to his death, leaving us to learn how to live. She looks at me like I am so much more than I am, and it stabs me in the heart because I am not worthy of her.

All my words choke me, so I kiss her again. Her mouth opens, and she lets me in, but then she lifts her hands and pushes against my chest.

"Was it really your mother?" she mumbles.

"Yes."

Kiss.

"Are you lying?"

Kiss.

"No."

Kiss.

"Is there something you aren't telling me?"

Kiss.

"No."

Lies. All the lies pour out of my mouth, but I shut them up as I kiss her, as I hold her, as I tell her I'm sorry. Only I don't use words. I can't. There is too much at stake. But I tell her over and over again through the night as I worship her body. I tell her I'm sorry, and that I don't mean to hurt her. And as I slowly enter her, as I mark her as mine, I know I have to leave.

Not today.

I'll leave tomorrow.

Just not today.

CHAPTER TWENTY-FOUR

Addison

EVER SINCE THE PHONE CALL YESTERDAY, SOMETHING HAS been off with Olly. He touched me like I'd never see him again. I'm not sure what happened, but I need to ask him if everything is okay today at lunch. Right now, though, I can't.

Today, the paperwork for the sale of the land in Wiltshire will be signed. A part of me is sad to see it go. A big part thinks I should keep it so I have a place close to Olly, but a bigger part, the part that has been hurt before, is afraid of what keeping the property will mean.

What I have with Olly, though I want it to be more, isn't. At least not yet. The thought is staggering. My feet actually fumble as I walk to the conference room.

I don't want this to end.

I'm falling for him.

When did that happen?

This is exactly why I have to sell. With how Oliver was acting yesterday, if this goes south, I want no ties to him. I could have allowed the Lancasters to build on it, but while on my trip, I fell in love with the village and couldn't imagine a hotel of that magnitude destroying the way of life there.

So no, selling is the only option.

With my mind made up, I continue my trek. Head up, back

straight, heels clicking on the marble beneath me.

I'm the last one in the conference room, and all gazes lift as I approach. Sitting on the far side of the table is a man and woman I have never seen. The man stands and reaches out his hand.

Now standing in front of him, I meet his hand with mine.

"Hello, Ms. Price. I'm the solicitor for the Dowager Countess of Lockhart."

I turn my attention to the woman still sitting and smile down at her, reaching out my hand. But she doesn't take it, nor does she offer me a smile. With everything I have, I refrain from making a snide comment as I move to sit beside my brothers and my own attorney.

Through the next few hours, the papers we have drawn up are signed. The atmosphere is much tenser than I would have expected from this type of sale, but then I remember that the countess belongs to a different generation, and I chalk up her rudeness to the fact she's an elitist. She's probably looking down on my brothers and me for being self-made new money.

When the final T is crossed and I is dotted, the countess stands, and without one more word, she leaves the room with the deed in hand. Her solicitor is quick to follow, leaving me and my brothers shocked.

"Well, that went well," Jax jokes. "How far do you think the stick is lodged?"

My shoulders slump forward. "Thank God that's over with. I despise when people like her look down their noses at us."

"Let's grab a drink," Grayson chimes in, but I can't. I have a lunch date with Oliver; the same date I was dreading before this deal.

"Sorry, boys, you'll have to drink without me. I have plans."

Without a word of explanation, I head out the door and to the restaurant.

When I see him already seated, I instantly know it's over. Eyes that normally dance with humor and delight are hollow, lacking the emotion I have grown to love in those blue irises, and I can tell he's distant as I approach.

"What's the matter?" I ask, but he doesn't answer and only shrugs. So I decide to go with a joke. "Is it food poisoning? By any chance, did you eat a hot dog on the way to meet me?" I tease.

That makes his jaw twitch. I expect a laugh, but he gives me a fake chuckle; one that is tight and doesn't meet his eyes.

"You can talk to me. You know that, right?" I ask, needing to hear it with my own ears that this is over. Needing to know what happened and why.

He sighs. "What is it that we are doing here?" he finally responds.

"I don't know. What do you think we're doing?" I ask back. He looks away from me, and every last bit of restraint I have in me breaks. "Just spit it out," I say through gritted teeth. "No need to prolong the inevitable."

"Addison . . ." He looks down and back up.

"What. Is. It." My loud and forceful voice has probably garnered an audience, but I don't even care anymore. He stares at me, his mouth opening and shutting a few times as though he's going to say something. He shakes his head to himself before his mouth opens.

"I'm going home tomorrow."

"Okay. Is this over?" My level voice betrays my emotions. It's all a lie, though, because as I wait for our fate, a piece of me is breaking.

"Don't you think this has run its course?"

I don't know what to say because inside I'm breaking. I can feel my heart seizing and the tears burning, but I refuse to let them fall. Not here. Not in public and not in front of him. I square my shoulders, inhaling deeply. "Did something happen?"

"My life is in London. Your life is here."

"Okay." I shrug.

Lie.

"I can't see a future."

I want to say we can try. I want to say so much, but my pride has me mute. I can feel the eyes of everyone in the room staring. Even if they're not, I feel them, nonetheless.

"I understand."

Lie. Lie. Lie.

I don't understand. I thought . . .

He lets out a sigh. "I'm sorry for leading you on. I realized I can't live in this fantasy world anymore, and I need to go home."

"When are you leaving?"

"I had my stuff moved to a hotel." He stands then and leans forward, placing a kiss on my lips. "I'm sorry, Addison." *Addison. Not love.*

The name cuts deep.

I walk back into my office in a daze.

"I can't believe the property sold so quickly," Jasmine says as I pass her on my way to my office.

"I can't think about this now." I walk past her desk into my office, hanging on by a thread, but once the door closes, I allow myself to fall.

My knees hit the marble as the weight of my body is too much for me to carry now.

It's over.

He ended it.

He doesn't want me.

The room around me begins to blur through the tears collecting in my eyes until I can no longer hold them back, and they burst like water from a broken dam.

They spill down my face and onto the floor below as if I'm bleeding out all my emotions.

I can't breathe.

It feels like I'm dying, like I'm breaking into a million pieces.

What's wrong with me?

And then it hits me, and I'm drowning in the revelation. The one thing I never wanted has happened . . .

Somewhere along the line, I've fallen in love with Oliver Black.

After my meltdown two days ago, I went home and decided to skip work. I also bailed on yesterday as well.

Today, I'm at the office, but there is no point being here. I can't think.

All I can think about is him, and why?

My nails tap against my desk as I try to understand what happened. How everything was perfect one minute and then imploded the next.

What am I missing?

I continue to drum my fingers until it hits me. He's lying about the phone call, which means he's probably lying that it was his mother. There's a good chance Oliver is a lying, cheating bastard too.

Standing abruptly, I head out of my office. My heels crash heavily against the marble as I push open the glass door down the hall from mine. I toss my cell phone on the desk, causing my brother Jax to look up at me.

"Is there a reason you're throwing your cell phone at me?" He doesn't look impressed with me right now, but I don't care.

"I need you to find out everything you can about a number."

"That could take some time," he responds. He acts as if that's the hardest thing in the world for him to do, but I also know he's full of shit.

"Fine. Take whatever time you need, but right now . . . I need you to tell me the location of this phone number for starters."

"Addison, what you're asking me to do is illegal." He raises a smug-ass eyebrow, knowing full well I'd normally give him shit for doing something so blatantly against the law. I grit my teeth.

"I know. Please."

He smiles. My bastard of a little brother smiles. If I didn't need Oliver's location so badly, I might be pissed, but I do.

He starts to type furiously into his computer, not looking up, brow furrowed. "He's at The St. Regis."

I thought he was leaving two days ago.

Why is he still here?

"Anything else?" I ask, crossing my arms in front of my chest and tapping my foot impatiently on the floor beneath me. He still doesn't look up as he continues to look for information.

"I got you a location. What more could you want?"

"Information." I roll my eyes. This isn't my first rodeo with Jax and hacking. Obviously, I need more than just a damn location and phone number.

"That will take me a bit more time," he says matter-of-factly, and I know I'm being ridiculous. What did I expect? He's good at what he does, the best, but even he's not a miracle worker.

I nod with a tight smile. "Thank you, Jax."

"No problem, sis. Keep your phone handy. I'll get you all the info you need."

And I know he will. My brother is the best at finding information people don't want known.

It takes me only fifteen minutes to get to the hotel. My phone rings, and I swipe it open when I see it's Jax. "Do you have the room number?" I ask as I step into the ornate lobby and walk past the reception desk. I'm greeted by the bellhop, but I lift a hand, shake my head, and continue my path.

"Yes, but—"

"Room number," I cut him off, not having time to hear anything else.

"It's 772. But, Addison—"

I start to walk to the elevator, pressing the button.

"Addison, you need to listen to me. He's not who he says he is—" The phone cuts in and out as the elevator climbs.

"What?" I can't understand him.

"Addison, can you hear me? I have to tell you—"

"I can't understand you," I huff, lifting the phone from my ear to check the reception. "Did you say he's not who I think he is?"

The call cuts in and out, then I hear a crackling, jumbled sound . . . "Not Black. Blackthorn."

Is that supposed to mean something to me? "Jax, what are you trying to say?"

"The estate . . ." The line cracks. "Door . . ."

"What?"

"Next door in Wiltshire."

What about the estate next door to the one in Wiltshire? An earl owns the estate next door to the property we just sold, the son of the Dowager Countess of Lockhart.

I have no idea what he's trying to say, and since it's not coming through, I just hang up. I can't deal with my brother right now, not when I have to talk to Oliver. I need to speak with him. This isn't what I do. I don't put my heart on the line like this, but something about Oliver makes me want to try. Because I know Oliver is worth it. And I'm willing to take the risk.

When I find his room, I knock on the door. It swings open, and I'm met with Oliver. But he doesn't look the same. Actually, he looks quite different. Gone are his scruff and unruly hair. He's no longer in his signature jeans and T-shirt. No, actually he's in a suit. And not just any suit—he's in a bespoke navy three-piece suit.

I expect him to smile, to show a sign of warmth, but he looks at me like he doesn't know me at all.

"Addison." His voice is cold, closed off, and when he doesn't invite me in, I'm instantly on edge.

"Aren't you going to let whoever is waiting in?" I hear, and now I push past him. Because if he did lie, if he is married, I'm going to kill him.

When I step inside, I walk through the foyer into the living room. My movements halt as I take in the person sitting in a cream wingback chair. What is she doing here? How does she know Oliver?

She narrows her eyes. "Ms. Price."

"Lady Lockhart." I meet her gaze. "A pleasure to see you so soon," I respond tightly, trying to hold it together as I figure out what exactly is going on. It feels like a loose thread on a sweater, one that if you pull on too hard, it will unravel everything, leaving a big, gaping hole. I'm scared of how it will rip, but it will.

Oliver steps over, lifting his hand. "Add—"

"May I present to you my son," she says, lifting her hand toward Olly.

Her son.

Lady Lockhart, The Dowager Countess son. If he's her son, then he is . . .

Lord Lockhart

He's Lord Lockhart.

He owns the estate next door. The estate next door to the property that she just bought. That he just bought.

"Was it all a lie?" I whisper, and I can sense him step closer to me. I turn to face him, and his eyes aren't hollow anymore. Instead, they look drawn and tired.

"Please," he says, his voice imploring me to listen, but I don't care what he has to say. "Sit so we can talk about this."

"Was this your goal?" I hiss.

"Please sit so we can talk," he says again, his hand rising toward me. I move past him. I need to get out of here.

"No."

"Addison—"

"No," I shout this time. "You don't get to do that. You don't get to talk to me like I mean something, like I matter. Just tell me this, was it always a lie?"

"No—"

"Of course it was, dear," his mother says, cutting him off.

I know it's true.

Without another word, I turn and walk out the door. I hear him calling my name in the distance, but I don't stop. I can't. If I do, he'll see me fall apart.

The door slams.

It closes on the lie. It closes on the deception. It closes on the deceit.

It closes on us.

CHAPTER TWENTY-FIVE

Addison

Three months later . . .

"YOU LOOK LIKE SHIT."

"Well, thank you, brother," I say as I meet Jax's gaze. His blue eyes are dark and narrowed. "You don't look too hot yourself," I mutter back.

He tilts his head and takes a step farther into the room until he's standing directly in front of my desk. "Sure, I do," he responds to my quip, and I shake my head.

"No, you don't. You look like you partied all night and then rolled in here before even taking a shower." My nose scrunches up dramatically, implying that he smells bad too, but Jax doesn't get insulted. Instead, his lips tip up into a boyish smirk, and a giant dimple lines his right cheek.

"That's exactly the look I was going for," he says with a straight face, his voice monotone and flat.

"Well"—I gesture my hand up and down, pointing at his disheveled appearance—"you got it, and it's not working for you," I deadpan.

"But at least I'm having fun." This time, I know he's not joking, and his words cut into me deeper than I think he was aiming for. I'm instantly on edge, wondering if this is when I once again get lectured.

"What's that supposed to mean?"

"Well, at least I'm living my life."

The word living puts a bad taste in my mouth.

Sour.

Pungent.

It reminds me of him. The liar.

The deceitful piece of . . .

I'd like to say it's been radio silence, but just the other day, I got another phone call from him. Before the phone had a chance to ring a second time, I sent him to voicemail. No part of me has any interest in speaking to him at all.

What's there to say?

He made a complete fool out of me. It's been months, and unfortunately, I haven't stopped thinking about him. I still remember what it felt like to have him in my bed, to have him hold me, and I hate myself for being so weak.

I guess it's karma, cosmic karma.

Maybe it's not as bad as what I did to Spencer—which was so much worse—but I was young, stupid, drunk, and didn't know what I was doing. Oliver was sober, not young, and an ass—or as he would say, an *arse*.

The message he left this past month said he wanted to talk. He said he wanted to explain things and he was in New York. But speaking to him wasn't, and still isn't, an option, so I didn't call him back. I didn't text. I pretended it never happened, and I've been sick ever since.

He wants to explain.

What's there to explain? He used me to sway my decision. But worse, he went behind my back, lied about who he was, and bought my property out from under me. If that isn't the worst form of deceit, I don't know what is.

It took me a full week to get over the shock and sadness of hearing his voice on the first message he left me. This last time, it took me only a few days, so it appears I'm doing better. I just hope he gives up now because I don't know how much more I can take. The pain I feel in my chest when I hear his voice is gut-wrenching.

I never wanted anyone to hurt me again like Oliver did. My heart won't be able to take it, and I refuse to allow myself to feel like this. It's not who I am. I'm the CEO of a company. I'm strong and smart, not some weak little girl who gets used.

So, because of this need to be strong, I've thrown myself into work. All day. All night. Weekends too. Never a break. Because if I allow myself to stop, I'll crumble, and I can't.

I won't allow myself.

I look over and find Jax standing in my office staring at me. God. I was so lost in my own mind I had forgotten I had company. "You're still here?" I shake my head, wiping away the thoughts of Oliver out of my mind.

"I'm worried about you," he admits, his voice dropping low.

"You don't have to be. I'm okay." I shrug.

"Okay is a horrible word."

"Then I'm fine."

"I might be a guy, but even I know 'fine' is worse." He laughs as he uses air quotes.

"Well, on that note . . ." I trail off, picking up my phone and hitting the intercom. "J, can you come to my office?" I say, and when Jasmine answers, I hang up. "I have work to do. Go back to your office and get out of mine." At that moment, Jasmine walks in.

"Ready?" I ask her, dismissing Jax, who then walks out of my office as Jasmine takes the empty seat.

"Addison—" she starts, but I lift my hand, silencing her.

"Don't."

"I'm worried about you too. You haven't had a day off in over two weeks. You work nights and weekends. Maybe it's time to do something for you. I know—"

"You don't know anything." Jasmine's lip trembles at my verbal attack. "I'm not trying to be rude"—I sigh—"but I have a lot to do. I don't have time for a social life nor do I want one. I can't . . . You don't understand." I shake my head and turn my back to her, peering out the window.

"I only don't know anything because you won't talk to me about what happened—"

"Jasmine." I cut her off, not wanting to speak about this now and certainly not here.

"We're friends. Please talk to me." Her voice is low and full of emotion, imploring me to open up.

"Here, we are not friends. Here, you are my employee, and there's nothing to talk about." I know she doesn't deserve my attitude, but if I allow this line of thought, I will fall apart in my office, which I refuse to do. Instead, I keep my internal walls up high, so high they are almost indestructible . . . almost.

"You say that, but whatever he did, changed you. For a moment, there was a different Addison. One I had never seen before."

"Well, unfortunately, she's gone."

"She doesn't have to be."

"Again, you're out of line, Jasmine. Remember where we are."

"I know, but I'm sorry. You barely eat, and you've lost so much weight. I know I should be quiet and bite my tongue, but I can't. You're more than a boss to me."

I inhale. "I know. And I know you're concerned, but there's no need."

"Please at least eat," she pleads.

"I eat."

"Please eat more."

"Fine," I hiss under my breath.

"And stop working so much."

I groan. "Miss having your weekends free, J?" I say sarcastically.

"You know I don't mind working, but you need a break. You're pushing yourself too hard."

"Fine. Any other requests?"

"Go out." She hopes if by making the mere suggestion I might actually consider it. I shake my head.

"No."

"Just consider it."

"Probably not."

"That's not a no." She smirks, and if I could roll my eyes any farther, they'd be out of my head.

"So what's on the agenda?" I ask, changing the subject.

"The purchase agreement for the land in Phoenix is almost ready. Grayson said he would touch base when the acquisition is done."

"Hmm, what else?"

"The Lancaster meeting is on Friday to sign the paperwork for Malaga. And—"

"And what?"

She bites her lip. "Lord Lockhart . . ."

"Yes." My voice is rougher than I intend, but it's the only way to keep my emotions in check. Even months later, when I hear his name, it's like twisting the knife in my back. The wound he inflicted is still raw.

"Nothing."

I nod and turn back to stare outside at the city beyond my window.

Bleak and gray, just as I feel.

Oliver has a way of getting to me like no one else can. He makes me weak and has the power to destroy me. No. I would rather exist than live and die at the hands of Lord Lockhart.

CHAPTER TWENTY-SIX

Oliver

TIME GOES SLOWLY WHEN ALONE.

After New York, I couldn't deal with my mother, and although I knew the importance of why we did what we did, I still had no interest in being in the same city as her, so I went back to London.

However, London was awful too, so now I'm back at my holiday cottage.

Unfortunately for me, it's not much better here.

The walls feel smaller than normal as if they are closing in on me. Needing a distraction, I decide to take a walk and clear my brain.

It's starting to get cold now, so I throw on a coat and set off to get fresh air. Heading outside, I allow my feet to carry me with no clear destination.

With each step I take, my back gets tighter. This walk should relax me, but it's had the opposite effect. Each gust of wind reminds me that the last time I was here, it was summer, and she was here.

The vision of her on my couch, in my kitchen, on my bed doesn't fade with the distance. No, the images become crisper.

Time passes with a memory of every second we spent together playing like an old-fashioned movie in my mind. I see each moment, I hear each lie, and before long, I'm so lost in my own torment of what I had done that I didn't even notice my feet stopped.

My chest constricts as I realize where I am.

Ms. Maddox's Bake Shop.

I push open the door and head inside. The chime telling anyone inside I'm entering.

"Oliver." I look toward the counter to see Ms. Maddox. Weathered skin and gray hair meet me, and a smile that tells me she's happy I'm here.

I allow myself to smile, but I know it doesn't touch my eyes by the way her own smile tightens. "Ms. Maddox, I hope you are well," I say in greeting.

"Very well, how can I help you, my dear? The usual?" She winks.

Under the glass, I can see the blueberry scones, and suddenly, the air around me is thin. I nod my response, not being able to summon words.

It feels wrong to be here without her.

Wrong to be without her in general.

The ground underneath me shakes as my heart cracks in half at the thought of never seeing her smile while talking with a scone in her mouth.

Of never watching her face blush, of not touching her again.

Bloody hell.

Bloody fucking hell.

I love her.

After my revelation, I have tried to ring her, and she won't answer. She won't give any inkling of ever answering.

A few more weeks have passed since then, I saw Nathaniel

briefly, and before that, I distracted myself by partying it up, but that's grown tiring as well. Now that I've finally admitted a truth I never thought possible, that I love Addison Price, I want to scream at the bloody injustice of it all.

Everything I did was for the right reasons.

For my mum. To help the one person who always took care of me, and in turn, I hurt the only person I've ever loved.

A part of me wants to march over to my estate and curse my mother for putting me up to it, but the truth is, she never told me to fall in love. She never told me to use Addison the way I did. She never told me to be the villain in this story.

No, I made that decision all on my own, and now I need to own up to it and get her back.

She wishes I were dead.

Therein lies the problem.

The first obstacle in my way to redemption is the land. However, my hands are tied with that. I own it now, and she will never forgive me for the deception I dealt to acquire it.

It's bollocks really because I had no choice.

She doesn't know that, though, and I can never tell her the truth, so it doesn't matter. Life, or at least my life, would be easier if I could tell her why I did what I did to her. I thought I could pull off this elaborate lie I wove, but I couldn't, and now I'm the only one punished for it.

I have the land, but I lost the girl.

Unless . . .

Maybe I can make her see reason.

Before I know it, I'm on a jet to New York, but I have no game plan. No plan at all. All I know is I need to see her, speak to her. What I'm going to say is beyond me right now, but I will make her listen.

I arrive in New York, exhausted and not entirely prepared. The moment I'm in my car, I fire off the address of her office. It will be five p.m. when I make it into the city, but I know Addison. She will still be in the office, so I plan to show up there unannounced.

The long and tedious car ride into the city is made worse by the horrific traffic. With each blare of a horn, I'm more and more annoyed. I watch the streets creep by at a turtle's pace, and then I watch the cars at a standstill as we try to cross the bridge.

At this point, by the time I pull up, she'll be gone. At this rate, I won't be there until tomorrow.

Finally, after thirty more minutes and an endless string of profanities, we make it to the bridge. The traffic on the bridge isn't much better, and the view is even worse. It's no longer summer in New York, and fall has passed too. I can't believe I haven't been here since the summer. It feels like a lifetime ago.

At first, I tried to drink the memory of Addison away, but now I don't know what I'm doing. All I know is I can't get the damn woman out of my mind.

I fucked up.

Royally.

I'm not sure what I hope to gain by flying here, but I need to see her. Maybe if I do, I can stop thinking about her and move on with my goddamn life. Because Lord knows I haven't lived these past three months.

We pull up to the massive and oppressive high-rise building. This was our ruin.

Who are you kidding? It was always destined to fail. That's what happens when the foundation of a relationship is built on lies.

My driver pulls over, but I don't wait for him to get out. I don't need anyone to help me. Fuck. Security is everywhere. No way will Addison let me anywhere near her, but even knowing that, I don't let it stop me. Instead, I head to the desk with my normal cocky swagger.

"Lord Lockhart to see Ms. Price," I say, arrogance dripping off my words.

His face doesn't budge. He doesn't even acknowledge I spoke as if my name has already been drilled into his head. I'm still standing there when I feel a person behind me. Turning around, I see a man who looks vaguely familiar. It's the eyes.

They're her eyes.

This man is about the same height as me, maybe a bit taller. I'd put him at about six feet two inches. He's older than me, though, probably late thirties with at least a week's worth of scruff but not a full beard on his face.

This must be Grayson.

"The brother," I say, looking him up and down.

"The liar," he retorts.

There is no reason to deny the claim, so I reach my hand out. "At your service," I say smugly.

He doesn't take my offered hand. Instead, he crosses his arms over his chest but not before I notice him make a fist. "What do you want?" He scoffs.

"To speak to her."

"Not going to happen. Give up already, you got the land."

"This isn't about the bloody land," I hiss. That's when I notice three security guards walking in our direction.

"I'm gonna need to ask you to leave now. I'm also going to

tell you to stay the fuck away from my sister. Do you understand me?"

"No."

"No? Did you just say no to me, Lord Lockhart?" He draws it out, his intention clear. He knows my title, and he will use it against me if need be. "I would hate for this to end up in the papers."

"Are you threatening me, Price?"

"Oh, no. I'm not threatening you. This is a promise. Stay away from my sister or all your exploits will end up in the tabloids. And if you think they won't, you're wrong. Don't underestimate me. I will ruin you."

With nothing more to say, Grayson Price turns around and walks back toward the elevators. The three security guards continue to approach, but I lift my hand.

"No need."

They step closer.

"I'm leaving."

Now that they are backing off, I walk out the revolving door and back out onto the New York City streets. A light snow hits my waiting car, but I can't get in just yet. I need to think. I take a step over until I'm standing at the side of the building with my foot flat against the concrete. I lean back and try to decide my next step. Go to her apartment or go back home? I'm not one to admit defeat that easily, so going home is not an option. I know where she lives, though, so I'm sure I could figure out a way . . .

"Lord Lockhart."

I turn to the left and realize I'm not alone. A woman's standing beside me with short brown hair cut in a bob and sad, deep brown eyes. I remember her right away.

"Can I help you?" I ask.

"I'm not sure you remember me. I'm Jasmine . . ."

"Yes, I'm aware." I lift my brow, waiting for her to tell me what she wants.

"Addison's assistant . . ."

"Yes, I know," I hiss out, my emotions still not reined in, but then a thought pops into my head. *This woman can help me.*

"What can I do for you, Jasmine?"

"I saw you with Mr. Price."

"Oh, you saw that? Are you planning to yell at me too?"

"No, I'm planning to help you."

Well, that was easier than I thought. "Why do you want to help me?"

"Because I think Addison needs closure."

CHAPTER TWENTY-SEVEN

Addison

I can't believe I'm here. I can't believe I'm doing this, but apparently, this was the only way. As Dua Lipa once said and then Jasmine apparently stole like an artist:

The only way to get over someone was to get under someone else, but jeez, this feels wrong.

I can't believe I let someone set me up on a date.

A friend of a friend. At least I'm not on a dating app. That's where I draw the line because I can't do that right now.

Too much work to sort through the profiles, but even though this is easier, it's still a bad idea. This date won't go anywhere. Most men who know me are intimidated by me. That, or apparently, they are using you for a plot of land.

No.

I won't go there tonight.

One night with Olly monopolizing my thoughts is already too much.

Fresh from the blow-dry bar, hair and makeup done, and still wearing a little black dress and knee-high boots, I walk into the lounge where I'm meeting Maxwell. I don't know much about him. He's also in real estate, but he works in commercial property, leasing corporate space. It's in the same field as me, but not directly, which Sarah, one of my college friends, argued was a plus because apparently, we'd have things to talk about.

Sounds awful if you ask me.

Why would I want to spend my time talking work? It's funny because I had liked that with Spencer, but after Oliver, it doesn't sound at all appealing.

I look around, but when I don't see anyone who fits his description, I walk over to the bar and wave at the bartender.

"What can I get you?"

I think about what I want and what to order. I decide not to have wine because, let's be honest, nothing is worse than red-stained teeth on a date. I might not date often, but even I know that.

A glass of champagne will work.

Because he's not here yet, I don't need to have the fight of who's buying. But the truth is, I don't need him to buy me a drink, nor do I want him to anyway.

"Glass of Dom," I say.

"We only sell it by the bottle," he responds matter-of-factly.

"Then I'll buy the bottle."

To this, he smiles and nods, then bends to retrieve it in what must be a fridge. My glass is full, and as I take a sip, I feel a presence. "Addison?" I turn around. This must be Maxwell. He's handsome and clean cut with blond hair and blue eyes, wearing a sport coat, button-down, and slacks.

He's not my typical type, but maybe that's good.

"Maxwell." I smile, placing my drink down and reaching my hand over to his. He takes my hand and shakes it.

"Pleasure to meet you." He smiles, and it's warm and inviting. I know I can't judge or trust appearances—case in point, Oliver—but he seems like a nice guy. I only wish my heart were more into this date, rather than just playing a part I don't really want to play.

One that even months later, I'm not ready to play.

"You as well," I say back.

"I see you started without me." He points at my glass.

"I hope you don't mind."

"Not at all."

"Good, because it's delicious," I say as I raise my glass and take a large sip. The bubbles flow down my throat, tingling as they course their way into my bloodstream.

"So tell me what made you decide to meet me?" he asks, taking me off guard. I'm surprised he knew how reluctant I was for this date.

"What's that supposed to mean?" I laugh. The liquid is already doing its job to loosen me up.

"I was just surprised you would agree." Dear God, if this man mentions my name or my money, I'm going to take my bottle and go home. "Just that I know you don't date."

"So then why did you ask?"

"Because I think you're beautiful. I respect you as a businesswoman. I figured I would never know unless I asked. Lucky for me, you said yes."

"I don't normally."

"I know, that's why I said I was lucky." He winks.

I think back to what I told Oliver not too long ago about my faults, and I don't feel like explaining myself again.

I could tell him what I want and why I'm here, but I don't bother doing that either. Because in truth, I'll never see this man again. I'm not ready for a relationship. I'm not ready for anything.

Slightly buzzed, the date is actually going much better

than I expected, but now I've excused myself because I need a minute to gather my thoughts.

As much fun as I'm actually having, I still feel a piece of my heart is missing, and the more I drink, the bigger the hole gapes.

I make my way to the bathroom. It's a private stall, and when I move to push it open, it's locked.

I hear the footsteps behind me, and I turn to tell the person there's a line, but when I spin around, I'm met with very familiar blue eyes.

Him.

Eyes I haven't seen in what feels like forever.

The one person I can't see right now.

The one person I don't want to see, but so desperately do as well.

As much as I tell myself I hate him, and I do, a part of me, a very big part of me, has missed him so much that it makes it hard to breathe. And now, with him standing in front of me, his presence is my oxygen. I'm finally able to breathe.

No, I tell myself. Put the wall you place over your emotions down.

"What are you doing here?" I hiss.

"I came to see you," he responds, and I had no idea what hearing his voice after all this time would do to me, but now that I've heard it, and now that I've seen him, I realize I'm much weaker for this man than I thought. I need to get out of here.

I look around, trying to find an escape. I'm on a date, but I can't stay. There has to be a back entrance somewhere. I push off the wall and start to walk.

He follows me.

I walk faster.

So does he.

"Addison, stop," he pleads.

"No." I don't turn. Instead, I keep heading to the door in front of me. The door that says exit.

"Please."

"Goddammit, Oliver. No." I push it open. "Don't follow me."

When I go to step through, his arm reaches forward and pushes the heavy door open. The cold air hits me first as I step out, then realize I have nowhere to go. I had hoped it would open to a busy street—one with a cab readily available—but it doesn't. It's a back alley if even that. More like a back courtyard.

Dammit.

The door slams behind him, and I finally turn to face him because he has me where he wants me. Although I could go forward and search for a path to the main street, going through the building would be easier.

"That better not have locked." My voice is harsh, and his jaw tightens. He pulls it open, and it's not locked, thank God, but he's still blocking the door.

"What do you want?" I finally say.

"I've been trying to speak to you."

"I know."

"I've been trying to explain."

"I don't care."

"I miss you . . ."

"Sounds like a personal problem because I don't miss you."

He inclines his head, and then a ghost of a smile forms. "If you don't miss me, then why are you running?"

"It has nothing to do with running. I just don't want to talk to you."

"So are you saying you don't still want me? That I don't still affect you?"

"Yes." I try to sidestep him, but my boot slips, and I'm convinced I'm going to fall. His arms reach out and bracket me to his side, and I shiver. I fucking shiver. I tell myself it's because it's winter, and I don't have a coat on, but I know that's bullshit. New York has been experiencing an unnatural heat wave, and it's fifty degrees right now. The shiver is all for him. It's my traitorous body agreeing with his words.

He moves me closer to him, turning me and stepping me back. "I miss you." His low and husky tone is raw, dripping with desire, but underneath the words, it's also laced with sadness.

The rough pads of his fingertips trace a pattern against my jaw, forcing me to meet his gaze. The sadness is there even more so in his voice.

There is no mistaking it.

My heart thumps rapidly in my chest because as much as I want to hate him, seeing him standing here sad and exposed makes me feel things I shouldn't. It makes me miss him too and makes me want to take away his pain, which is crazy and irrational because he's the one who started this battle.

His lies.

His deceit.

So then why do I feel sadness, and why do I feel desire all at the same time? The two conflicting emotions run havoc in me as his hands slide down my jaw, across my throat, trailing to the hollow of my neck.

I feel hot.

Even with barely any clothing on, in the middle of winter, outside as the cold air tickles my skin, I feel hot.

And needy.

Confused.

He steps closer to me, and I try to get away, but the hard brick stops my escape.

"I miss you," he says again, and this time, his voice is rough. "Tell me you miss me; tell me you miss this."

Our bodies are so close now, and I can feel the outline of his hard erection pushing into my stomach. "No," I say on a breathy whisper. He bends his knees until his face aligns with mine, and he's so close that if he leaned in a mere inch, his lips would be on mine.

Then I would for sure be lost.

"Tell me, Addison. At night when you're alone, do you think of me?" His breath tickles my lips.

"No."

"Liar."

"I don't. And you're the liar here." The word comes out of my mouth harsh, but I'm silenced by his mouth as it descends.

As soon as I feel his lips on mine, I'm completely lost. I don't remember anything but this. All rational thought disappears, and I can no longer think of a reason not to do this. My own mouth opens, fully under his hypnotic trance. His tongue slides in, and our tongues collide. Unspoken words are spoken through this kiss.

It tells him I'm a liar.

That I miss him.

That I want him.

What it doesn't tell him is that in the time apart, I realized I wasn't whole. It doesn't tell him that what I actually learned is that I have fallen in love with this man, nor will it. Because as lost as I am to his touch, I will allow myself this one moment before I let him go forever.

Closure.

His hand slides from the hollow of my neck, running down my chest to the sides of my hips. I forgot how amazing this felt.

"Don't say no," he mutters against my lips as I feel his hands under my skirt. His kiss deepens, desperation filling each stroke of his tongue. He doesn't have to worry about me saying no, though. All thoughts of that are gone and replaced by the need to have him inside me, claiming me one last time.

"Please," I beg against his lips, and that must be enough because his fingers tighten around the lace of my thong, pulling the flimsy material aside as he breaches me with a finger.

A moan escapes my mouth. Before I can think twice, I hear myself utter a word I shouldn't. "More."

His finger still inside me, he lowers to the ground in front of me. I feel him remove his finger, and before I can even comprehend what I just begged for, he's fucking me with his mouth, and I'm grasping his head, pulling him closer.

I need him to go faster. To make me forget everything but this.

"Make me forget," I plead.

And he does, his tongue licking me at a punishing clip. He owns me with each swipe and movement of his mouth. Makes me believe the lie I tell myself that this is nothing more. That after, I will be okay. That after, I will be over this sick obsession I have with him, and this will be my closure.

He's just as desperate as I am with his ministrations to tell me the same. That he too needs to believe something. What, I don't know. I don't know what he's deceiving himself with, but it doesn't matter because right now, this is all that matters.

The world around me begins to fade, and soon, with a tremble that runs the whole length of me, I feel myself come undone. I tighten my hold and fall apart around his finger, around his tongue, around the notion that for a moment I can still feel bliss with this man. But like all things, this too has come to an end, which means reality comes crashing in as my breathing regulates.

The haze lifts, and he moves to nuzzle my thigh, but I place my hands on his head and push him away. "Never again," I bite out as I readjust my clothes and put myself back into place. I step away. His eyes are wide, stunned by the turn of events. I take advantage of the fact he's still kneeling on the floor, and I make my escape. Back into the lounge, into the bathroom, and then . . .

Back to my date.

CHAPTER TWENTY-EIGHT

Oliver

I'M A BLOODY BASTARD.

I truly am.

When Addison's assistant told me that Addison was going to be at the lounge, I didn't even think before I showed up. Now I'm standing here, my dick hard, and Addison gone. *That went well.* I never did get a chance to talk to her, and now, knowing her, I won't.

I didn't really think this through.

As amazing of an idea as making her come against a brick wall in a back alley was, now with the haze gone, and her as well, I realize I probably officially cocked this up. Not that it wasn't fucked to begin with, but at least she still needed closure, but when she looked at me, right after she came on my tongue, that's exactly what I saw in her eyes.

She was done.

Leaving me nothing to work with.

Once I right myself, I make my way back into the building, hoping to make this right. I stride through the corridor by the bathroom and walk into the lounge. Looking around, I find her at the bar. She's still with him. Drinking champagne.

Anger courses through me, and my hands fist by my sides. It takes every last bit of energy not to walk up to this bloke and bash his face into the bar top. But seeing as the press would eat that shit up, and my family can't handle the scandal, I don't. She catches me staring, and then she does something I never thought Addison Price would do. While holding my gaze, she places her hand on his shoulder, leans in, and places a kiss on his lips. Her eyes never leave mine. Instead, they narrow, and her point comes across loud and clear.

She's done.

I have two choices, confront her or leave . . . make that three choices. Choice number three is to get drunk.

I choose option three.

As I turn my back to her, I let it be known that her message was delivered.

Once I'm back in the city air, I pull out my mobile and swipe until I find Nathaniel's name. When the phone stops ringing, but before he can say hello, I speak. "I'm in New York," I state.

"I'm starting to think you're following me, mate." He laughs.

"Nothing to think about," I say, but the truth is, nothing could be farther from the truth. I'm here for her, but I don't say that. One of the benefits of having your best mate in the same city as you, is that you can lie.

"Seriously, what are you doing in New York so much?" he asks, obviously knowing me better and calling me out on it.

I think about how to answer. "Visiting a friend," I finally respond.

"Does this friend have a name?" Nathaniel is relentless, like a dog with a bone, when he wants to find something out. Unlucky for me, I'm the recipient of his pursuit.

"Don Julio . . ."

"You're such an arse."

I let out a throaty chuckle. "But seriously, are you going to meet me?"

"Yes."

Thank fuck. After watching Addison place the lips I had just kissed on another man, I need to drink, and I need to drink now. "That took a lot of convincing."

"I'm working with all women. I need a night out with my best mate," he responds.

"See, aren't you happy I stopped in New York now?"

"I am, but don't you have work to do? Or is it all just fun and games to be the sixteenth earl to whatever your damn title is?"

"See you soon." I laugh through the phone.

At eleven, Nathaniel rolls up to the private lounge. On the table, a bottle of Don Julio 1942 waits for him. "It's a tequila night, I see?" He lifts his brow.

"It is."

"Want to talk about it?" he asks. I shake my head.

A waitress comes over and smiles. "Can I get you something, sir? A shot, perhaps?"

"Sure. I'll have a shot but also get me a bottle of Grey Goose."

"Mixing." I shake my head in mock disapproval. *Amateur.*

"I'll be fine." He laughs.

A minute later, the waitress brings my vodka and a shaker. Sitting here, I can't stop thinking about what Addison did. I know she hates me, but to let that man touch her . . .

Would she take it farther?

Would she let him fuck her?

The Addison I know wouldn't. But she told me about her past and her failed relationship with Spencer Lancaster. Is it that hard to believe that maybe she would?

I shake my head, trying desperately to get the image out of my mind.

Opening my eyes, I catch a tall blonde staring at me. She is the opposite of the woman haunting my thoughts. I should ignore her. It's obvious what this woman wants, and there's no way I would do that. Not now. Not when I can still feel Addison wrapped around me. Not when I can still smell her, taste her.

No, I won't be fucking anyone tonight. That's for sure.

Nor do I think I'll even be able to get it up for another woman for a long time, not until I speak to her at least. Because she might have closure, but I sure as fuck haven't said my piece. As the blonde smiles, I find myself gesturing her over, and she approaches, perching herself on my lap. It would be so easy to erase the memory of Addison right here, right now.

But I won't.

At the end of the night, this woman will go home alone, and so will I, but I don't tell her to get off my lap either because, although I won't touch her, she distracts me. And right now, with the only thought of heading back to the bar and killing someone going through my head, I need a distraction.

CHAPTER TWENTY-NINE

Addison

IT'S TIME TO GO HOME.

I have never felt more disgusted with myself. I need to shower and wash tonight away. Wash Oliver away.

After I kissed Maxwell and pulled away, I noticed Oliver was gone. The job was done, and he had left, so I pulled away from the kiss, and now hours later, we're finishing the bottle.

"Are you okay?" Maxwell asks all while giving me a knowing look, and I'm not sure how he knows, but he does.

"Yes, of course," I answer too fast.

"Listen, I'm not dumb, Addison. I figured you didn't want to talk about it, and I was going to respect you. I wasn't going to ask but—"

"But what?"

"I watched you polish off that bottle. Obviously, you're not okay."

I let out a long drawn-out sigh. "I'm not."

"What happened?"

I lift an eyebrow. "Do you really want to know?"

"No, I know what happened. It's pretty obvious you're nursing a broken heart, and the kiss was your way of trying to get over whoever hurt you."

"God. I'm an idiot and so embarrassed. I didn't mean to use

you like that. I'm not that woman." I place my hands over my head and want to die of mortification. Not only did I just kiss this man at the bar, but I also almost fucked Olly in a public alley.

I'm so incredibly stupid.

A story like this could easily be sold to a tabloid for serious bucks. Not just because of me, but Oliver is a goddamn earl, for crying out loud. What were we thinking?

"Don't worry. Your secret is safe with me," he jokes. "I won't tell anyone you have emotions."

"Really?" I raise an eyebrow. Most of the time there's an ulterior motive for niceness. This man has seen me at my worst, and he could easily spread the story of the emotional billionaire.

"But it will cost you," he says, and I'm instantly on edge. Here it goes . . .

"Don't worry, nothing like that."

"Then what?"

"Another date." He smirks, and when he does that, an adorable boyish dimple pops up.

"Let me get this straight. You want to go out with me, knowing what you know? Knowing I'm not over whoever broke my heart."

"Yes."

"Even though—"

"Yes, Addison, I do."

"Why?" It makes no sense at all.

He takes my hand in his. "Because you're smart. You're beautiful. You're not like other women, and I'd be a fool not to see that. And whoever he was who broke your heart."

"And you think you can mend it?" I ask honestly, knowing full well some men have a hero fetish. He might be that type of guy.

"I want the chance."

He is. But is that a problem? All my life, I've taken care of myself—pushed myself—so would it be so hard to let someone take care of me for once?

I think long and hard about what he says. "I might not be ready for a relationship for a long time."

"I'm okay with that."

"I won't sleep with you." I need him to know that I'm not just going to hop into bed with him.

He nods his agreement. "I'm okay with that too."

"I don't get it," I admit on a sigh.

"What's not to get? You're worth the wait."

I'm worth the wait.

It's odd how one sentence can resonate within you so much. I wasn't worth forgiveness from Spencer, and I wasn't worth the truth from Olly. But this man who's practically a stranger is willing to wait for me to be ready. In those four words, I can actually feel something inside me fuse back together, and I feel a little less broken.

"Okay."

The next day comes before I know it, and just as I suspected, Jasmine is in my office waiting for me. I really should rethink this idea of making my assistant my BFF, or whatever she calls us.

When they say don't mix business and pleasure, it's not just for relationships, it's also for friendship. I think I'm going to have to give her a promotion and transfer her out of my office, because we spend so much time gossiping these days; I swear we don't get any work done.

Add that to my list of things to talk to Gray and Jax about. She's smart and hard-working, so she can easily transition to any position here. Then I can approach her. It's not that I don't love her. I just love her more as a friend than as an employee. And as I can't have both, I choose a friend.

"Tell me everything."

"Before I do, how would you feel about a promotion?"

"Wow, way to segue."

"I'm not."

"You totally are. Tell me what happened."

"Oliver was there . . ."

She looks down, guilty. "I know," she mumbles.

"You know? How do you know?"

"I might have been the one to tell him where you would be."

"What? How could you?" My voice is louder than I want, and I'm visibly shaking.

"I'm so sorry. I thought—" Her chin trembles, and it looks like she might cry. "Don't be mad at me."

"I'm not mad." I sigh. I take a deep breath to regain my composure. "Why did you do it?"

"I thought you needed closure."

"It wasn't your place."

"I know. Addison—"

I lift my hand. "What's done is done. I got my closure. He didn't. I don't want to talk about Oliver again."

"Okay, we won't. And I'm sorry again. It wasn't right. Especially knowing you were on a date. I just . . . I was just so mad at him. I wanted him to see you were moving on; I wanted him to get hurt. I never thought he would speak to you. I'm sorry if it ruined your date."

"It's fine, J, and it didn't. Maxwell actually asked me out again. Even though I was a mess and he knew I was still getting over someone."

"That's odd . . ." Her brow furrows. "Isn't that odd?"

"Yes, but then he explained himself."

"And what did he say?" she asks.

"He said he would wait and that I was worth it, and the way he said it was actually kind of amazing. I believed he would."

"And are you going to go out with him?"

I nod once, and her eyes widen considerably. "Really?"

"Yep." I shrug.

"Even though you just got over what Olly did to you?"

"Here's the thing, J. This man can't hurt me because I am already too broken. My feelings aren't involved. At this point, what's the harm in going? Best case, he makes me forget Olly completely, and we fall in love." I roll my eyes. "Worst case, it's a distraction. Worst case, I'm bored. And bonus points if I'm photographed with him." I laugh.

"Why is that?"

"Because maybe *he'd* see, and then maybe, just maybe, he'd feel half the pain I've felt."

"Maybe you should talk to him."

"No. He lied. He used me. He was willing to scheme . . . I can never trust him again."

"But—"

"No buts. I'm living my life, and he's living his."

"But you're not living."

"Well, I guess that's where Maxwell comes in."

"Well, you know what I always say. The only way to get over someone," she says, and then we both say in unison, "is to get under someone new," before bursting into laughter.

I'm ready to move on and try to live again.

No matter what.

Five weeks later . . .

Sitting at my desk, I look over the work I still have to do, and then I look over at the clock.

Five thirty p.m.

I'm going to be late. Saving the file I'm working on, I head out the door, barely stopping to talk to Jasmine.

Once outside, I head down the block until I'm in front of The Conroy. Standing on the corner, Max waits outside for me. He's leaning against the wall with his coat pulled tightly. He's staring down at his phone and has a small frown on his face.

I wonder what's bothering him, and if he's annoyed that I'm late, but then he sees me, and his face morphs from a frown to a giant smile.

When I'm finally standing in front of him, he leans down and places a soft kiss on my lips.

"I'm so sorry I'm late." I'm still trying to catch my breath after my speed walking.

"No problem. I have you now. That's all that matters."

"About that . . ."

"You have to cancel dinner?" He laughs.

"Am I that predictable?"

"You are, but it's fine as long as you have a drink with me first and tell me what you're working on."

"Today won't work at all, actually."

"This must be big. Can't wait for details," he says as he pulls me again and places another chaste kiss on my lips. "Breakfast?"

"Breakfast works."

"Okay, then off to work . . ."

This is why I like spending time with Max.

He understands.

He doesn't expect me to stop or work any less; hell, he barely even bothers me during the week. It's pretty perfect actually.

It's still new, but I can already tell he's different than Olly.

He understands my need to work. Olly would have told me that sitting behind a desk isn't living. He'd convince me to ditch work, or maybe . . .

Maybe Olly wouldn't. Maybe he'd tell me to work, and he would show up with a delicious home-cooked meal. My eyes close of their own accord.

"Are you okay?" Max's voice cuts through my thoughts, and I grimace at the images swirling around in my brain. Images I shouldn't see anymore.

"I was just . . . I was just thinking about . . ." I start and stop, not sure what to say.

"It's okay to think about him," he says, and when I tip my head up, he smiles at me. A smile that doesn't reach his eyes, but I'm sure it's 'cause he caught me thinking about Oliver. But that's the thing about Max . . .

He doesn't judge.

And most importantly, he's not a liar.

CHAPTER THIRTY

Oliver

MONTHS HAVE PASSED. AND THERE HAS BEEN NO contact with Addison. I attempted to see her again. I even found myself celebrating my birthday in New York just on the off chance I could get her to speak to me and get her to come, but even though I invited her, she never showed. So instead, I drank myself to a stupor. I played the part I needed to play, but it was hollow. It still is.

I'm early, but I needed to get out of my flat. It's too silent. Too quiet. I despise it now. Just like I hate everything.

I walk into Blacks to our table and take my seat.

"The usual, Lord Lockhart?"

"Yes, Winston. Harrington won't be here for a bit, so could you get me something to read?"

Winston arrives with a bottle of scotch in hand, two glasses, and a copy of the *New York Times*.

I've started to read that *specific* periodical now more often than usual. What was once a weekly occurrence is now an everyday one. I like to keep up to date on America.

Or on one certain American.

When I shuffle through the pages, my stomach drops at the headline in bold ink. I'm used to a headline for business deals and whatnot, but this isn't in that section at all. This is in the society section, and my fist clenches as I read it.

"ADDISON PRICE DATING CEO OF STAR ENTERPRISE. A ROYAL COUPLE MADE IN MANHATTAN; SOURCES CONFIRM. MAXWELL WAS RECENTLY SEEN AT CARTIER. ARE WEDDING BELLS IN THEIR FUTURE?"

I ball the newspaper in my hand; the sheets crinkling loudly in the quiet space. There is a picture of them, and even though the image is wrinkled, I can clearly see who it is. It's the bloke from the lounge. The one she was on a date with.

The one she kissed.

What in the bloody hell is going on?

Karma. That's what. *You ruined her, and now she's out to ruin you.*

"Olly," I hear, and I lift my gaze to see Nathaniel walking over.

"Nathaniel," I respond, standing and heading over to him, giving him a one-arm hug. "It's been too long," I joke.

"Bollocks. I just saw you."

"Yeah, mate, except you bailed."

"Only because Cecile was there."

I shake my head. "Would that be so awful? If I remember correctly, she was a right good shag."

His turn to shake his head. "She was, but she was also a big cock-up on my part."

"Don't be so hard on yourself. You couldn't possibly know she was fucking all of England." I wink at him.

"Not all of it."

"Just your best mate."

"Sod off."

Sitting back down, I reach over and take the bottle of scotch and pour him a glass.

"Ready for me, I see?" he asks.

"Always."

We both lift our glasses and take a swig. "You coming tonight?"

"Maybe," he responds.

I look down at him over my glass.

"What's going on with that?" he asks, pointing at the crumpled newspaper.

"Just a thorn in my side."

He lifts a brow at my nondescript answer. "Anyone I know?" he asks.

"Just an American," I hiss. Not wanting to talk about it, I change the topic of conversation to him. Before long, he has me convinced I should show up at his event tonight. I don't want to go, but as the crumpled newspaper in the trash bin reminds me, she's already moved on. Maybe I should try too.

You have been trying.

But have I really?

I've been to a few clubs, yet I haven't slept with anyone but Addison since New York. I haven't touched anyone else. I haven't thought of touching anyone else.

I'm starting to wonder if I ever will.

This is awful.

I need to get over this woman.

Tonight.

Tonight, I will go out. I will go to the cocktail party hosted by Nathaniel's company. I'll take a model back to my hotel room and shag the memory of Addison right out of me.

This is a bloody good plan.

The plan did not go the way I imagined. Yes, there were plenty of models, but no, I didn't go home with any.

Instead, I drank myself into a stupor, then woke up this morning with a blaring headache and no blonde beside me. I'm going to have to come up with a better plan. Because this plan isn't working at all.

Distraction. I'm going home to the country, and I'm going to work on estate matters. Only one problem. My mother is there.

Okay, next plan.

Travel?

Work?

Get drunk every day?

Yes.

I think that's the only plan that will work.

CHAPTER THIRTY-ONE

Addison

"HAVE YOU SEEN THIS?" JASMINE RUNS INTO MY OFFICE.

"I have no idea what you're talking about." I lift my eyes from my computer and see she's holding her iPad. Her eyes are wide, and she just stands there waiting for me to say something. "Are you going to tell me what I'm missing?"

"TMZ . . ."

"J, you know I don't read that shit." Not anymore anyway. Not since the Spencer debacle. The crazy thing is, it's not because of him that I stopped. I no longer have a fear of seeing Spencer and Olivia. Now, I fear seeing a certain earl.

Luckily for me, he's the "Elusive Earl." Never photographed. Never mentioned. He stays out of the limelight completely, and for that, I'm thankful.

"Well, according to this, Max is looking at rings."

"What? Show me?" Jasmine flings her iPad in my face, and there on the screen is a picture of Max leaving Cartier. I stare at the image for a minute, waiting for a reaction from my body. Something. Anything.

"Are you dying?" Jasmine asks, mistaking my quiet for shock. And I am shocked.

Is he really going to propose? And the better question is . . . do I want him to?

What would our life look like?

I stare at his handsome face, one that makes me smile and laugh. It's not an all-consuming passion, but it is love.

A safer type of love.

It might not burn as hot as what I had with Olly, but this type of love will never *burn* me. And what I've learned from my past is I will never allow myself to get hurt again.

"So what do you think?" Her question pulls me out of my haze, and I look up and smile at her. I open my mouth to answer when Jax walks in.

"Word around town is you're in love."

"Jeez, you too, Jax?" I shake my head at him. "I thought you were better than reading the gossip columns."

"I have an alert set to anytime you're mentioned in the news. I don't follow tabloids." He shrugs, and I roll my eyes. "Well, do you think it's true?"

"How would I know? Men don't usually tell women things like this."

"Need me to hack his credit cards?"

"No," I say too quickly. The idea of finding something on Max is too scary for me to even comprehend.

I would rather live in ignorance this time.

Ignorance *is* bliss.

CHAPTER THIRTY-TWO

Oliver

Four months later

I HAVE SPENT THE PAST FEW MONTHS PARTYING UNTIL I'M drunk, not working, and basically cursing my fate. Today I'm a bloody mess.

I spent the whole night at some private party. Drank enough to kill someone and then woke up in the bathroom. When I woke up at three in the morning, somehow I wound up in my bed.

But enough is enough.

I fling my legs out of bed and pad my way into the bathroom. Lucky for me, there are no remnants of my stay. I brush my teeth quickly and splash some water on my face, then I go to grab something to eat.

A little while later, I'm sitting at the table with a cup of coffee. I have my mobile in my hand, and I decide to check out the local news. Nothing interesting. So I click on the American news. The mug I'm holding drops to the table, smashing and spilling the coffee across its surface.

"OUR PREDICTIONS WERE CORRECT. NEW YORK'S FAVORITE COUPLE IS TYING THE KNOT."

CHAPTER THIRTY-THREE

Addison

SITTING IN MY OFFICE, I HAVE MY HAND RAISED IN THE AIR. The early morning sunlight bounces off the facets. The ring is beautiful, and everything any girl would want. A perfect four-carat cushion cut for "Manhattan's princess of property" apparently, or so says *Exposé's* latest article about me. It might be the right ring, but is it the right guy? Was I acting impetuously when I said yes?

No. You love Maxwell.

He's done so much for me. How could I not?

"Let me see it," Jasmine squeaks, stepping into my office. She might not be my assistant anymore, but her office still faces mine, so she's always in here.

I lift my hand. "Like it?"

"Like it. Try, love it. It's perfect. And Page Six agrees."

I groan. "It's all over the news?"

"And every magazine cover. Your picture was on TMZ, for crying out loud."

I lift my hand and cover my face. "What am I doing?" I mumble.

She takes a seat directly across from me. "It's an amazing ring, and Max is great, but . . . it is a bit soon?"

"I don't know. Truth?"

"Always."

"I don't have any idea what the fuck I'm doing."

She places her hands on my desk and leans forward. "If you're not sure, you don't have to marry him."

"You don't understand."

"So make me understand."

I had no way of explaining it. "I do love him. Truly, I do."

"But not as much—"

I stop her right there. "What I have with Maxwell is different, and I love him." I don't say the truth. The truth is, he saved me. He healed me. He made me remember what I wanted from life before I got distracted and lost my way. I will never allow myself to get lost again.

The phone on my desk starts to ring. Pressing the button, I answer.

"Yes."

"There is a Lord Lockhart here to see you," the security guard for the building says.

Oliver is here. Why is he here? *Because despite everything, you knew he would show up. You knew that a public engagement would make all the major newspapers. You knew it would get back to him, and you hoped . . .*

I shake my head.

No.

I never hoped.

Lies.

The lies we tell ourselves are useless because no matter how much you say it, the voice is there, screaming in your head about all the lies. It screams the truth not just in your mind but also in your heart.

You hoped.

And now he's here.

Now what?

"Send him up," I say before I can second-guess myself.

Closure and all.

Maybe this can be the closure we both need.

Marrying Maxwell should be enough, but a part of me knows that's not true. It's just another thing I'll try to tell myself in the future, so instead, I say yes.

My heart pounds in my chest as I wait. It's been so long, and I have tried to convince myself that I was over it, that I no longer felt anything, but that isn't true. My hands are shaking. I know I need to get myself in check because I can't let him see me like this. Oliver is way too observant.

The seconds pass slowly. I concentrate on inhaling and exhaling.

Calming myself.

Finally, the moment is here. The door pushes open, the creaking of the hinges making sweat break out against my nape.

You are not affected by him anymore.

He walks in, and I don't look up. I keep my eyes focused on the computer in front of me as if he is of no importance at all. As if he is nothing.

Like the way he treated my feelings.

I hear the padding of his shoes and know he's getting closer. With each step he takes, the oxygen in the room diminishes further. On top of the desk, I'm cool and collected, but underneath the desk tells a whole different story. Under the desk, my nails bite in the skin beneath the hem of my skirt. The pressure is hard enough to break the skin, and it wouldn't surprise me at all if I find blood when all is said and done.

"Addy . . ."

I still don't look up. I refuse to, so instead of acknowledging him, I lift my hands from my lap, bring them back to my computer, and just start to type. I'm not typing anything important anyway, just a memo to myself.

"Love."

With that, I glance up with a scowl on my face. "I am not your love."

He nods before taking a seat.

"Did I say you could sit?" I lift my brow.

"You didn't say I couldn't."

He has me there. "Why are you here, Lord Lockhart?"

"Lord Lockhart." He leans back on the chair and nods. "Don't you think that's a bit formal?"

"Seeing as we're not friends, and you're no one to me, the appropriate way to address you is by your title," I snip back. "So now I ask you again, why are you here . . . Lord Lockhart?"

He leans forward and cocks his head to the right.

"Yes?" I lead him. "Because if you're here just to stare at me, I will kindly ask you not to waste my time. If you won't, I'll be forced to call security, so please state your business and then leave," I say coldly.

"I saw you in a magazine with your boyfriend," he finally says.

His words make me grit my teeth before I raise my hand. The reflection of the large diamond flashes against the surface of my desk. "Fiancé, you mean?"

"So the rumors are true."

"This time, the tabloids are right." I shrug and force a smile. "I'm getting married."

"Then I guess congratulations are in order?" he asks, but

the tone of his voice and the dark circles around his eyes tell me that his words are hollow.

"Thank you. Is there anything else you wanted to talk about because if not . . ." I stand and signal to the door.

He doesn't stand. He just stares at me. "Why are you doing this, Addy? Why are you marrying him?"

"Because he makes me happy." My eyebrows furrow.

"That's it?" He crosses his arms over his chest.

"I love him," I answer, and even though I know that's a lie, and I don't necessarily feel that way, I am committed to my decision. I'm committed to marrying Maxwell and being happy.

Or at least as happy as I can be.

"You don't love him," he whispers, and his words are almost inaudible. But I hear them anyway, and I refrain from even giving him the luxury of an answer.

"I do." I inhale. "Max is great, and he makes me very happy."

"You don't love him, love." I watch as he swallows, and his Adam's apple bobs. "Your first response was that he makes you happy, not that you're in love." Oliver cracks his neck, and a sly grin grows on his face. "So then why are you marrying a man you don't love?"

"I'm just taking your advice." I lean on the table for support.

"And what advice might that be?"

"I'm living."

"This is how you want to live?" He purses his lips. "With a useless excuse of a man."

"He is exactly how I want to live. And where do you get off coming here and saying otherwise? You don't know me. You don't know what I want."

He stands, walking right up to me. "I'm what you want."

"No." I shake my head with anger. "He is what I want. And further, he's not a liar." My words cut through him, and he looks down at me. "You have no right to come in here and say anything. I never meant anything to you. All you ever wanted was your precious fucking land."

He steps in so close his body almost touches mine. "You don't know how much I wish I could take it all back. You mean everything—"

"I don't care. I don't want to hear any more bullshit out of your mouth." I swallow and hope that my tears don't betray me. "Go back to England. Go back to your country. Go back to your estate and all your property, and while you do . . ." I start to walk past him to the door, which I swing open. "I'm going to move on with my life. Now leave."

"No." Oliver stares me down. "Not until we speak."

I shake my head, my fists balling at my side. "There is nothing more to say."

Oliver reaches into his pocket and pulls out that damn coin. "Then let's leave it to chance . . ."

He starts to flip it in the air, but I reach my hand out and grab it. I look down at the coin that played such an impact on my life this past year. That made me do things I wouldn't have done.

The coin stares back at me, old and weathered. Heads. I flip it over, and my stomach drops.

"It's a double-sided coin." I scoff, but I'm not at all surprised.

"You can't blame me for trying . . ."

"Not only are you a liar, but apparently, you're also a cheat."

"Addi—" he pleads, but I raise my hand and cut him off.

"Leave," I say as I place the coin in my pocket.

"This isn't over," he states.

"You and I are so over, Oliver. Go home and please don't come back."

He walks out the door, and when he's through, I slam it shut and slide down the wall, burying my head in my hands and letting out all the emotions I was holding.

Fuck.

It only takes a few minutes for the knock on the door I've been expecting. I want to be alone. I don't want to discuss how I feel after seeing him after all this time. I don't want to think about it either. But I do know if I don't answer the door, Jasmine will continue to annoy me. She's a pesky little thing. Like that gnat that keeps flying around until it gets what it wants. Unlike the bug, she's not trying to hurt me. She only wants what's best for me. So on the third knock, I give in.

"You can open it," I yell through the door. It swings open beside me, and she takes a step in and then turns her head a few times, looking for me.

"Down here."

She moves toward my voice and then looks down. "Jeez, Addison. What are you doing here?"

"I don't know."

"You don't know why you're sitting on the floor?"

"Yes. No. I don't know." I lift my head from where it's buried in my hands, this time tipping it up so I can meet her gaze.

"That bad?"

"Yes." My throat feels tight, like I'm choking and I can't swallow.

Jasmine lowers herself to eye level with me. "Then why are

you doing this?" she asks. Her voice is soft and tentative as if I'm a wounded animal, and she's afraid of my reaction.

"Because I have to." I bury my face in my hands.

"That sounds ridiculous," she says, and I lower my hands and lift my head. "You must hear how ridiculous it is."

I do, but I won't admit it. My pride won't allow me to.

"It really isn't. You just don't understand," I fire back, my voice rising a little too loud. She doesn't deserve it, but her comment makes me feel trapped against a wall.

"Then make me."

"Maxwell and I make sense. He's nice and caring, and together, we work. We complement each other." I swallow hard as the words leave my mouth.

"And? Don't make me say it, Addison."

"Then don't," I implore.

"You're scared, and he's easier."

"You're wrong. Watch your place, J."

"I'm just looking out for you. Sorry that I care, and I think you're making a huge mistake."

"Is that all?"

"Yep. That is all." She scoffs and walks out.

I know I've pissed her off. And while I know I should care, I can't. I'm too frazzled. I already have seeds of doubt, but her words have made it so much worse.

I know I look weak to her and she thinks I'm settling, but I'm not. This is me being strong and putting myself first. Yes, I don't want to be alone, but that's not all. Max and I will be happy. Deep down in my gut, I know it.

Maybe the passion isn't the same, and maybe it's not a life-altering love, but I do love him.

You're just not in love with him.

As of recently, I don't spend time with my college friends very much, but if there was ever a time to reach out, it's now. Now that I'm engaged. And now that I need support that Jasmine won't give me, I need them; I start a group text.

Me: I'm engaged!

Sarah: I saw. Congrats!

Sarah: Let's celebrate?

Me: OMG! Yes.

Julie: Wedding time!

Me: Hahaha drinks tonight?

Everyone shoots back yes. And after that, I send them the name of a private lounge I like to frequent. I'm feeling better already. This is what I need. I need friends who are excited for me. Not Debbie Downers like Jasmine.

The drinks can't come soon enough.

I'm all out of sorts by the time I make it to the lounge and to the table I reserved for tonight. Bottles of champagne and tequila are already waiting, as is my table host.

"Ms. Price," she greets. "I hear congratulations are in order."

"They are, Sabrina. Tonight, I'm celebrating with my friends."

"Is there anything I can do to make tonight more enjoyable?"

"Make sure there is never a shortage of drinks."

"That would be my pleasure," she says.

I smile at her and nod. No one in my family is a stranger to this club. It's one of the most exclusive private clubs in the city. So she knows I'll tip her royally if everything goes right.

Before I know it, all the girls are sitting around the banquette, gushing over my ring. They're planning my shower and my bachelorette party. Hell, they're planning everything. As they talk about Max and how perfect he is, how perfect he is for me, I know I made the right choice.

He's nice.

He's stable.

He's a good guy.

In real life, the princess doesn't marry the prince. She marries the normal guy. I'll marry the normal guy.

And I'm okay with that.

I smile.

I dance.

I beam.

None of it touches my soul, though, but I push that thought down.

I'm determined to enjoy myself even if it's pretend.

I wake the next day in my apartment, my heart beating rapidly in my chest and my whole body covered in sweat. Frantically, I try to shake myself out of the haze.

Olly.

I need Olly.

I reach for my phone and stop myself.

No, Addison.

You can't call him.

My heart feels like it will burst out of my chest, so I close my eyes and will it to calm. In my head, I can hear his voice . . .

"You're okay,"

"You're going to be okay."

"Inhale, Addison."

"Exhale, love."

As my pulse regulates, I take stock of myself.

I'm okay. It was just nerves.

Nerves that Oliver's voice calmed.

I can't think about what that means right now, so instead, I stretch my arms into the air.

I'm tired and worn out. Last night helped me get my thoughts in check, but it didn't cure the dilemma completely.

This wedding.

It was impulsive when he asked. Even more so when I said yes.

We were having coffee together. It felt so natural and easy, and he turned to me and said we should get married. I thought he was joking.

Then he lifted up my hand. And slipped the ring over my finger.

I was going to say no. But the words died on my tongue.

Why shouldn't I say yes? For once, I was being put first. I was his world. Why shouldn't I take for once, instead of always being the one to give?

The next day, it was all over the news. The next day, Olly was standing in front of me.

I have been engaged for four days, and I'm already lost.

I need Jasmine to talk me off the ledge, but unfortunately, I pissed her off enough yesterday that, as a friend, she won't answer, and as an employee, well, I would never do that to her. Hopefully, by the time we are at work and I apologize, she'll forgive me for being a bitch.

Since I can't call her now, I reach for the phone and call my fiancé. The phone rings once.

"Hey, sweetheart," he answers.

Even the nickname doesn't make me feel anything.

It will. You just need to see him smile at you. Show you that dimple you love so much. That will make you forget again.

"Hey," I mutter into the phone. "Are you free?"

"For you? Always." His voice is soft as if he's trying to tame a wild animal. Maybe that's how he sees me, but it doesn't matter; he always calms me regardless.

"Okay, great."

"Do you want me to come over?"

"Let's meet at Sarabeth's for breakfast."

"Sounds great. Thirty?"

"Perfect."

I hop out of bed and quickly get dressed. Once at the restaurant, he stares at me from across the table. His arms rest on the surface, and his head tilts slightly to the right as he watches me.

"How was yesterday?" he asks, and the muscles in my back tighten. How was yesterday? Does he know? How could he?

There is no way he knows Oliver came to see me. Right?

"Yesterday?" I ask.

"The girls."

"Oh." I had forgotten that I told him about that. I had forgotten so much. The only thing I hadn't forgotten was the one thing I needed to.

"It was fun. You know, drinking. Talking. Planning."

"What were you planning?"

"The shower. The bachelorette party."

"How about the wedding?" He smirks, and the dimple is present, and it makes all the corded muscles in my back loosen.

"We just got engaged." I laugh, lifting my mug to my mouth and taking a sip. My throat is parched from where this conversation is going. It feels like I swallowed honey, or something sticky, and I can't speak.

"That doesn't mean we can't start planning."

As the liquid pours down my throat, it loosens my tongue, and I place the mug back down. "When were you thinking?" I ask.

"The sooner, the better."

Thud . . . Thud. The beat of my heart starts to pick up.

"How soon?"

"A month."

Thud. Thud. Thud. Thud. I swear, I've stopped breathing. My heart is hammering so hard in my chest, I might be having a heart attack. "Are you crazy? I can't plan a wedding in a month."

"One, I'm not crazy, and of course, you can."

"Where would we even get married?"

"The Lancaster," he says as if this is something I would consider, but what he doesn't know is with one word everything comes back . . .

The Lancaster wedding. England. The coast. Falling in love. The lie.

Why am I waiting?

The faster I marry Max, the faster it's all in the past.

CHAPTER THIRTY-FOUR

Addison

Dad used to tell me, "Time may be free, but it's also priceless. Don't waste it on people who don't make you want to freeze time and live in this moment forever." But as I walk into Price Enterprise's annual gala for inner-city youth with Maxwell by my side, I don't want to freeze time. I want to speed it up—to fast forward through the night as bored people with more money than they can spend pretend to care about people they'll never understand.

I glance around the room. Walls decorated by art, exposed beams, dark lighting, and a stark white interior make this space sublime for this reception. The disparity between the tones makes the art pop and leaves an air of seduction. It looks like the perfect place for an illicit tryst or even better yet, the ideal backdrop to indulgence. Neither would surprise me as I look at the people meandering. Like me, they have too much money. Unlike me, they are unmotivated and bored, apparently.

With a glass in my hand now, we venture farther into the gallery. My eyes wander around the room, and I feel Maxwell squeeze my hand to get my attention.

"I'm going to the bar. Do you want to come?" he asks, but since I already have a drink, I shake my head. With a quick but chaste kiss to the top of my head, he walks away to get a drink.

I watch as he stands at the bar, and I can't help but admire how handsome he is. In a charcoal gray suit with no tie, he looks every bit the sweet and wholesome CEO.

Our eyes meet, and he smiles, and then I go to look at the artwork. I'm halfway through the space when something, or rather someone, catches my eye.

It couldn't be.

Could it?

As if he can hear my thoughts, Oliver turns his head as he laughs, his face now in perfect view. He is simply breathtaking and every bit the earl in his black three-piece suit. My heart lurches in my chest, or maybe it stops altogether. I'm not sure, but all I know is as I watch him, my breathing becomes ragged.

He's not alone.

In, out.

In. Out.

He's with a woman.

My pulse races so fast, I'm dizzy. I might hyperventilate. I need to move. I can't let him see me. My eyes focus on them. The blonde he's with looks like a model. Tall and lithe, her hand is on his arm as she speaks to him. Laughing and smiling, he's moved on.

So have you.

I swallow and hope and pray he will not see me. She laughs again, and this time, her body moves closer to his.

My stomach knots as I watch them. A voyeur yet I can't pull away. I need to. I will myself to move, but I'm too slow because I tell my body to stop betraying me. He looks over, his blue eyes locking on mine, his gaze lighting me on fire.

Leave.

It finally works. My feet remember how to move, and I do.

With my shoulders pulled back, I walk with dignity and confidence as if I wasn't affected by that display of affection. As if I didn't care.

A perfect lie . . .

I find a quiet alcove, and finally, I'm alone. Alone with my thoughts. Alone with the vision of him. Alone with my shaking hands and ragged breath.

Time passes . . .

Minutes.

Seconds.

And then I'm no longer alone. I don't see him at first, but I know it's him. I would know him anywhere.

I suck in air quickly as he makes his approach, as he steps out of the shadows and into the dimly lit refuge I've found for myself. His gaze penetrates me with each step he takes until he stands so close before me that I swear I can feel the heat of his body on mine. I breathe in deeply to calm my already shaky nerves.

"Why are you here?" My voice is barely a whisper, raspy and confused. "Why are you following me?"

"I'm here to donate money," he responds, his voice holding a challenge. I feel my heartbeat pick up in my chest as he leans forward until his lips graze my ear. "When I came here tonight, I had hoped I would be able to get you away from your fiancé to have a word, but it seems it was much easier than I thought."

I pull back and look at him. He looks at me like a hungry predator stalking his prey. "You need to leave me alone," I breathe out again in almost a whisper as his fingers skim my waist.

"I miss you." He trails a pattern down my torso, stopping at the curve of my hip. I shudder, and my breath hitches as his hand turns me around. His eyes glaze over with desire, and he leans forward. "Tell me you don't miss me, love." His face is a mere inch away from mine.

"I don't miss you."

"Now who's the liar?"

My heart slams against my chest. "I was never the liar. That has always been you," I say through gritted teeth.

"Yet . . ." His lips hover over my own, his breath tickling my lips. "You're lying now." I shut my eyes and will this to end. "By the way your heart is beating, I know you're affected by me. So tell me what you want, truly."

"I don't want you." But even I don't believe the words. Suddenly, his body presses against mine completely. I'm not sure how he did it, but he's maneuvered us against a wall.

My breathing grows frantic and choppy. His mouth nearly descends onto mine, but it doesn't connect. Instead, it just hovers.

Waiting. Teasing. Toying.

"No."

I push away.

Run as far as I can . . .

From him.

From the memories.

From the feelings.

From everything.

CHAPTER THIRTY-FIVE

Oliver

I'M STILL IN NEW YORK. AND SHE'S STILL GETTING MARRIED.

I can't let her go through with it.

It's ironic that this is how it all began. She came to England to move on from her ex, and she was able to, but I know without a shadow of a doubt, there is no one in this world for me but her.

I will never be able to let Addison go.

A part of me came here on a whim, not sure what I would find, but I knew I needed to see her. To see if she's in love with him. To see if she's happy.

She's not.

I was a dick to her, that much I know, but even though I can be a wanker, and yes, an arse, I'm not that way when I care about you, and I care about her. If she had been in love, and if she was marrying him for the right reasons, I would have left. I would have walked away and given her what she wanted.

But she doesn't.

So I don't leave.

Again, this might make me a prick, but I can't find it in me to care. Not one bit.

Since I'm in the city, I should ring Nathaniel, but I'm sure he's doing things with Madeline, his girlfriend. I could go out, but that feels hollow, so instead, I think of a plan.

The next day, I find myself at her building. There's no way she'll allow me up to her office, but I show up, nonetheless.

Before I walk inside, I notice the assistant standing along the wall of the building. She's talking to a man. From my angle, I can't make out who it is, but I can see Jasmine shake her head. The man continues to speak, but since I can't see him, I watch her. She looks visibly upset. Her lips puckered, and her back slightly bent. She looks like a scolded child.

I start to walk over when the man turns to leave. That's when I notice who it is.

The fiancé.

Why is he talking to her assistant?

And why does she look upset?

As soon as Maxwell is gone, I approach Jasmine.

"Are you okay?" I approach her, speaking calmly.

Her eyes lift from the floor. "I'm fine," she responds too quickly and then before I can ask another question, she turns on her heels and leaves.

I wonder what that's about?

CHAPTER THIRTY-SIX

Addison

A FEW DAYS HAVE PASSED, AND I HAVE DISTRACTED MYSELF with work. When I approach my building, I find Maxwell waiting for me. I probably should make him a key to my apartment, but I haven't. I don't know why. Jasmine says that means something, but I tell her she's just being dramatic. I've just been busy.

Walking right up to him, I stand on my tiptoes and place a chaste kiss on his lips. It's good to see him after the past couple of days. I feel like I'm losing touch with myself, losing touch with reality almost, but Max grounds me. He reminds me of what I want from life. This.

Together, hand in hand, we make the way up the elevator. Opening the door, we go straight through the foyer into the kitchen. He takes a seat at the island, and I open the fridge. Grabbing a bottle of water, I turn to him.

"Want one?"

"Sure. So what do you want to do for dinner?"

I sigh. "I really don't want to go out."

"Is there a reason?"

I don't want to tell him. The truth is, I don't want to see anyone. I'm too afraid I will see him. "To be honest, I'm beat. I just wanna put on pajamas and eat a home-cooked meal."

He laughs at that like I said something crazy. "And by a home-cooked meal, you mean we're going to order it, right?"

"No, I mean let's cook something."

"You know how to cook?" he asks.

"I mean, not really. Do you?"

"Why would I know how to cook?"

"I don't know . . ." I don't know what to say. Every thought brings me to Olly. Everything I want to say gets lodged in my throat. "What would you like?"

"What do you have in your house to make?"

I think for a minute, and the truth is, I have nothing. I have eggs. Yogurt. I walk over to my phone and call Jasmine, leaving the room.

"Hi, Addison. Everything okay?"

"Can you . . . this is awkward. What's the delivery service you use for groceries?"

She laughs in the phone. "What do you need? I'll place the order for you."

I proceed to tell her the ingredients for the only dish I can make. An hour later, the buzzer goes off, and then I hear the knock on my door. Maxwell stands from the couch and goes to answer the door. A few minutes later, he walks into the kitchen carrying a box.

"What are you making?"

"I'm making lobster risotto."

His eyes go wide, and I swear his mouth opens. "Wow," he says, dumbfounded.

"Don't be too impressed." I laugh. "It's the only thing I know how to make."

"I'm very impressed, but I can't say I'm surprised."

"You aren't? Why?"

"Addison, you are an incredible woman."

My face goes warm at the compliment because he means

it. With every word and compliment he says, not only does he mean it, but to him, I'm everything.

It's a good feeling.

After all I've been through, after the nerves I have felt, I need to hear that. I needed what only Maxwell can give me right now.

But as I stand here, there is a pang in my stomach because I remember standing in front of the stove with Olly behind me. I sauté the vegetables. Once they are done, I start to make the risotto. As I stand in front of the stove, memories flash in my mind.

His arms wrapped around me.

Stirring.

His breath. His body. The beat of his heart against my back.

I can feel his hands on mine.

My own heart picks up, swirling around and around in my chest. My eyes well. The memory so fresh and vivid, I don't know how I cook, how I move the rice, how I pour in the broth. My legs feel weak.

Time has passed, but has it? It still feels so fresh. The wounds so deep, that as I stand here, I don't know how I can breathe.

I feel sick with guilt. I hate myself for the thoughts flashing through my mind.

Maxwell doesn't deserve this.

He doesn't deserve to be compared, but I can't help my train of thought as I feel Max behind me. His arms don't feel the same. They don't heat my body the same. He doesn't smell the same, but as he moves behind me and places a kiss on my forehead, I feel his warmth and strength.

I push the guilt aside and focus on what he gives me.

Peace.

He gives me something Oliver doesn't.

I never thought I would need anyone else to boost me up,

but right now, I welcome it. Right now, I admit my confusion. Admit my treacherous heart for missing something that was never mine. I welcome the feeling of him, and I use it, pulling him into my back, and take what he gives me.

I take it all.

It might be selfish.

It might be wrong.

But I don't care.

I need him.

He makes me forget.

It's Wednesday, so like all the other Wednesdays before, I let myself go to shit for a man, then I stand from my desk and pat down my skirt and head out the door.

Jasmine lifts her hand with a wave.

"Have fun."

For a while there, I wasn't showing up to the weekly lunch with my friends but after the haze of depression Oliver left me in, I've been back at it.

We meet at the restaurant right down the street from my office building. It's a nice brisk walk, not far enough that I need to change my heels, but far enough that I don't have to worry about running into anyone I know, other than the friends I want to see.

Like always, I use the time during my walk to mentally tabulate the things I need to do this week. My mind never turns off. Occupational hazard, I guess. I'm so distracted when I walk in the door and head to my table that I don't notice him.

Until he says my name.

"Addison."

I look up from my seat, and there he is. As handsome as ever.

"You have to be kidding me! Are you stalking me?" I hiss.

"If stalking means I have been here at the restaurant you always go to every day this week hoping to see you, then yes . . . I'm stalking you."

"I'm surprised you remember that I told you I eat here every week." I glare at him. My cold voice lacks all the previous warmth it's ever held for this man.

"I remember everything," he says, his eyes boring into mine.

"I remember a lot too." I narrow my eyes. "I remember you being a liar. I remember you using me for a business deal. I remember being a means to an end."

"That's not what you were," he says.

"Oh, no? Then what was I?" I run my tongue along my lower lip. "A quick lay?"

"You were, you are, everything."

"You know what? I can't hear this. My friends will be here any minute. You can't be here."

He doesn't leave. Instead, he looks at me. His eyes that have always made me feel things do the same right now even when they aren't supposed to. They make me feel remorse, but I shake the feeling away. He lost the right to make me feel.

Squaring my shoulders, I hold in all the emotions that swirl inside me. I puff out my chest in defiance and drop the cool charade I place over my demeanor when I need to.

I don't care about him.

Not anymore, not ever.

I repeat those words in my head, forcing them to be a reality and for me to believe them. "You have your land. Go back to it," I hiss.

He inclines his head, watching me intently. He's trying to peel back my layers and see what's beneath, trying to see if I still care under it all, but he won't find anything.

I don't care about him. I don't care about him.

"Addy. Love, please—" he starts, but I lift my hand.

"Go away."

"I want to talk."

"We have nothing to talk about."

"Of course, we do. We have unfinished business."

"You already took my business."

"I meant about us."

I fist my hands on the table. "There. Is. No. Us." I pause between each word, making sure my point comes across loud and clear. "It was just a lie. And you fooled me once, but you know that old saying. Fool me once, shame on you, fool me twice . . ." I let my words trail off. "Do you really think I'm that stupid? Now leave before someone sees you."

I watch him, and he nods and walks back toward the door. I expect him to look back, but he doesn't, and that bothers me. I don't think about why, though. I can't go down that rabbit hole again.

I stare down at the table, wondering how my life got so far off track. I was once able to keep my emotions out of everything. After Spencer, I didn't let anyone in. I'm trying so hard not to let him affect me. Trying so hard not to let the walls crumble and let him penetrate them. Every time I see him, I hate him a little bit less, which isn't a good thing.

No. It's not. Not at all.

I can't control how I feel. The future is unknown when he's around, and I hate it. I want the stability I've had the past few months with Maxwell back. If only Oliver had stayed away.

You knew when he found out, he would come back.

You hoped for it.

Prayed.

I shake my head violently. *No. No. No.*

"What's wrong? Something in your hair?" I hear Sarah say as she takes a seat in front of me in the chair Olly occupied only a few moments earlier.

"Oh, I thought there was a fly."

"Got it. I hate flies."

The rest of the girls file into the restaurant, sitting in the seats we always occupy, and our waitress, Beth, brings the usual round of Bellinis. Everything is back to normal and right as I lift it to my mouth and take a drink.

Everything is simple again. Like it's meant to be.

I sit back and listen to the excitement. The oohs and aahs about the wedding plans. We laugh and drink. We talk about flowers and music. About the orchestra, and what jewelry I'm going to wear, and by the end, I'm excited.

"Next weekend, dresses," Sarah exclaims, and I smile. Dresses mean my mother is in town. I haven't seen her since we announced the news.

When lunch is finally over, I head back to the office with a huge smile on my face and my confrontation from only hours ago long forgotten. Excitement for the future hovers so close I could reach out and touch it.

Soon.

This wedding has occupied every single minute of my time. The truth is, it has taken up so much time; I want to take a vacation from wedding prep. It's not that I don't like clothes shopping, but the idea of trying on an endless supply of wedding dresses seems awful.

It's like I'm going through the motions. I wonder if other brides feel this way, or if something is wrong with me.

Oliver.

The name is sharp in my brain, and I actually want to claw at my own head to get it out. I swore I was done doing this, yet here I am again, doing something I should be happy doing, and his damn name pops in my head.

Today, my mother, who is staying at the apartment we keep in the city for when she visits, is meeting me outside the building.

My driver pulls up to the street, and when I see her standing with the doorman, she's escorted to the car.

"Are you ready for today?" she asks.

"I am." I smile back.

"You're going to make a beautiful bride," she says as she takes my hand when we sit beside each other.

Within ten minutes, we pull up to our location. The couture designer will be designing my one-of-a-kind gown.

We step into the study, which looks more like a boudoir lounge. Adorned with upholstered couches with gold ornate trim, chandeliers, and coffered ceilings, it's magnificent.

Once my friends arrive, champagne is passed around, and I'm stripped to my bustier and panties. One by one, I try on simple designs that the designer will customize only for me. By the time I'm on the third, the champagne has worked its way through my bloodstream.

This gown is French lace, high in the neck, and sweeps down in layers to the floor. My arms and my back are exposed, but the rest of me is covered. It's beautiful.

I can hear the gasps when I turn to face my friends and family.

I turn to look at myself. To see what they see.

This is the first dress I really look at. For the other dresses, I didn't like the feel of them, so I didn't bother. But this one, I do.

Turning toward the mirror, I stare.

I'm a bride. I'm going to get married. My large cushion cut diamond sparkles and bounces off the reflection in the mirror.

"That's the one," I hear someone say, but the voice sounds like it's underwater. I don't know who says it.

Sweat breaks across the skin beneath the lace. I reach my hand to my neck, to where the soft lace no longer feels soft, to where the neckline chokes and suffocates me. My skin feels balmy.

"Is it hot in here?" I ask as I start to pull at my neck.

"No," someone says, but again, the words sound like a hum. My heart pounds as the walls around me close in.

"It's so hot." I hear the humming in my ear, my legs becoming unsteady as I try to suck in a breath. "This dress. I can't breathe in this dress."

"Are you okay?" my mother asks. I register her frail, cold hands on my skin.

They feel good, calming, but not enough. "It's suffocating in here."

"I think she's having a panic attack," someone says.

My legs buckle under the weight in my chest.

My eyes focus in and out on the picture before me. Me in the dress.

Me walking down the aisle.

Me with Oliver.

Everything goes black.

My eyes flicker open.

I'm lying on the settee with a cold compress against my now exposed neck. "What happened?" I whisper, confused.

"You passed out," my mother says, her tone concerned and wary.

"I don't—"

"You said you were hot," Sarah adds. "I think you just got dizzy from the heat," she says, not admitting what really just happened. And I'm thankful. My mother nods, but her eyes continue to stare, her head cocked, analyzing me.

"I didn't eat," I lie.

"Well, that's it." My mother smiles. "Low blood sugar."

"Yep," I agree. I have to agree, and I have to lie because the truth is far worse. I know what I saw in the mirror. I know the vision that haunts me.

And I know without a measure of a doubt it will always haunt me.

But that's not reality. That's not how this story ends. It's okay, though. It's okay. I stand from my position on the settee and right myself.

"Sorry about that, ladies." I chuckle. "Next time, I won't try to diet before dress shopping. Apparently, it can backfire." I wink.

"Silly girl," my mother says, standing over and helping me up. "You don't need to lose any more weight," she whispers in my ear. "You're already too thin."

"Mom," I start.

"I know, I know."

I start to walk back to the platform set up for me to try on dresses. I feel a hand touch mine and find my mom looking at me, really looking. "Are you sure?" she whispers so low only I can hear. "Is this what you want?"

"Of course, it is, Mother." I scoff. I go to move past her, but she doesn't move.

"Addison—"

"I'm fine, Mother." This time, she lets me go, so I go to find a dress.

CHAPTER THIRTY-SEVEN

Oliver

Something feels off with this man. I can't get the look in Jasmine's eyes out of my head. The way she looked down at the floor and how uncomfortable she was. Before I can think twice, I pick up the phone and dial a number I never expected to dial.

"What do you want?" he answers.

"It's Oliver," I respond. I didn't need to say who I was. Jaxson answered the phone knowing full well it was me. There is little this man doesn't know.

"I know it is. Why don't you get to the reason for this phone call."

"I'm concerned about your sister."

"It's a bit late for that, don't you think?"

My back muscles tighten at the implication. I know I was an arse to his sister, but I'm trying to redeem myself. "I think something is off about—"

"Whatever you're going to say, I don't want to hear it. I know my brother has said it before, but I'm going to say it again. Stay the fuck away from my sister."

The line goes dead.

Well, that went well.

I guess I'll have to look into Maxwell myself.

CHAPTER THIRTY-EIGHT

Addison

Today is the day of my wedding shower. It's all approaching so fast, I'm not sure where the time has even gone.

I'm not ready.

Yes. You are.

My stomach roils with nerves, but I tamp it down.

I'm making the right decision. No matter how I felt when I saw him, I'm making the right decision. Maxwell is your best friend. Sure, things haven't been the same since Oliver walked back into your life, but they will go back to normal.

They have to.

After the wedding, Oliver will be gone, and I'll be able to love Maxwell the way he deserves to be loved. *Not the way you love Olly,* a persistent and unwelcome voice says in my head.

I brush it off, shaking my head back and forth. I can't think thoughts like that today. Not when I'll be leaving soon for the luncheon.

My hair and makeup are perfect. My long brown locks are blown out in a sexy beach wave, my makeup soft and graceful.

Today, I chose to wear white. A bit apropos since, at this point, I'm basically a born-again virgin. I can't believe how long it's been since Max and me . . .

Oliver.

This is the problem. Even when I think about Max and being intimate, I can't because the damn Brit keeps popping into my head. How can I sleep with him under false pretense? I need to get my shit in order before I can.

At least I bought myself some time by telling him that I wanted to wait. I wanted to spend the next month not being intimate to allow myself to get rid of my past once and for all was a great idea. When I do finally come to him as his wife, I'll be able to.

Yes.

Once I'm at the restaurant overlooking the park, I see everyone who has gathered to celebrate my nuptials. My friends, Jasmine—although I think she's still mad at me—and my mother. I'm happy she's here. With her not living in New York, it's hard to see her. Plus, she hasn't been well since Dad died. It's like she lost a piece of herself that day. I can't imagine being like that. Seeing her reminds me so much of how weak I was once. Now, I'm putting myself first, and that's okay.

She's frail in the corner. Her brown hair cut short and blown out straight. She's wearing a Chanel suit and flawless makeup. But she's hollow, and beneath the makeup, I can see the lines. She no longer sleeps. Hasn't since he died a year ago. It's sad.

And this is why I won't be here in the future.

On the other side of the room is Maxwell's mom and his aunts. He has one sister, and she stands talking to my friends, probably discussing next week's bachelorette party if I had to guess. She's younger and still in college, so I imagine this will be fun for her. I can't think of anything I'd like to do less than go out and get drunk, but I know it's all part of the fun.

My friends had shot down my suggestion to go to a spa, so

then I proposed a trip, like a shopping trip, but apparently, it wasn't conducive to their schedules. So we are going clubbing in New York next week instead.

Sounds like trouble waiting to happen, but what can I do?

When we sit to eat lunch first before we start the presents, a Waldorf salad is served. I push the food around my plate during the whole meal because I can't eat. The idea of food makes me feel ill. Instead, I reach for the tall flute filled with a mimosa and take a sip. It's divine against my tongue, and by the time dessert comes out, I already feel my cheeks warming and my nerves settling.

Once the plates are taken, I see my friend Sarah stand. "Time to open presents," she says cheerfully. And I'm happy someone feels like this. I, for one, still feel like the vise around my chest keeps tightening.

From the corner of the room, Maxwell strolls in. When I see his large and contagious smile, I find myself smiling for the first time since I've been here. Maybe this is all I need. Maybe I just need him to be with me more often, then I'll be okay.

The thought is sobering, though, because who is this person speaking in my head? I'm not an unsure person. I don't need anyone to hold me up, and suddenly, I feel like I can't stand without him.

I need air.

But unfortunately, I can't get it now.

"Hello, sweetheart," he coos, leaning down and placing a kiss on my lips.

"Hi, Max," I say, pulling back. His smile falters at how fast I stop the kiss, so I quickly speak. "No time for kissing. Time for presents." I wink, and his smile reemerges.

Hand in hand, we walk over to the table setup. My college friends open each gift and pass it to us. I hold them up, then Max and the crowd ooh and aah.

Once each present is unwrapped, we start to say our goodbyes. As Jasmine approaches me, I see she's holding one more box. "What's that?"

"There's one more."

"I didn't know. I can tell them to come back . . ."

"No, it's okay. Open it at home."

"Don't be silly. I'll open it here."

Without another word, I take the box from her hands and set it on the table in front of me. Most everyone has left, but I pretend they haven't. I open it slowly. Over dramatic. I'm trying to lighten the mood between us, but it doesn't work.

"Addison, I think you should open it at home. I don't think—"

"It's fine. All the old people are gone." I wink. "They won't see anything sexy."

"Addison—"

But I don't listen. Instead, I pull off the top, reach my hand in, and pull out what's inside.

Odd.

It's not lingerie. It's something round . . .

Soft.

I pull it out, and my heart pounds faster, the clips so fast, I feel dizzy.

"Where did you get this?" I hiss under my breath.

"It's from him," she responds.

As if a cold draft hits me, I shiver. "H-he gave you this to give to me?"

The walls around me, the clothes on my back, everything

feels tight. It feels like my lungs, my chest, and my heart are being squeezed to the point of pain.

"What is it, sweetheart? What did Jasmine give you?"

I can't show him this. I can't look at him, but when he reaches his hand out and takes the box, I have no choice but to watch as he pulls it out.

"Scones?" he asks, perplexed.

"Yes."

He lifts the box toward his face and smells. "Is that blueberries?"

"Yes."

"Is there anything special about those scones?"

"No," I say forcefully before turning my back and moving toward the door. A hand reaches out and stops me.

"Are you okay, sweetheart?"

"I'm fine," I lie. I'm anything but fine.

"Are you sure?"

"I just need air."

"Do you want me to come?"

"No, if you can please stay and make sure . . ." I think I might pass out.

"No problem. You go take a walk, and I'll meet you back at your apartment."

"Okay," I say and head out the door, my feet taking me Lord knows where.

Before I know it, I'm outside the park. And as if by some wicked twist of fate, I'm standing in front of the goddamn hot dog vendor. It feels like yesterday that I stood here with Olly when he fell to the ground and made me laugh. Made me feel.

I walk over to the vendor before I can stop myself, needing to remember even if just for a moment.

"What can I get you?"

"She'll have a dog with just ketchup," I hear from behind me, but there is no mistaking the British accent.

I don't turn. I can't. Instead, I stand and wait for my food. Once it's in my hand, I feel him turn me to him.

"How did you know I'd be here?" I hiss.

He doesn't seem shocked by my anger. If anything, that infuriates me more. He knew coming here would make me feel this way, and he did it anyway.

"I needed to see you," he responds. "I had to speak to you about—"

"Today. Today, of all days, you needed to see me? Today, you need to speak to me?" I fire back.

"Yes. Today. Your fiancé—" This time, I hold my hand up.

"Stop right there. Don't you dare speak to me about Maxwell. You have no right. Just like you had no right to send me the scones."

"I needed you to remember."

"Oh, I remember all right. I remember everything," I hiss. He looks down at my hot dog, as if he understands, and I hate myself for being so transparent.

"Why can't you leave me alone? You already have the land. It's yours. Why are you doing this?"

"'Cause I love you." His words knock the air from my lungs. Shaking me to my core, seeping into my soul, tugging at my heart until I can't breathe.

No.

Not now.

Not after everything.

I shake my head.

"Don't marry him," he implores, and my head moves fast as

if I'm trying to block out his words. "He's not who you think he is. Something's off."

"Oh, that's rich."

"Please, Addison."

Tears fill my eyes. He reaches his hand out to wipe the stray tear on my cheek and then moves them down to cradle my face. Stepping closer, he tilts it up.

"Don't," I say, putting my free hand to his chest and pushing back. "He doesn't deserve this. And I don't deserve this."

His gaze sears mine. It tells of everything I never wanted to hear, but in his eyes, I see the truth. He loves me.

But it's not enough.

Don't marry him.

I walk past him straight to the trash bin and throw the hot dog out. Throw out the memory.

I have to.

CHAPTER THIRTY-NINE

Oliver

I don't find out very much about Maxwell on my own. The only thing that stands out is that shortly after dating Addison, he got a promotion. But that's not alarming.

Something still doesn't sit right with me, though.

Without her brothers' help, there isn't anyone I can turn to. So I spend my time in New York trying to figure out what has me concerned.

I'm sitting at my hotel, laptop in my lap, when I receive an email from a business colleague. I had inquired if he knew anything about Star Enterprise.

The only thing I was able to find out so far is they had just relocated their headquarters to New York about six months ago, which was around the time Addison and he started dating.

Opening the email, I read it over.

Greetings Mate,

Hope all is well. In regards to the matter you asked, there isn't much to tell. What I did find is that Star Enterprise is apparently low in funds. Talks of a hostile takeover are underway if they can't raise capital and soon. Not sure if this is what you are looking for, so let me know if there is anything else I can be of service on.

Sean

Low in funds?

Hostile takeover?

And a speedy engagement to Addison Price . . .

This can't be a coincidence, can it?

The email from Sean haunts me all week. I try to reach out to Addison to discuss it, but she refuses to take my phone calls.

I try to reach out to Jasmine too, but like Addison, she ignores my calls.

Finally, after trying all week, I catch a break when she answers.

"What do you want, Lord Lockhart? Don't you have more pressing matters than to harass me?" The bitterness in Addison's voice spills through the phone line.

"Your fiancé is lying to you," I say matter-of-factly.

"The only liar here is you," she fires back.

"Addison, don't you find it peculiar that his company is low on funds?"

"Not particularly. But I'm not sure why any of this is your business?"

"I just want you to be happy."

"And if I'm happy with him . . ."

I let out a long-drawn-out breath. "Then I would let you go in peace."

"Then do that. Because I am. I am happy, Oliver. Please stop trying to find information on Maxwell. He's a good guy. He helped me. When you broke me, he helped me. Haven't you brought enough pain to my life . . . ?" Her words hit their intended mark; I'm a bloody wanker.

"I'll stop."

"Thank you."

But I don't want a thank you. I want an *I need you. I miss you. A screw you. A fuck you.*

Literally anything that shows me she still cares.

CHAPTER FORTY

Addison

It's been the longest week of my life. Oliver has left me alone since the phone conversation, but the more time I've had without him pestering me, the more time I've had to think.

And all I can think about now is him. The scones, the hot dog, and most importantly, the words he said that I never wanted to hear. I love you. I never wanted to hear them because the truth is, I so desperately *wanted* to hear them. But timing is everything, and it doesn't matter now. I'm with someone else, and even if I wasn't, it still wouldn't matter. I don't think I can trust him again. No, I know I can't. Can I?

This isn't the right type of thoughts to have when I'm getting ready to go out for my bachelorette party to marry someone else. I can't be thinking about this. I can't be thinking about him. Not now, not ever. Picking up my phone, I dial Max. My one true constant.

I let out a deep sigh as I wait for him to answer. "Hello, sweetheart," he coos in the phone.

"Hi," I say back.

"I can tell you're super excited for tonight."

"You have no idea."

"You know we could always elope."

"We could."

"Addison, why don't we?"

"Typical man. That ship has sailed in the form of a large deposit."

"I'd happily burn all the money just to be married to you," he says, and a smile lines my face because he means it; he really does. He loves me with all his heart, and I love him. My mother always said to find a man who loves you a little bit more. Some might argue that that's the wrong response, but to me, it makes sense. I don't know much about when my parents first started dating, but what I can tell you is that my father doted on her. He loved her just a tiny bit more. And I want that. With Maxwell, I'll have that.

"Trust me, I would if I could."

"I'll do anything you want."

"I love you, Max. What would I do without you? You truly are my best friend." I laugh.

"You already sound better. Now go have fun."

"I will."

"I love you."

"I know," I respond before hanging up the phone.

Now to get dressed. Two hours later, I'm dressed in a skin-tight black bandage dress with my hair blown out in beach waves again, but this time, I traded in my nautical makeup for a smoky eye and red lips.

I look like a sex goddess, and I'm ready to get drunk.

The lounge is dark, which is perfect. No one can see how I feel. Tonight, instead of thinking, I'll be drinking champagne and doing shots of tequila. Don Julio 1942, to be exact.

Olly's favorite.

Shit.

Why did I think that?

Once his name touches my brain, it's like a raging fire I can't escape, and it's all I think about. So I do what any person would do when they're trying not to think about something. Every time he comes into my brain, I take a shot to chase away the memories.

Before long, I'm dancing on the banquette with a glass of champagne in my hand, swinging my hips to the beat of the music. All my friends are here, and they're all dancing with me, screaming along with the beat.

The alcohol's coursing through my body. It's hot, and I feel dizzy. I turn to my left and see Sarah. Apparently, she's brought over a man. As if my bachelorette party is her wingman. She's sitting on his lap, leaning into him. His arm is wrapped around her, his hands fanning her back the way Oliver used to hold me. Oliver. Olly.

Before I know what I'm doing, I'm sending a text I should have never sent.

CHAPTER FORTY-ONE

Oliver

I'M IN MY HOTEL ROOM, WHICH, AT THIS POINT, HAS BECOME my residence. I haven't seen Addison since last week. Not since I sent her the scones. Not since I showed up at her shower and followed her to the park. I haven't spoken to her since I told her I would stop harassing her.

My moves have been a bit stalkerish. Ringing her, showing up . . . the scones. But the fact she went to the hot dog cart means it worked. Or at least I hope it did.

I just want a chance to try. A chance for her to see that the prick I acted like when I was with her wasn't really about her.

I'm in a no-win situation, not without me airing a story that's not mine to tell. Because in the end, I had no choice. Maybe I could have come clean, maybe I could have told her I needed the land, but when I first met her, I didn't realize how much I would care and how much I would fall for her.

How much I would love her.

It doesn't make what I did any less shitty.

But maybe she would understand why. My last shot is making her remember, and I hoped the scones would do that.

That was a better time, one when we were happy. Even if I was deceitful, I was happy.

Lifting my tumbler to my mouth, I take a sip of my drink.

The taste reminds me of her. Fuck. Everything reminds me of her. I need to try again—just one more time—and if it doesn't sway her, then I need to let her go. She deserves that.

She deserves for me to let her go now.

Nope.

One more chance.

As I'm sitting drinking, staring out the large window at the city, knowing she's out, having fun and not even thinking of me, my mobile vibrates across the table.

Addison.

A text has come through from Addison. It's as if she knows she occupies my thoughts, and now I know at least a piece of me occupies her thoughts as well.

Addison: I miss you

Not just a piece, but apparently a fairly substantial piece. It vibrates again in rapid succession.

Addison: I'm the liar.

Addison: I'm not happy.

Addison: I don't want to do this.

Addison: Why did you have to ruin what we were?

Me: Are you okay?

I send back a text because this isn't like her. Addison would never show her cards like this. Addison wouldn't pull back the curtain and let me, the enemy, into her inner thoughts.

Addison: Just drunk.

Me: Bachelorette?

Addison: Yes. They're all happy. Why can't I be happy?

Me: Why aren't you happy?

Addison: It's so bad.

Me: What's so bad?

Addison: You know how bad it is . . . it's sooo bad. I'm so broken, I'm saving myself for marriage. That's how bad you broke me.

Me: You haven't slept with him?

Addison: That's not what I meant . . . I just haven't since . . .

Me: Since what?

Addison: Since you came to my office.

Me: That means something.

Addison: It means nothing, Oliver. You hurt me.

Me: No . . . it means everything. I wish I could take it all back.

Me: Where are you?

Addison: Wouldn't you like to know . . .

I don't need her to tell me where she is. I know where she'll be going eventually. Home. Well, if she doesn't go to his place. But seeing as she just admitted that she hasn't shagged him since I showed up at her office, I highly doubt she's going there. I stand, quickly pulling off my sweats to replace them with jeans and a jumper, and then I head out the door before I can think twice.

Even if I have to wait there all night, I will.

Addison: Olly? Are you still there?

I hadn't responded. Too quick to jump up, I had forgotten.

Me: I am

Addison: Can you forget I said anything. I'm sorry I messaged you.

Me: Can you really forget me?

Addison: Never.

I like this Addison, not because she's drunk but because her inhibitions are gone, and she's speaking her mind. Maybe this is who she was before I ruined her, but now that I have her open, I don't want the door to close. No, I want to grab a sledgehammer and break down any walls still up. I want to strip her bare so we can rebuild together.

Opening the door, I head out of the hotel and walk the three streets to Addison's apartment. This is why I decided to stay at this hotel. Proximity.

It doesn't take me long. I see her doorman, and he looks over at me. I don't walk in, though. No reason to since she's not here. But I'll get her home.

Me: Addison, you should go home

Addison: Why?

Me: You're drunk.

Addison: Maybe you're right. Sleep will do me good.

I laugh to myself. Even after all this time, she doesn't fight me. I stand with my leg bent, leaning against the side of the building and watching traffic. Watching people mill by at this hour is also interesting.

Even in a prime property in New York. Across the street, though, is a different story. Right across Fifth where the park is, there are rambunctious kids obviously not sober. I wonder if that's what Addison will look like.

It takes about twenty minutes, but that's when I see the familiar Mercedes pull over in front of her building. I watch as the driver walks around the car and opens the door. Her legs come out first, long and lean, and all I can think about is how badly I want them wrapped around my waist.

I push off the wall and head to meet her by the door. She steps out, and I'm there standing in front of her. The moment she looks at me, I can't help but chuckle. Her green eyes are wide as saucers.

"Oliver?" Her mouth now hangs open.

"Yes, love."

"Why are you here?"

"Where else would I be?"

"Maybe in England, on my land," she retorts. She's the sharpest drunk I have ever met.

"Come on, I'll take you in."

"I'm not going anywhere with you."

"Are you okay, Ms. Price? Is this man bothering you?"

I slowly bring my hand to touch her. She stumbles, and I catch her with one hand while holding her steady. The faint smell of liquor wafts up at me as I frame her face. "Please," I mouth and her big eyes continue to stare at me until she nods.

"I'm okay," she tells her driver.

Stepping closer, I lace her fingers in mine, and together we walk to the door. The doorman opens it for us, and we move past him and ride the familiar elevator to the penthouse.

The place is exactly the same as I remember. I let my gaze span the room, looking for any piece of him, but I don't find anything. It might have been odd, but after her drunk confession, it makes complete sense. And it spurs a need in me to claim what's mine.

She opens the door, and I pounce . . .

Caging her in right there in her foyer.

Her breathing becomes ragged, and I feel her hand push on my chest.

"Why are you here? Why are you doing this to me? Why can't you just leave me alone?" Her words are slurred.

"You texted me," I remind her, looking directly into her eyes.

"I might have texted you, but I didn't tell you to come."

"You texted me, so of course I would come."

"I'm supposed to be getting married, and you've officially ruined me."

I grab her face to make her look at me. We stare at each other, and it's as if we are in a silent argument. Battling in a war we will both lose. Who will surrender first? Who will throw themselves on the sword?

Neither of us moves. We just stare. Breathing. Wanting. So I take it. I pull her toward me, tilting her chin, and kiss her with force, a passion I have never felt before.

I plunder her lips, telling her without a measure of doubt how I feel. How much I love her.

She kisses me back, answering without words my unspoken questions. She loves me too.

She needs me too.

I just hope it's enough.

Our foreheads touch, and I think maybe it is. Maybe it is enough . . .

But then I feel it. She's pulling away.

She pushes off me. I watch as her eyes move from lust to anger and her breathing once controlled by her need turns to rage. "And now you have made me worse than you. You might be a liar, but I'm a cheater again. I told you I would never be that person, and you just made me go back on a promise I made myself."

"Not if you don't marry him."

"What do you want, Oliver?" She sighs.

"I just want to talk."

"Don't you think the time to talk was a lifetime ago?"

"I've tried, love."

"No. I mean, don't you think the time to talk was before?" She crosses her arms over her chest as if that will protect her.

"I had my reasons at the time. I did what I thought I had to do."

"Still cryptic as ever, I see."

"You don't understand. I can't."

"Oh no, I remember. It's not your story to tell." She scoffs.

I nod. Though I desperately want to tell her, to make her understand, I can't.

"So you would do it to me all over again? If the land were still mine, you would do it all over? So this is all for nothing."

"You don't understand," I say, trying to make her see.

"No, I understand perfectly." She moves past me toward her bedroom. "Leave."

"No. Not until we speak."

"Leave, or I will call the cops."

"I'm not going to leave tonight. We need to talk, and you need to be sober."

"You know what? Come, go, I don't care. Stay the night. It won't change anything. Nothing. You might have made me a cheater, but nothing has changed. And I will never be with you."

She flings herself on her bed and buries her head in her hands.

No matter what she says, I won't leave until she's heard me out. I'll leave her be for the night, but come tomorrow, this ends.

CHAPTER FORTY-TWO

Addison

I WAKE THE NEXT MORNING WITH A SOUR TASTE IN MY MOUTH. It's like there is cotton on my tongue, and I can't open my eyes. I haven't felt this hungover in forever.

Since Olly.

Olly.

Oh, my God.

Olly.

With my eyes still closed, I remember everything. The kiss flashes behind my lids.

I did the one thing I swore I would never do again. I cheated.

You stopped it.

It's like he places me in a hypnotic trance, and I can't, for the love of God, decide what to do. I just can't.

Now, the next day, I feel ill about what transpired. I'm an awful person. I lied and cheated. I'm so much worse than the man who hurt me. Years have passed, and I'm still the little girl who got scared and sabotaged a relationship. Here I am years later, thirty-one years old, and still making the same mistakes.

I cover my face with my hands and pound on my skull. My brain hurts from the booze, but I need to wipe the memory clean. I need to forget what I did.

"Headache?" I hear from beside me in the bed, and my body goes rigid. I hadn't realized he was still here.

"Why are you here?"

"Do you need me to get you ibuprofen?" he asks, ignoring my question.

"I asked you a question. Why are you still here?"

"I didn't want to leave you alone when you were drunk."

"Well, now that you can see I'm fine . . ."

"I want to talk."

"So talk," I whisper.

With my eyes still closed, I feel him move closer to me and sit down on my bed. I can feel his hand on my skin, lifting my hands that cover my eyes. "Can you please look at me, Addison?"

"No," I grumble.

"Please."

"Why do you need me to look at you?"

I can't look at him. If I look at him, I'll cave. I'll forget everything other than him. I won't remember what brought us here.

I won't remember Maxwell.

Maxwell.

"Why won't you look at me?" he asks.

I shut my lids tighter. "Because I can't. I might not be able to say what I need to say."

"And what is that?"

"That this, everything with you was a mistake. And that I can never see you again."

Saying that hurts. It physically hurts, but it's what needs to be said. He's no good for me. His lies have destroyed everything, and if I let him, he'll pull me down further.

"Because of him?" he asks, sounding angry despite having no right.

"No. Yes. I don't know."

I squeeze my eyes shut harder, needing the headache to go away and wanting this conversation to be done. It's too hard.

"Talk to me. Open your eyes and talk to me. Be honest with me."

At those words, my eyes fly open in rage.

"Oh, that's funny coming from you," I spit.

"Yes. It is. I'm a liar."

I'm lying here, unable to move and unable to form words of how to deal with the situation. I can't look at him. I feel dreadful. It's like a dark cloud has lifted from me, and all the stuff from last night has faded, yet everything is still wrong.

I can barely remember why I called him. All I remember is sending the text. Then like an idiot, I let him come upstairs with me.

I needed to feel his lips on mine. I just needed to feel. I needed to live, and although for a moment I did, it's over now.

Last night, I felt alive, and I remembered. I remembered what it was like to come alive when his mouth touched mine and to feel the spark of life when he looked at me. But this morning in my bed, regret swelters in my blood.

What have I done?

We kissed.

"Addison, can we please talk?" Oliver says or pleads more like it.

He is just as beautiful as always, and I can't deny that he owns a piece of my soul, but it's not enough. I've said all there is to say.

"I can't, Oliver."

"I know I hurt you, and I know I lied. I'm so sorry."

"I truly believe you are, but it's not enough."

"Why can't it be enough? Why can't my love be enough?"

"It's not worth the risk."

"And living isn't worth the risk?"

"This isn't living."

"No, this isn't living." He grabs my face and kisses me abruptly, forcefully, making me forget the argument lodged in my throat. "When I kiss you, I know. I feel it. I see it."

"What do you see?" I mutter against his lips, unable to pull away. I'm drawn to him like a moth to a flame, and he'll burn me any moment. I know he will, but hell if I want to stop it.

"I see our lives together. Our home, our wedding. You walking down the aisle to me. When I close my eyes, I see our children. We have two. A boy and a girl. He looks like me, but she . . . she has your eyes. Green with little specks of amber. I can see it all." I close my eyes to his words, allowing the vision to penetrate me, invade my heart, and make me believe. It's all there. The fantasy, the promise, the . . .

Ring.

Ring.

Ring.

My eyes snap open, the dream fading away. What is that noise? His mobile.

I can see when he picks it up that it's his mother, the same woman who told me so poignantly how little I meant to him.

"Aren't you going to answer it?"

"No."

He pulls me toward him again, and before I can say anything else, he shuts me up. He kisses me; he touches me; he breaks me apart right there and then until everything I've just done and said are gone. I give in, and I kiss him back with everything I have. I'm bleeding out in front of him, my heart on the table, every part of me saying how much I love him, but I know this is the end. I know once this is over, I'm going to say goodbye.

I eventually pull away.

"We can't do this," I say on a sob.

The look on Olly's face tortures me more. The desperation I see almost has me caving. Almost.

"Don't. We can't be over."

"That's where you're wrong. We never started," I say, sadly.

"Does this feel like we never started?"

He grabs me again. Kissing me. Owning me. Claiming me. Breaking me apart and putting me back together all at the same time. Our mouths come together, frenzied and primal.

Each kiss says goodbye. He knows it now, and I know it. Tears leak out of my eyes with each swipe of the tongue. By the end, I'm nearly sobbing. I don't want to say the words I'm going to say but have to.

We are toxic.

I'll never be the same once I say goodbye to him, but I have no choice. My pride demands that I end it to protect my heart. It demands that I close it off but not yet. Just a few more moments of this lie, I tell myself. A few more moments when I let myself believe in the future where there are no lies, and we can live our lives together, not exist apart.

"You're mine, Addison. Admit you're mine. Not his. Not anyone's but mine."

"And that's where you're wrong, and that's where you've always been wrong. I'm not yours, and I'm not his. I am my own person, and I don't need you or him. This is my closure."

"I can't live in a world where I only exist. I'm yours." His voice is hoarse with emotions.

"Will you choose me?" I ask. But as if divine intervention, before he can answer, I see the phone ring again, and the word "mother" appears on the screen again. And right then, I know the truth. I know he won't. He'll always pick her. So I do the only thing I can.

I move away from him.

"That might be so, but I deserve better. I deserve to be more. I deserve to be first. Please leave."

I see the moment when he concedes. His face falls, and then he does exactly as I asked. He turns his back and leaves.

After I hear the door close, I know Oliver is gone. I make my way back into the bathroom and turn the water to scalding hot. I burn him off my lips, scrubbing hard and fast, making my mouth shake against the friction. When my skin feels raw, I turn the water off.

No matter how I feel about Oliver or what I say to the contrary, I do love Max. He saved me when I was sure I'd never be able to breathe again, so I owe him so much. I owe him the truth.

Throwing on my bathrobe, I dress, and then I get back into bed. When I wake up, everything will be okay. When I wake up, none of it will have happened, or at least that's what I tell myself.

I hear the buzzer go off. My eyes open, and I'm not sure how long I slept. Looking over at the clock, I see that it says it's after four p.m. I stand and answer it.

"Hello," I say.

"Maxwell is here to see you."

It's funny I had never told my doorman to let Max up without asking. I thought about it, but I didn't. Now in hindsight of what I've done, I'm thankful because if he had shown up any earlier, it could have been worse. Nothing could be worse than telling your fiancé you can't marry him, other than if he had walked in on Oliver and me.

I walk to the foyer and open the door, waiting for him in my pajama pants and a robe. He walks off the elevator into my apartment. "Must've been some night," he says as he appraises me, and instantly, guilt descends upon me. "What's going on?" he asks, my silence speaking a thousand words. "Are you okay?"

When I walk to the living room, he trails me. Once inside, I turn to face him. Suddenly, he looks a little sad. He knows this is coming.

"We need to talk."

"Okay."

"Last night . . ." I start but stop. I can't say this. How do I say this? How do I knowingly crush him? I swallow a few times, trying to wet my tongue. Trying to force the words out that I don't want to say. "Last night I did something." My eyes fill with unshed tears. "I can't marry you."

He doesn't react right away. His eyes stay trained to mine. After a moment of silence, he finally speaks.

"I love you, Addison. Whatever you did, it doesn't matter."

"But I—"

"I don't care."

"You don't understand."

"Yes, I do."

I lift my gaze to study him. What I'm met with makes my chest feel tight as though a vice is tightening around it.

Sadness.

Pity.

He knows.

"I let him kiss me," I admit on a sob.

"But you stopped it?" he asks, and I nod.

He wipes the tear that is trailing down my face—

"I forgive you."

My heart hammers in my chest at his words. It's too easy. I don't deserve his forgiveness.

It makes no sense.

"I will make you happy. I will give you the life you deserve," he promises.

At his words, tears stream faster down my cheeks. I don't deserve his forgiveness.

"Max. You helped me when I didn't think I could feel again. You made me happy when I couldn't." I run my hands across my cheek to stop the flood of tears. "You made me smile and laugh. I'll never forget those things."

He smiles, making my chest tighten.

"I love you, Addison," he says with a smile.

"I love you, Max." I take a deep breath, willing myself to finish what I started. "But I'm not sure I'm in love with you."

"One night with *him* and you're ready to throw away everything?" he grates. "Have I not given you everything?"

"This has nothing to do with him, Max. This is me being honest because you deserve that."

"Don't tell me what I deserve, Addison. You don't get to tell me anything."

I stay quiet, giving him a moment to calm down. He needs to collect his thoughts. Whatever he's feeling, I owe it to him to hear him out. His anger slowly ebbs, and in its place is sadness. It breaks my heart to see this man crumple in front of me.

"Please don't do this. Give me a chance to make you happy. Give me a chance to take care of you," he begs, tugging at my heart.

As horrid as I feel, I can't give in. This is what's best.

"I'm not sure if I can."

"You'll always be first to me, Addison. Can you say the same for anyone else?"

I think about what he's saying. I can be first to him. Have I ever been someone's first before? I wasn't Spencer's, and I sure as hell am not Oliver's. From the first time, since as long as I have known Max, I have been the most important person for him. Can I really give that away? For what?

Guilt.

You kissed Oliver.

"You'll hate me one day."

"I won't," he reassures.

"You'll resent me for what I've done."

He narrows his eyes. "Are you going back to him?"

I shake my head. "No. That's over."

"Then I can forgive you for anything. After the wedding, our slate will be wiped clean. Be with me. Marry me."

His forgiveness reaches out like a balm to my troubled soul, and Maxwell pulls me into his arms, his lips meeting mine. "Marry me."

He loves me. He asks nothing in return. He will put me first. He will always be there.

I can trust him.

Don't I deserve happiness? Maxwell can be my happiness.

"Yes," I whisper.

As the word escapes my lips, a small part of me aches. I push it down and bury it.

CHAPTER FORTY-THREE

Addison

WITH THE WEDDING FAST APPROACHING, I'VE TAKEN some time off from work. I'm relaxing on my couch with a glass of wine when I hear a knock on the door.

Instantly, my back goes ramrod straight. Part of me wonders if it's Olly, but I know it's not. My doorman would buzz, and on top of that, he's gone. I finally did what I set out to do. What I wanted. So why do I feel this way? I stand from my chair and make my way over to the door. I don't bother looking through the peephole because it's either one of my brothers or my mom. When I swing the door open, I see it's not one but both of my brothers. Grayson and Jax are both standing there, Gray still in his suit, and Jax in what he considers formal attire . . . jeans and a graphic tee with a blazer over it.

"Aren't you going to let us in?"

"Shouldn't you guys be working?" I ask.

"It's after five." Jax smiles.

"Fine, come in." I push the door wider, and they enter. With them now in tow, we head toward my living room.

"Drinking alone? Is it time for an intervention?" Jax says, lifting a glass off the drink cart in the corner of the room and helping himself to a glass before plopping down on the side chair.

"Yes, please stay and drink my wine." Sarcasm drips off my words, and he lifts his glass and takes a sip.

Once he's done, he smirks. "Don't mind if I do."

"To what do I owe this honor?"

"Can't we just want to come here and check on our sister?" Grayson asks.

I lift an eyebrow, and Jax laughs.

"Because you often stop by unannounced?"

"She does have a point, bro," Jax says to Grayson, and then Gray shrugs in response. "I guess we should just cut to the chase . . ."

"Please do, Jax. Just cut to the chase," I chide.

"Are you really going through with this?" Grayson asks.

My mouth drops open at the balls of Grayson and Jax. Even though he's not the one talking, they are both here and both saying this to me only mere days before my wedding.

"Of course, I'm marrying him!" I shout back because as much as I want to rein in my emotions, I can't.

Every muscle in my body is tense from this exchange, and I feel like I'm wound up so tight I might burst.

Gray steps closer. "Addison—"

"No. Don't you dare Addison me."

"Listen, we let this go on long enough. You didn't want to talk to us. But now—"

My head shakes back and forth. They can't do this to me now. Not when I'm hanging on by a thread. I know Maxwell will make me happy. I just need to marry him. Once we're married, everything will be okay.

Everything will make sense again.

"Did you know he used your name to secure funding?"

I didn't . . .

But it doesn't matter.

"So what? So fucking what! He's my fiancé, so why can't he use my name to secure a loan? He's family. That's what family does if they need to."

"Not yet, he's not. Until he signs those papers, until you sign them, he's nothing. And he's been using your name since the beginning."

"I don't care. Maxwell might have done those things . . ."

"Not might. He did."

"Again, I don't care. And neither should you. We have all used connections to get ahead in business. All that matters is that he loves me."

"We just want you to know the facts. And be sure."

"I am sure. Now, please leave, and I expect you on board with this wedding."

Grayson looks over at Jax, and they both nod, standing. Gray opens his mouth to speak, but I silence him with my hand.

"No. Right now, I want to be alone."

Without another word, they respect my wishes and leave, and I pour myself another glass.

I'm making the right decision.

But the thing about doubt is that once the seeds are planted, it grows and spreads until that's all you see.

Back in the office, all I can do is think about what my brothers said to me. My hands visibly shake, as I try to figure out how to confront Maxwell. I don't doubt that he used my name but is that all I am to him?

Stop.

I chastise myself for allowing another man's betrayal to

tarnish my trust in Maxwell. It's just . . . he didn't tell me. Why wouldn't he tell me?

"Are you okay?" I hear from behind me, and I turn around to see Jasmine standing there. Her lips are tight.

"I'm . . . fine."

"You don't seem *fine*."

"I'm getting married. I'm stressed," I say.

"Yeah . . . about that. You sure that's what you want?"

It doesn't take a rocket scientist to know that she doesn't support me, and she doesn't agree with my decision to marry Maxwell.

A part of me wants to talk to her about what I heard, but at the same time, what if Maxwell has an explanation and what if I decide to still marry him? Could I risk my friendship? What if she says something to me that she can't take back?

"I'm sure," I lie.

The truth is, I don't know what I'm going to do yet. If it turns out Maxwell is using me, he won't ruin me. I'll be all right.

I'm too strong to be ruined.

I will never let anyone ruin me again. Olly almost succeeded but he didn't. I'm still here. As strong as I am, just thinking his name makes my hands shake more. My whole body wants to shake at the emotions swirling inside me.

"What's going on?"

Despite my earlier concerns, the internal pep talk has me feeling stronger. I decide to tell her because I need a confidant.

"My brothers told me something about Max . . . They said he was using me."

Jasmine's eyes dart away from mine and look toward the floor.

Odd.

But what really has me worried is when she bites her lip.

"Do you have something you want to say to me?" I walk over to my former assistant, someone whom I once considered my best friend before this wedding. "What is it? You can talk to me."

She doesn't speak. And I wonder if this is because of us or her job.

I lift my hand. "Whatever it is, I won't hold it against your job. You'll still have your promotion. I won't take that away from you."

"This has nothing to do with my job. I consider you more than a boss, so right now, I'm going to pretend you aren't one, and I'm going to say something regardless if you want to hear it or not. Max is not worthy of you."

"What are you—"

"Your brothers are right. Olly is right."

I know she's speaking the truth. Deep down, maybe I always knew, yet I chose to ignore all the signs. But now looking at Jasmine, I'm no longer blind. I see it all.

What I once thought was endearing was indifference.

The things that appeared genuine were ungenuine.

I was so desperate to move on from Oliver that I pretended. I buried my head in the sand, but now everything makes sense.

He wasn't supportive of me working. He was supportive of what my work could do for him.

With a deep inhale, I finally allow myself to speak the words I never wanted to. "Tell me everything."

She nods in understanding and then sits down in the seat across from me.

"I don't even know where to start."

"The beginning, I guess?"

"One night, I went out . . ." she starts and stops, taking a deep gulp before continuing. "It was at the fundraiser." She doesn't need to clarify which one because it's where I saw Oliver . . . "I drank too much, and well, I went home with one of the developers who happened to be bidding on a project for us." She bites her lower lip, and it doesn't take a rocket scientist to know where this story is going.

"You went home with Seth Mason?"

She nods, the implication heavy in the room. She went home with the man we awarded the multi-million-dollar contract to.

"I didn't know you would choose him, and I didn't tell him anything to help him land the contact," she whispers. I hold my hand up and give her a reassuring smile.

"I know. I would never think you did."

"Maxwell must have seen us."

"What did he do?" I ask, my stomach hollowing as I wait.

"He approached me. He wanted information, threatened to out me, not just to you . . . but also to our competitors. He wanted to ruin me.

"He wanted insider information?" She nods at my question.

The feeling in my stomach spreads inside me. "He wanted to use the information to hedge bets," I whisper more to myself than to her. "He wanted to know who would win the contracts . . . whoever won . . . the stock would go up . . . He wanted to use you for insider trading."

She worries her lip, and I know I'm right.

"Why didn't you come to me?"

"I know I should have, but you knew how I felt about him. How I wasn't supportive, and I didn't think you'd believe me."

I lean forward and reach my hand out, taking her hand in

mine. "I'm sorry I failed you. You should have felt safe coming to me."

"It's not your fault. You deserve the truth, and I'm sorry I never told you, and I'm sorry I didn't trust you. Because you deserve more from me. You deserve more period . . ."

"What do you mean?"

"You deserve to be someone's everything."

She's right, and I see it now. I refuse to be hurt again. I will do what I need to, to put myself first.

Standing abruptly, I make my way out the door.

"Where are you going?" she asks from behind me, but I don't answer. I'm already in the hall.

It only takes me two minutes to find who I'm looking for.

Sitting at the conference room table are my brothers. They both look up at me as I step into the room. When I slam the door behind me, Gray lifts a curious brow.

"Tell me everything," I demand.

Jax's mouth spreads into a large grin, as he turns to Gray.

What is going on?

"I told you she'd come around." Jax chuckles and Gray shakes his head as he reaches into his pocket and grabs a wad of cash and hands it over to our younger brother.

"Did you really make a bet on me?" I ask because, clearly, that's what's going on here. They made a bet, and Jax won. "On if I would come around and ask about Max?"

Gray shrugs and Jax places the money in his wallet.

I let out a deep breath. "Fine you were right, is that what you want to hear?" They both nod. "Now grow up and tell me everything."

I don't bother to knock as I storm into Maxwell's office an hour later. Maxwell stands only a few feet away . . . I stare at his features, and the kindness and his soft eyes are gone. Now that the veil is lifted, I see him for the snake he is.

Worse than a liar.

He is nothing more than scum.

I square my shoulders and stand as straight and tall as I can. My carefully constructed facade is pushed down. "We need to talk," I hiss and then slam the door behind me.

Maxwell's eyes widen at my tone. "Okay."

I stand in front of his desk, peering around the space. What I notice first is the faded coat of paint on the barren walls. Next, my gaze stops at the cluttered desk. How had I never noticed the disarray before now?

You were too busy clinging to a fantasy to notice anything.

"Tell me the truth. What did you expect to get from me?" I pause, my hand resting on my hip. "Money. Power . . . all of the above?"

He looks shocked at first, but he schools his features.

"Does it matter?" He shrugs. I can't believe I didn't see him for what he was the whole time.

An opportunist.

"You used me," I said. "For what marrying into the Prices would bring you."

"Don't play innocent, Addison. You used me, too."

"How dare you? I might have used you to get over someone, but I genuinely cared. You, on the other hand . . ." I trail off, trying to find the words.

He steps closer to me and reaches out his hand. His fingers touch mine, and for the first time, his touch makes me feel cold. "We can still be the power couple of Manhattan."

I pull my hand back. I slide the ring off my finger and drop it in his open hand.

"Being with you would just be existing." And with that, I leave.

CHAPTER FORTY-FOUR

Oliver

I'M BACK IN LONDON. THERE WAS NO REASON FOR ME TO STAY in New York.

I thought there might be a chance we could make things work, but then, I knew. I knew when I saw the tears that she was done. Nothing I could say would get her to change her mind. I had ruined her, she sobbed, and the last part of me that was still intact broke too. But I still thought maybe, just maybe, there was a shot.

I look down at the text I just sent her.

Me: Addison. We need to speak.

She doesn't answer, and I feel dead inside—as though a dull, serrated knife is carving out my heart—but now, here at my estate, I don't know what to do with myself. Nathaniel is in New York, my mother is God knows where, and Addison is about to get married.

In one week. One fucking week and she will belong to another. Her heart will no longer be mine.

I reach for the bottle of scotch and bypass the glass completely. Instead, I bring the bottle up to my lips and drink. I drink and drink. I take my mobile in my hand and stare at her name. I stare at the last text she sent on the night it all went to shit.

The last night.

The end.

I sound pathetic. Never in my life did I think it was possible to fall this hard and to hate myself this much. Because I do. I hate myself for being stupid enough to lie to her. I hate myself for thinking I could be happy. I hate myself for being too loyal.

I don't deserve her, though. Not now. Not ever. Regardless of what I do to show her how I feel or why I did it, she'll never understand. She'll never forgive me.

Tell her everything.

Tell her why you lied.

I shake the voices out of my head, begging me to get on a plane and head back to New York to confess the secrets that are not mine to tell.

I know I can't, so I lift the bottle back up and take a long swallow. The scotch courses down my throat on its warm path to the pit of my belly. To the empty part inside me. It doesn't take long for everything to fade away and for me to feel warm. I keep drinking, and it keeps fading until I barely remember what brought me back home.

This lie has turned families against each other.

This truth has ruined lives.

This property has hovered over too many people and destroyed them for too many generations.

I keep drinking.

More.

More.

More.

Until I'm barely able to hold my head up, and my whole body is numb.

"Oliver. Oliver," I hear from beside me. My eyes are heavy, and I turn to the voice. I turn to my mother's voice. That, right now in my drunken state, seems shrill to my ears. "Wake up, Oliver."

"What do you want, Mum?" I mumble out.

"You need to stop this. You need to stop drinking."

"No." I laugh. "I like scotch." I lift the bottle off the table and go to lift it back to my mouth.

"No," she shouts, grabbing the bottle from my hand. "No more. You are self-destructing, and you can't do this. You have responsibilities. You have been here drunk for days. Have you even bathed?"

"What's the point?"

"The point is, you are an earl. This property—"

"Fuck the property. Fuck my dad, and you know what? Fuck you," I hiss. I hear an audible gasp, and I realize in my inebriated mind what I have just said. "I'm sorry, Mum, I didn't mean it." I groan, lifting my hand to my head and grabbing my hair. My head starts to pound. Throbbing as the memories I had previously rid myself of come back.

"Pass me the scotch."

"No. You need to go to bed, Oliver. Everything will look better in the morning."

"How will it look better? She's getting married. I lost her."

"You'll find somebo—"

"Don't you dare! I will never find another. She's everything to me. Do you hear me? Everything." I jump up before she can stop me and grab the bottle from her hands. "If that will be all . . ." I stumble out of the room, the liquid splashing out of the bottle as I swing it, leaving a trail behind me, a bread crumb to where I'm going.

Once in my bed, I continue to drink, and eventually, when the bottle is polished off, I'm out.

CHAPTER FORTY-FIVE

Addison

After Maxwell, I walked home, blocks and blocks to clear my brain. It took me three hours before I stepped into my apartment.

Now alone, I know it's time that I put myself first and figure out why?

Why had I allowed this to happen not once, but twice?

Picking up my cell, I fire off a text saying that I will be taking the rest of the day off. Then I shoot back another text to my brothers telling them I'll actually be taking the rest of the week off.

Gray: Are you okay?

Jax: What happened?

Me: It's over.

Gray: Do you want us to come over?

Me: No. I want some time alone. To think.

To feel.

To decide what I would do now.

Gray: Would you like us to make a statement to the press?

Me: No. Not yet. I don't need speculation and gossip right now.

I needed to figure out what I wanted from life, and I can't do that if the press stands outside my building hounding me for a story.

Gray: Take all the time you need. We will be here when you're ready.

Me: Thank you.

Jax: We're proud of you. Dad would be proud of you.

His words filter over me like a balm over the wounds inflicted on me. Jax doesn't realize how meaningful his words are.

All I have ever wanted was to be respected and valued, the way my father valued me.

To prove to everyone I was worthy of the job he entrusted in me. But there was so much I forgot on this road to success.

The problem has always been that I've been scared to allow myself to be happy. To allow myself to be more than just Addison Price, the CEO of Price Enterprise.

But now that my eyes have been opened, I have seen everything I need to. And now I have to decide what I'm going to do with that information.

I spend the first day of my self-proclaimed exile in my apartment. I clean. I cook.

I do all the things I never thought I could, or at least never tried to do.

It feels good to stand on my own two feet. As much as I know I can run a boardroom, it empowers me to know that I can run my own house as well.

On day two: I venture out, dropping off food at the local shelter that I had cooked.

As I stand at the counter, now helping serve food, I notice a young man in his late teens in the corner . . .

His eyes are downcast, his face swollen with tears. I step away from the food and remove my gloves.

With tentative steps, I approach him.

"Do you want to talk about it?" I ask, but I know the answer before he even shakes his head. I'm at a loss for how to break through to him, but then I feel something weighing heavy in my pocket.

"Heads you tell me what's troubling you?"

My comment has him snapping his gaze up, and he looks at me like I'm crazy. I can recognize the look anywhere; it's the same way I felt the time Olly told me to live.

"Heads, you let me buy you lunch, and we talk." I try again, and this time I see his lip twitch up.

Pulling the coin out of my pocket, I hold it away from the boy. Flipping it like Oliver would and then place it on my hand.

When I show him the heads, I wink. "So what are we having for lunch," I say, and he laughs.

The young man laughs a beautiful laugh and makes my eyes tear.

Many months ago, I was lost. I was sad, and Olly made me feel alive, now almost a year later, I'm back in New York. Once again alone, but this time, I realize I'm happy. I'm strong. I'm not defined by a man or how they love or treat me. I'm defined by how I love and treat myself.

It's okay to be vulnerable.

The reason I pushed him away was that I didn't want to feel weak, but loving someone is never a sign of weakness. It's a sign of living, and that's what Oliver taught me to do.

I realize that now.

Oliver was right. I simply existed.

That was until now.

CHAPTER FORTY-SIX

Oliver

WHAT DO YOU DO WHEN YOU LOSE THE WOMAN YOU love? Well, other than the obvious of getting pissed, there really isn't anything else. So after you exhaust every pub in London, you move onto greener pastures or, in my case, the blue waters. I couldn't stay in London or at my estate. I refuse to even turn on the telly for fear that Addison's upcoming nuptials will be all over the news as if she were royalty.

So instead of trying to avoid the flagrant news coverage I knew would ensue, I decided to leave and go to the Greek islands. It might not be the ideal time of year to go, but in my opinion, the weather is lovely. The water is cold this time of year, but that is a different story.

So here I am, on my yacht anchored off the coast of Santorini. From where I'm perched, I have the perfect view of the pebble beaches and the towering cliffs. But it's the ocean that does me in. Because as far as I am from her, every time I look at the damn ocean, I see the green of her eyes.

This was not a well-thought-out plan.

I'm supposed to be so drunk I don't remember her eyes, but as the setting sun bounces off the clear glass waters, she is all I can think about. I turn my body so I don't see it and stare at the throng of people around me.

The party I'm having tonight on my yacht is in full swing. The tourists who flock to the islands to drink and party are on board. The music blares from the surround sound, and everyone is dancing. Drinks are flowing. Women are plentiful. It's a right good time, and I wish I could get over the way I feel. Because as I hold down court, sitting on my "throne," I look around at the hordes of people, of the naked women dancing, and I feel nothing. There is no excitement. There's no need to partake. Instead, I sit with my bottle of Don Julio and go shot for shot with no one in particular. To be honest, half the time, I drink alone to drown my pain.

Finally, after I'm fully gone, I decide to go join the crowd. Maybe tonight I will find a woman to shag.

I should.

I need to.

Right now, she's preparing to get married to the wanker of a fiancé. So why shouldn't I bury myself in someone new?

Taking the steps down, I make it to the large sundeck. My gaze scans my options. At one end are a mix of people dancing. At the other end and a floor lower, I can see women on the deck leading to the ocean. Only women. Naked women about to skinny dip.

That's where I'm going.

I stumble my way over to them, and they all start to sway their bodies seductively. I glance from one to another, to the next, and eventually land on one who seems promising.

I head over to her, she smiles, and I lift my bottle in the air. She nods. Placing the bottle directly to my mouth, I drink and then pass it to her. I'm dancing now—moving around as if I know what the hell I'm doing—but I'm so drunk it doesn't matter. The world is spinning, and I must be spinning too.

Laughter erupts from my mouth, and then I feel myself flying . . .

Or falling.

And splash.

Another series of laughs escape.

I fell into the ocean. Everyone on the boat is pointing, and I wave my hands in the air to my adoring fans.

That's when I see the flashes.

Snap.

Snap.

Snap.

Shit.

Damn paps.

I wake up the next day, and I'm not even sure how I got in my bed. I can barely remember anything after my late-night dip other than I was caught on film.

Bloody hell.

Opening my eyes, I see I'm alone, and I'm thankful for the fact that even in my inebriated state, I didn't fuck someone. As drunk as I was, I would have gotten myself into trouble. With my luck, it would have been a pregnancy or some other scandal I would never live down. It's bad enough that I was caught falling off the boat. I move around my bed and see I have three missed calls from my mum.

This is not good.

I dial her back. "Hi, Mum." I groan.

"Is that all you have to say for yourself? You're a mess, and worse, you're a mess all over television."

"Mother . . ."

"Don't 'Mother' me."

"Why do you bloody care? This is all your fault. I lost her because you . . ." With nothing more to say to her, I hang up. My stomach growls, and I know I need to ring for food. Instead, I decide to head up and see about coffee on the aft deck.

Luckily for me, the boat has cleared out, and no stragglers remain. I'll have to tip my staff extra when I vacate the premises. For now, though, I'll settle for just telling the head steward a thank you.

As soon as I sit on the deck, my coffee is brought to me, and then my eyes widen when I see I have a guest. "Nathaniel."

"Oliver," he says, but his voice is not welcoming. I have a blaring headache, but the look in his eyes is enough to sober me up.

"To what do I owe the honor?"

"This, mate, is your 'come to Jesus' moment. It was only a few months back when you did one for me, so I'm going to do this for you. You are a bloody mess, and I want to know why. Because in all the years I have known you, this has never happened." With that, he flings a tabloid on the table, one with a picture of me taking my late-night swim. "So tell me who she is and what you did."

"Who says I did anything?"

He raises his brow, and I lift my hand in surrender.

"Fine, fine."

Over a large coffee, I tell him everything. Every horrid detail of how I lied and betrayed her, how somewhere along the line I fell in love with her, and how I had lost her.

I bury my head in my hands and groan. "Now what do I do? She's getting married."

"Then you have to stop her."

CHAPTER FORTY-SEVEN

Addison

As I'm walking to grab a bottle of wine from the fridge, I hear the buzzer go off. "Yes?" I ask my doorman.

"There's a Lady Lockhart here to see you."

"Tell her I'm busy."

"She's rather persistent." By the clip in his voice, she's probably driving him insane or insulting him.

I let out a sigh. "Fine. Send her up." I step out of the kitchen and head to the door. When she gets off the elevator, I'm waiting with the door cracked and my head peeking out. Just seeing her in my hallway makes my body go ramrod straight.

"What are you doing here?"

"Can I please come in and talk?" Her voice is weak and unsure, and it makes my stomach tighten at the sound. She doesn't sound like herself and come to think of it, she doesn't look like herself either. Or at least she doesn't look the same as when I last saw her.

Her cheeks are gaunt and her skin pale, but what is more alarming is the way she worries her lower lip. Last time I saw her, her shoulders were pulled back tight, and she looked regal. Right now, she looks everything but that.

"You have horrible timing. You do know I'm getting married tomorrow," I lie.

I don't know why I do. Maybe I don't want Oliver to know. Perhaps some petty part of me hopes he's somewhere suffering over my nuptials.

"I will only be a minute."

"Very well." I open the door to my apartment wider, allowing her the space to walk in. The apartment is quiet. Painfully so. The clicking of her heels echoes in the space like the hammer pounding against my heart.

Once we are in my living room, I don't sit, and I don't offer her a chair. Instead, I tap my heel, placing my hand on my hip. "What can I do for you, Lady Lockhart?"

"Please call me Elizabeth."

"No, thank you," I reply sharply. She's not my friend. She's quite the opposite. She's my enemy. The moment she went after my business and tricked me, she lost her chance at anything more. She is nothing. "I have a party to get to, so if you can make it quick."

"I'm not sure that I can," she whispers, and then I'm on edge. As if everything will change because of this moment.

"Take a seat," I reluctantly say. "Would you care for a drink?"

She nods, and now I'm really wary of where this conversation will go. "Scotch?"

"Yes, please."

Like mother, like son.

I walk over to where I keep my best scotch. My hands shake as I pour her a glass, and by the time I hand it to her, they shake further. I'm making myself one before either of us speaks.

She drinks hers faster than me, but after we both have had a few sips, she places her tumbler down, so I do the same.

"Oliver . . ." she starts.

"Is he okay?" I ask, hating my treacherous heart for being concerned.

"He's not."

"What's wrong?" I ask almost frantically, the rhythm of the blood pumping through my veins accelerating to a faster clip.

"I-I don't know how to say this. He reminds me of his father," she stutters.

"I don't see why this is my concern. If he's unwell, please tell me, but if he's just an asshole—"

"He's drinking."

"So?"

"He's inconsolable."

I shake my head. This is none of my business, so why is she telling me this? "Why are you here?"

"It's my fault. It's all my fault. You're not a mother yet, so you can't imagine the pain to see the one you love most in the world be devastated and to know you're the cause . . ."

"He made his choice. This has nothing to do with you. He chose to lie. To be deceitful. He chose to use me. Hurt me. He chose to destroy me."

"It's not his fault."

"Nothing you can say will change things," I hiss.

"I killed his father," she blurts out, and I stumble back in my chair at her words. "I killed his father . . . and his body . . ." She trails off as tears start to flow freely off her face, her body shaking uncontrollably with sobs.

"His body?" I press.

"It-it's . . ." She starts to shake again, but then I see her take a deep breath, her chest rising and falling. "He's buried on the plot of land. The plot of land you once owned."

The one they were desperate to buy.

My mouth hangs open. I can't possibly . . . she couldn't possibly have just said that? "His father?" I say, confused, trying to understand the whole picture.

She nods. "I think I need to start from the beginning."

I reach for my glass and take another drink. "I agree."

She proceeds to tell me the history of the land. Of the entail. She tells me a story dating back to World War Two. Of war debts and property taxes. She tells me how Oliver's grandfather, the former Earl of Lockhart, was forced to sell off the entail property piece by piece.

She tells me about her father, who had new money but no title, and how at the time, doors were closed to him because he was merely a merchant, making his vast fortune in shipping and trade.

Her father, like my own, dreamed of rising above his humble beginnings and making something of himself, but where mine continued to work hard, hers decided there was a faster way to be legitimized in the eyes of the British aristocracy.

Her father bought one piece of land when she was a mere child and hung the fortune over Lord Lockhart. An arranged marriage was forged, all for money, land, and the need for acceptance into the good old boys' club. Her father, like my own, had lofty dreams, but where mine put me first, she was merely a bargaining chip. And in the end, at the ripe age of seventeen, she was forced to make the ultimate sacrifice for her father.

I never understood why Olly would do what he did, but now I do. When she gets to the part about my father, every muscle in my back tenses.

"A card game. He lost this property in a card game . . . and he was so angry. So he drank. He beat me. The more he lost of our money, the more he beat me. The day I—that day, he had found out that my father wouldn't bail him out, that his well had officially dried up, so he dragged me to the property. He hurt me. I truly thought he would kill me. I was on the ground, and he was so close, his hand wrapped around my throat as he said I was useless, that it was my fault. I grappled for anything to stop him. There was a large rock. I hit him . . ."

I didn't know what to say, but I felt my own tears leave my eyes.

"After I realized . . . I ran back to the house and got a shovel the groundskeeper had in the greenhouse. I wasn't thinking. It was dark, and I didn't know where to go. I was so scared of what they would do to me or to Oliver, so I buried him on the property. But in the night . . . I couldn't drag him. He was too heavy. I was distraught and a mess. After a few months, I waited. I waited to hear from the surveyor about the land, about what they would build. I also waited for the cops to come, but they never did, so I filed a missing person."

"Why didn't you mark the grave? Move him later?" I ask.

"It was too dark, and I was too scared. By the time I came back—eventually, I dropped a shoe of his off the cliff. I said that he had gone out drinking by the coast. They thought he fell to his death . . .

"With no other evidence, and with him not showing up, I filed a presumed death. Without a body, it took seven years. That's when the title passed to Olly. In those seven years, my own father died, passing his estate to me. Oliver's father might have been broke, but I was a wealthy woman. Piece by piece, I bought back all the land. All but the most important one. The one that held the key to my future."

"Our land," I whisper, and she nods.

"I tried so hard . . . I rang your father. For years, I tried, but he never returned my calls. I hated your father for years, but that didn't give me the right to behave as I did. I'm sorry for how I treated you, but I was desperate. I couldn't let you build, and fear made me lash out. Fear made me hate."

My heart rattles in my chest as I finally understand. "How did you know I was going to build?"

"I had the surveyor on my payroll. And I begged Oliver to follow you."

It feels like every piece of the puzzle has fallen into place. I can see her story play out in front of me just as if it were my own, and in truth, it is.

An old family strife. Two families wanting the same land. My father hated her husband for looking down on him and refused to sell, and her mother hated my father for not selling.

A hate fueled by the land

Only one piece is missing. And that's the piece where I fell in love and became collateral damage.

I feel sick.

Confused.

I've come so far in finding my own strength that I'm not sure what this new information means for me and Olly.

Everything in my life has been clouded by deceit for so long, and now I needed time to think.

"Thank you for trusting me," I say, trying to calm my emotions.

"Ol—"

I lift my hand and shake my head. "Thank you for telling me this, and I'm so sorry for all you've been through . . . While I understand why he did what he did, I need some time."

"But—"

I lift my hand and silence her. "I just need more time. Your secret is safe with me."

Time I get. No one disturbs me for days, and before long, it's the eve before what would have been my wedding day.

I'm dressed in PJs and staring at the copy of *Romeo and Juliet* Olly bought me. Time has passed, but I'm still not sure what to do. I love Olly. I've forgiven Olly, but I'm not sure I want to open myself up to future weakness. I'm strong now, stronger than I've been for a long time, but am I willing to risk it?

As if conjured by my thoughts, I hear a knock on the door, so I stand and swing it open.

In my doorway is my mom, who for the first time looks like the woman before my father died. She looks like herself, her skin no longer gaunt, and it has its warm rosy shade again. I lift my gaze. Although she looks beautiful, her eyes are sad.

"Hi. Is everything okay?" I ask her.

She tilts her head and worries her lip. "I want to talk to you."

"Okay."

"I want you to know how much I love you and your brothers."

"I know—"

She holds her hand up. "You are the great loves of my life. You and your father."

"Mom—"

"No, let me speak. I loved him; I still love him. There is no one else but him for me, and there never will be. I want you to marry someone you feel that way for."

"I will, Mom," I whisper, my voice low and not convincing.

"Sweetie, I'm your mother, and I know you. I know you

better than yourself." She gives me a small, sad smile. "I see you now, and you look good, and you make me so proud, but something is missing from your eyes, from your voice. Do you know what that is?"

I shake my head.

"Love. I want you to find love. Even if that means putting your heart on the line because if what you had with Oliver is even a fraction of what I had with your dad, then it's worth fighting for. I want you to have what I had with your father. It's all we would want for you. It's the only thing your father wanted for you. For you to be as happy as we were."

"But you're so sad. So broken. I can't do that again. I can't risk it."

"Don't be scared."

"But how can I not? Look at you."

"Yes, maybe that's true, but I would rather spend the rest of my lifetime missing him and cherishing the memories, than never loving him as my husband and never knowing his love. Life is short, Addison. Don't spend your time existing."

I look at my mom, really look at her. "What did you say?"

"Don't just exist. That's what I'm doing. You deserve more."

I let my own lips part, giving her a soft smile.

I place my hand in the pocket of my dress and touch the coin. Oliver's coin. The coin I keep with me always.

She's right.

I deserve more.

I deserve to love and be loved in return.

And I'm ready now.

I stand from where I'm sitting abruptly, making my mother's eyes go wide.

"Where are you going?"

"To live." I wink, and for the first time in a long time, she smiles. Not just any smile but a large and contagious smile.

Then she does something I don't expect . . . she laughs.

My brow arches, "Why are you laughing?"

"Your father."

"My father?"

"All he ever wanted was for that land to belong to you and your husband, so he must be smiling up in heaven."

"Let's not get ahead of ourselves, Mom."

"You'll see." She winks.

CHAPTER FORTY-EIGHT

Oliver

It feels cliché, but here I am, on a plane flying across the ocean to see about a girl. And not just to see about her but to stop her wedding. My foot taps impatiently on the floor. I know it can't fly any faster, but I need to get there. Now that the haze of my perpetual booze has worn off and I'm sober, the reality of what is about to happen hovers around me like a smoky cloud. It makes it hard to breathe or even catch my breath.

What if I'm too late?

What if I'm not?

It's a ballsy move, but I'm not one for subtlety.

The plane touches down at midnight New York time. I tried to ring her quite a bit, but alas, she didn't answer. What did you expect? It was her rehearsal dinner.

Lord, I really am awful.

Technically, it's already her wedding day.

It takes thirty minutes to arrive in the city, and I head straight to her apartment. When I walk in, the doorman looks shocked to see me. I imagine I'm quite the fright, to be frank. I've been up for twenty-four hours and traveling for nine. I haven't shaved or showered. But truly, what did he expect? It's not every day you crash a wedding. At least I had the decency to try to do it in private.

"She's not here," he responds curtly.

"No? You know where she is?"

"I do not. But it's often customary for the bride to stay at the location of the wedding."

I feel like a bloody idiot. Of course, it is. Which means she's where? At the Lancaster? I still can't believe she chose there of all places. Once I get her back, I'll have to ask her that story because I'm sure there's one.

The Lancaster is only a few blocks away, and I walk straight to the front desk like I own the place. "How can I help you, sir?" the man behind the front desk says, but before I can even get a word in edgewise, I can hear the sound of someone approaching from behind. I turn around and am met with Grayson Price.

"You have some nerve showing your face, Lockhart." He sneers.

"I'm here to stop Addison from making the biggest mistake of her life."

He narrows his eyes.

"I love her. She's everything to me. She can't marry him. I made a mistake, Grayson, a mistake that will haunt me for the rest of my life, but Addison is it for me."

He lets me ramble, and when I'm done, he shrugs with no emotion on his face. "She's not here."

I lift my hand to my hair and pull on it with a groan. "Don't you just want your sister happy? She doesn't love him. She loves me, but her pride won't—"

"Jesus, man, do you ever stop? I'm not saying she's not here to be a dick. I mean she's actually not here."

"It's one in the morning. Where the fuck is she?"

Then it hits me. She's with him. A feeling I have never felt before coils in my stomach, and I think I'm going to be sick. "I understand," I mutter, defeated. This was my last shot. The last chance I had.

But she's not here.

She's gone.

Moving on.

My legs give out, my footing stumbling.

"Easy, man." He steadies me and helps walk me over to the chair in the lobby. I bury my face in my hands.

He doesn't say anything as I sit on the chair, trying to right myself. Trying to come up with a way to live a life without her when I can't come up with anything. I finally lower my hand.

"She's on a plane."

On a plane? Was I too late? Did they already get married? Are they on their way? My jaw lifts, and I look at Grayson. "When did they do it?" I whisper, and he looks serious.

"Do what?" he asks me.

"Don't make me bloody say it." My voice cracks with emotion. "When did they get married?"

"Married?" He shakes his head. "Where the hell have you been?"

"What do you mean?"

"They didn't get married. Jeez."

"What?" I stare, dumbfounded. Heart hammering in my chest, I'm not sure I heard what I think I heard. *Scared to believe.* "What do you mean they didn't?"

"The wedding was called off," he answers as if I should know this.

"You couldn't lead with that?"

For the first time since we started this exchange, his face cracks, a smile forming. "That wouldn't have been as much fun. Plus, I had to know." He smirks.

"Had to know what?"

"If you were good enough for my sister. If you loved her. If you deserved her." His words make me ball my fists. But punching the tosser probably won't be a good idea.

"And do I?" I sneer.

"What do you think?"

"I think I don't care what you think. I'm the only man for her."

With that, his smirk turns into a full smile, laugh and all. "Good."

CHAPTER FORTY-NINE

Oliver

I ANXIOUSLY WATCH THE ROAD AHEAD OF ME, MY FINGERS tapping on the steering wheel as I get closer to the destination. The sound of my tapping echoes through the space the closer I get to Addison.

When I found out she had called off the wedding, I knew I had to find her. Turns out she was on her way to London.

On her way to me.

I'm not sure what changed her mind. I'm not sure how she decided to forgive me, love me, but what I know is I need to get to her, and I need to get to her now. I have lost so much time with her. I refuse to lose another minute.

So now I'm trying to get to the place where it all began for me. Where it began for us. Where I realized we were more than I was letting on, but I was just too stubborn to accept it.

The drive is longer than normal, or at least it feels that way because of my nerves. As I take each winding road, I get closer until I see the cottage where she is waiting in the distance.

As I pull my car to the house and step outside, I hear the sound of the door to the cottage creaking. Then I see her. She jumps forward through the door and then shocking me; I see her run.

The next thing I know, she's throwing her arms around my neck. Climbing up my body and wrapping her legs around my waist, she kisses me on my neck, my jaw, my chin, and then my mouth.

"Excited to see me, love?" I chuckle against her lips.

"Shut up and kiss me, Oliver." She laughs back, and the sound warms my heart.

Slowly, I place her on the ground and look at her, really look at the woman who has turned my world upside down, who has changed me and who I love with all my heart. She watches me watch her, and suddenly, the realization that we are standing in front of each other now is falling over her. I can tell by the way she leans forward on her feet and shifts uncomfortably.

I stop her movement by reaching out my hand and placing it over hers, covering it completely. We both look down at our interlocked hands. Neither one of us is able to speak by the profoundness of the moment. Her hands begin to shake, and I lift my gaze to meet her stare. Her eyes fill with tears as we look at each other.

"Why are you crying?" I ask.

"I-I never thought we would be here again," she admits on a sob. "D-do you still love me—"

"Stop."

I pull her toward me with one hand and place her against my chest. With her encased in my arms, I place a kiss on top of her head.

"I will always love you. I have never stopped loving you. I loved you then, and I love you now. Do you understand me?"

"Then?" she whispers, confused.

"Here. Even back then, when we were here the first time, I loved you. I was just too damn stubborn to admit it. But I did, and I still do, and I will love you forever."

I hear her whimper beneath my touch, and I move back

and tip her head up. "I love you."

"I love you too."

"Thank fuck," I say, placing my lips on hers. She starts to laugh, and together, we walk toward the cottage.

I open the door and push us forward until we make it to the bedroom. "We should talk," she says.

"Later," I say. "First, I need to taste you, to love you. Fuck, I need to be inside you." I push her body down onto the bed, and her breath hitches. "Did you miss me, love?" My hand reaches down, and I begin to stroke her jaw, down her neck, to the hollow of her throat, and then I unbutton each button on her shirt. "Did you miss kissing me?" I place a kiss on the skin where my finger had just touched.

Slowly, my lips trail my hand's movements. Licking each spot. Finally, when she's naked, I place my lips to the apex of her thighs. "Did you miss feeling me inside you?" My finger dips inside, and she trembles. "Because I missed it all. Every day we weren't together, I missed you. I craved you. I felt dead without you, but now I'm alive again."

Pulling my finger out, she whimpers from the absence. And then where it all began, I show her just how much.

Sometime later, once we are both fully satisfied, we sit together on the couch. She nuzzles into my chest, and we watch the waves crash from the bay windows.

"So are we going to talk about it?" she asks.

"What's there to talk about?"

"Maxwell."

I turn my head and look down at her. "There's nothing to say, love."

"All this time wasted. I almost married him. This almost was never—" She chokes out. "We almost didn't end up together because of me."

"No, none of this is your fault. The fault lands on me. You were hurt and confused, and it's my fault for putting you in the position. Can you forgive me?"

"I already have."

"You have?"

"Your mother told me everything. And while that is not the reason for my forgiveness, it made me understand."

My eyes widen at her admission. My mum told her? Everything?

"What did she say?" I ask.

"She told me why you lied."

"I'm so sorry. If I can take it back, if I could go back and be honest with you, I would. It's no excuse, but she was all I had before you, and I felt I had no choice. But once I realized that you were nothing like the person my mother described, I should have trusted you. Please forgive me."

"I do forgive you, but that forgiveness isn't why I am here."

"So then what was the reason?"

"I realized when you love someone the way I love you, you need to accept them for the good and the bad, and you need to love them not just for the good but also for the bad. I know why you did it, and while I don't approve of your lying, I can't imagine a life without you."

"Thank you," I say, leaning down and finding her lips.

"Just don't lie again."

"Never."

"I know. And I trust you."

And then again, for the second time since we've been back together, I show her she can trust me, love me, and be mine.

EPILOGUE

Addison

"Lord Lockhart, what are you doing?" I giggle as he lifts me into his arms, cradling me to his chest. He starts to walk, and I hear the gravel of the driveway crunch beneath his shoes.

"Carrying you over the threshold, Lady Lockhart." He laughs as he continues to walk toward the door of the beach cottage.

It's our first time back since our wedding, and apparently, that means as my husband, he has to perform this ridiculous tradition. I close my eyes, loving the feeling of being enveloped in his arms. With my eyes closed, all my other senses intensify. I can smell the sea and the fresh blooms.

Soon enough, we are walking into the foyer straight into the house and then into my bedroom, our bedroom. He places me down on the bed, and his lips find mine. "What should we do first?"

"I thought that was pretty obvious." I smirk.

"You don't want me to cook dinner?"

I shake my head adamantly.

"Is that a no?"

"That most certainly is a no. Stop playing around, Oliver."

He starts to kiss my neck. "Is there something else you want me to do, love?" He pulls away and looks down at me with a smirk. "Come now, I have a surprise."

I groan.

"You always love my surprises."

"I'm pretty sure it's actually the opposite. I'm pretty sure I don't."

"You loved the amusement park. You loved that time when I surprised you in New York . . ."

"I'm pretty sure I didn't." I raise an eyebrow.

"Of course, you did 'cause it led you here."

I roll my eyes. "I do love you, though. I love it especially when you—"

"No distractions."

"Fine." I stand and readjust my dress and follow my husband out of our bedroom.

My husband.

It's certainly been a crazy trip getting here. But we got here nonetheless, and although there were hurt and pain along the way, I wouldn't trade one second if it means I can be here right now with him.

When we reach the path overlooking the water, the oxygen leaves my body as I see what he's done, what he's set up. There overlooking the water is a table set with fine china, linens, and a bottle of champagne. It's perfect and romantic and everything.

"Oliver," I whisper.

"Do you like it?"

"It's amazing. When did you do this?"

"I had the staff take care of it," he says.

"The elusive staff. Why are they never here when I am?"

"That's the way I like it, always have. When I'm here, I'm not Lord Lockhart, and I'm not Blackthorn. I'm just Olly."

"Well, I love all of you, but this is who I love the most," I admit.

"I know, and that's what I love about you most."

The food is still hot, and together under the stars, we eat, drink, and laugh. Once we're done, Olly stands and lays a blanket on the grass.

Stripping me bare, he lays me down. Kissing my shoulder, he trails his tongue along my skin. And right there on the cliff where it all started, and I realized I was falling for him, he makes love to me.

And as he kisses every inch of my body and we become one, I savor every second, every minute, every moment.

Because in this moment, I've never felt more *alive.*

ACKNOWLEDGMENTS

I want to thank my entire family. I love you all so much.

Thank you to my husband and my kids for always loving me. You guys are my heart!

Thank you to my Mom, Dad, Liz and Ralph for always believing in me, encouraging me and loving me!

Thank you to my in-laws for being so cool and supportive!

Thank you to all of my brothers and sisters!

Thank you to everyone that helped with Deceit

Lawrence Editing

Jenny Sims

Indie After Hours

My Brother's Editor

Marla Esposito

Champagne Formats

Lori Jackson

Hang Le

Special Thanks to Livia Jamerlan for helping me with the content and plotting of Deceit.

Thank you to Jon Wong and Christian Hogue for the most perfect image of Oliver EVER!

Thank you to Shane East, Lucy Rivers and Lyric for bringing Deceit to life on audio.

Thank you to Candi Kane PR

Thank you to my AMAZING ARC TEAM! You guys rock!

Thank you to my beta/test team.

Melissa: You're the best! Thank you for ALL you do for me.

Leigh: You dropped everything for me in order to make sure this book was perfect . . . Thank you!

Sarah: Your input and feedback was so amazing! Thank you!

Jessica, Kelly and Becca. Thank you for your wonderful and extremely helpful feedback.

Thank you Parker S. Huntington for listening to my crazy.

Mia: Thanks for always talking plot with me.

I want to thank ALL my friends for putting up with me while I wrote this book. Thank you!

To all of my author friends who listen to me complain and let me ask for advice, thank you!

To the ladies in the Ava Harrison Support Group, I couldn't have done this without your support!

Please consider joining my Facebook reader group Ava Harrison Support Group

Thanks to all the bloggers! Thanks for your excitement and love of books!

Last but certainly not least . . .

Thank you to the readers!

Thank you so much for taking this journey with me.

BY AVA HARRISON

Imperfect Truth

Through Her Eyes

trans·fer·ence

Illicit

Clandestine

Sordid

Explicit

ab·so·lu·tion

ABOUT THE AUTHOR

Ava Harrison is a *USA Today* and Amazon bestselling author. When she's not journaling her life, you can find her window shopping, cooking dinner for her family, or curled up on her couch reading a book.

Connect with Ava

Newsletter Sign Up: bit.ly/2fnQQ1n

Book + Main:
bookandmainbites.com/avaharrison

Facebook Author Page:
www.facebook.com/avaharrisonauthor

Facebook Reader Group: bit.ly/2e67NYi

Goodreads Author Page
www.goodreads.com/author/show/13857011.Ava_Harrison

Instagram:
www.instagram.com/avaharrisonauthor

BookBub:
www.bookbub.com/authors/ava-harrison

Amazon Author Page
amzn.to/2fnVJHFF